Durjoy Datta was born in New Delhi, and completed a degree in engineering and business management before embarking on a writing career. His first book—*Of Course I Love You . . .*—was published when he was twenty-one years old and was an instant bestseller. His successive novels—*Now That You're Rich . . .*; *She Broke Up, I Didn't! . . .*; *Oh Yes, I'm Single! . . .*; *You Were My Crush . . .*; *If It's Not Forever . . .*; *Till the Last Breath . . .*; *Someone Like You*; *Hold My Hand*; *When Only Love Remains*; *World's Best Boyfriend*; *The Girl of My Dreams*; *The Boy Who Loved*; *The Boy with the Broken Heart* and *The Perfect Us*—have also found prominence on various bestseller lists, making him one of the highest-selling authors in India. Durjoy also has to his credit nine television shows and has written over a thousand episodes for television.

He lives in Mumbai. For more updates, you can follow him on Facebook (www.facebook.com/durjoydatta1) or Twitter (@durjoydatta) or mail him at durjoydatta@gmail.com.

Maanvi Ahuja was born in New Delhi, India, and did her post graduation in finance from IIM, Kozhikode. She is the author of two books, *Of Course I Love You!* . . . and *Now That You're Rich!* . . ., both of which have been on various bestseller lists. Currently residing in Mumbai, she works as an investment banker at a leading banking firm. To know more about her, you can mail her at maanviahuja@gmail.com.

# Of Course I Love You

## Till I Find Someone Better

# DURJOY DATTA
## MAANVI AHUJA

**Penguin**
metro reads

An imprint of Penguin Random House

PENGUIN METRO READS

USA | Canada | UK | Ireland | Australia
New Zealand | India | South Africa | China

Penguin Metro Reads is part of the Penguin Random House group of companies
whose addresses can be found at global.penguinrandomhouse.com

Published by Penguin Random House India Pvt. Ltd
7th Floor, Infinity Tower C, DLF Cyber City,
Gurgaon 122 002, Haryana, India

Penguin
Random House
India

First published by Grapevine India Publishers 2008
Published in Penguin Metro Reads by Penguin Books India 2013

28  27  26  25  24 23  22 21

This is a work of fiction. Names, characters, places and incidents are either the
product of the authors' imagination or are used fictitiously and any resemblance
to any actual person, living or dead, events or locales is entirely coincidental.

ISBN 9780143421603

Typeset in Adobe Caslon Pro by Eleven Arts, Delhi
Printed at Manipal Technologies Limited, Manipal

www.penguin.co.in

# Acknowledgements

Were it not for these people whom we thank below (and an active God), this book would still be languishing in the *My Documents* folder of our computers. These people might not be literary superpowers, but they always made us feel that our book was Booker material, often without reading the manuscript. Needless to say, we took them seriously.

To start the list with somebody who was dying to see his name in print just as we were, we would like to thank Sachin Garg, first and last, for thinking that we are small Rushdies in the making.

Stuti and Mayank, who are still in a state of shock upon hearing that we can write and, worse, get published! There are others, most of whom have led strange lives and ended up, willingly or unwillingly, contributing to the book:

Megha Sharma, Kanika Suri, Deepika Kapur and Sheetal Shishodia—the four of them who thought it was a long joke until they realized we were not actually rolling on the floor laughing, or, as they say, ROFLing.

Nishit Bhatnagar, Neeti Rustagi, Archit Garg, Abhishek Sachdev (Thanks! You rock!), Nitin Verma, Nikita Singh, Naman Kapur, DVYRAS (partly)—who put up with our strange ways, and all of whom wanted a free copy until they knew they would be on the opening page. Now they want two.

All our fellow bloggers, and the people on Facebook for all the appreciation they showered on us—and still do—despite hating us for the mindless things we write.

Our batchmates at our alma mater(s) who unflinchingly provided us with proxy attendances whenever and wherever needed.

Our families, and especially our parents, who constantly supported and encouraged us, even as they grappled with nightmares of the two of us leaving all material pursuits (read *careers*) and ending up as intellectual paupers. That is, until they read the book and realized we were up to no good.

And finally our sisters, Rituparna Datta and Tanvi Ahuja, who have inspired us and made us believe that this is our calling in life—besides finding ourselves jobs, pursuing management degrees, having kids, taking out the garbage among others—and this is what we should continue doing.

We also thank Sri Sri Ravi Shankar, whose blessings were always with us.

We are glad to have come out of this ordeal of writing a book together, with just a few bruises here and there. We thank ourselves.

# 1

*This is perfect. This is perfect*, I kept telling myself. It had been twelve hours on the trot. I had already spent my entire month's allowance on her and there were no signs that I would be treated to any sort of guilty pleasures other than the expensive and the utterly fattening ones any time soon. The fact that Smriti looked smoking hot in her floral spaghetti and the short, pleated skirt that ended inches below her butt, wasn't doing me any good either. The very purpose of the skirt's existence—easy accessibility and eventual *get rid*-ability—was being defeated that night.

It had been a long day and I was ruing the moment I had asked her out tonight. I had missed all my classes that day, all in vain.

'So, what next?' she asked.

*What next?* For starters, she could fry my bloody head and chomp it down. Oh no, wait! That won't cost me *anything*. No doubt, she would order her *third* cocktail that evening to wash it down. Now if only she would get tipsy, start seeing things in double and eventually be oblivious to my rendering her clothes useless. I might be a jerk, but many guys would agree with me on this: nudity suits girls.

'I don't know,' I said, plastering a dreamy look on my face, one that screamed that I needed nothing but her. I hoped it would work this time, though it was the millionth time that day and she had not even blown a kiss, let alone do it real time.

I wondered why I had decided to be in love with her. I could have lived with the tag of an ugly but *lucky* jerk with a one-track mind. For a guy who looked as bad as I did, it was surprising that I had dated a few girls before Smriti. However, none of my relationships worked and apparently every break-up was *my* fault. This time, I had vowed that I would make it work.

*Why?*

Because I was tired of the nonsense being said about me. That I had no respect for women. It's not true at all. I was losing every bit of credibility on the dating scene. Soon, no friend who would set me up with anybody, which itself happened very rarely. Being a perennially struggling-to-save-money-for-dates student of a nerdy engineering college, in my world relationships were more than about partying each night and drinking oneself to sexual inability. People around me wanted love, care and long conversations, whatever that meant.

It was time I fell in *love*. I had to find somebody to love. Or at least somebody I would not hate after the first few weeks. And somebody who wouldn't dump me either. Smriti fit the bill. I was lucky I got her.

She was not too hard to handle and was low on maintenance. At least, that's what I had thought when I started pursuing her. But the *most* important thing—she was busy. As a medical student, she did not have a lot of time to spend on long phone conversations. She spent more time examining other people's crotches than mine. Although that made me uncomfortable, at least I didn't have to endure sleepless nights yakking on the phone.

She was a little too fair and a little too thin, compared to my bulky five-foot-ten frame, and consequently a little less endowed in the places I would have liked. But what the hell, she was beautiful. Not like the ones you would fantasize about till you were blue and frothing at the mouth, but the kind you would take home to your mom. Although in our case, I could never imagine *that* happening.

Something kept her from reaching the dizzying heights of dollish beauty. It was either her smile that extended from ear to ear, making her look like the little pug from a television commercial, or her slightly long, crooked nose. Whatever it was, there was something wrong about her. I guess I would find out in due time and find her not likeable. For now, I had to concentrate on getting her to kiss me.

I was not in a position to comment on something such as looks, anyway. The only redeeming feature on my face was the patch of unmanaged beard that covered my chin and took away attention from the below-average features I had managed to crowd my face with. The unruly mop of hair on my head helped too. The basic idea was to hide as much of my face as possible. Okay, well, I had a dimple, too, but more or less, I was ugly.

It had been almost a month since Smriti and I had accepted that we loved each other, but so far there was no physical proof to back it. We had not even kissed. However, a night-out was *exactly* what I needed to weave my magic, and weave her clothes off her. If I failed, I would tell myself it was pure, untainted love that I was after. As 50 Cent preached in one of his songs—*Be a Gentleman*. It was tough, though; she was not letting me be a *man*. Gentle, I never was.

Anyway, I had managed to put my arm around her and land a peck on her cheek during the wretched movie we watched earlier, gold-class plus popcorn. Moreover, the peck was so woefully devoid of passion, it could have graced a greeting card rather than a *Cosmopolitan* centrefold.

How was I supposed to know she would find *The Chronicles of Narnia* so interesting that she would fail to notice the stolen kiss on her cheek? She was a doctor, all right. But not a vet! Definitely not Dr Doolittle. Ideally, she shouldn't have been interested in a talking lion, let alone cry for the damned thing.

'It's closing down. Let's go to a place that will be open all night,' she suggested.

Nightlife in Delhi in those days was pathetic, to say the least. I suspected even a tribal region in Sikkim showed up more on the US military radar systems than Delhi did. We'd have to go to Comesum, the only all-night place that I could afford since the money in my wallet had hit rock bottom that boring night. Comesum was where all the inexpensive night-outs invariably ended, amidst lots of pathetic food and mosquitoes. Nevertheless, its large and empty parking space and low *do-not-disturb* bribe rates excited me, and many others who spent the night acting funny behind tinted car windows.

Sex was engulfing every part of Delhi, having long replaced television as the favourite pastime. The only people who refused to accept it were the ones not doing it. However, it was all around. The geeky girl in your class, the stud, the backbencher Sardar—however incapable you might have thought them to be, morally or physically, they were all doing it. If you had a girl, then you would be doing it. Sex was everywhere—schools, office backrooms, movie halls and parking lots. Secluded places were paradise. Illegal though they might have been, tinted car windows were *in*. In a few years, *not having* a girlfriend became as odd as *having* one had been, a few years back. The Delhi Public School MMS scandal of 2004 was just the tip of the iceberg.

'How about going to *Comesum*?' I asked a seemingly stupid question in response to a seemingly stupid suggestion.

Still, I did not blame Smriti for her naivety. The girl I had dated before her was so astonishingly boring when we weren't making out that I had to look for interesting places that one could go to in Delhi.

'We can go to Aura. It's in Hotel Ashoka. I heard it's fine, too. Lots of girls! I bet you will like it,' she said and nudged me. Sure, I could have leered at wiggly tits in a club, but an option like that is more alluring when you are no longer trying to get inside your girl's shirt. It had been ten months since I had broken up and it's not very easy convincing people to still be in contact, especially physical.

'I have been to Aura. It's not as good as people say it is. It just has a few drunken local brats dancing. That's it. And it's anyway not worth it, driving that far,' I said.

'Your call. After all, it is your treat. You decide.'

*Thank god for that.*

I loved Aura. Especially on evenings when stags weren't allowed, it was heaven and an expensive one at that. I had to shoot either the plan down or myself. *I loved myself.* So we headed off to Comesum, driving off on a drunken auto driver's directions. His breath was in no way different from Smriti's. It's amazing: *I paid for her bad breath and she isn't even drunk!*

We had to ask directions of whoever we came across, thanks to two of my most feminine attributes combined with a masculine one—I couldn't remember roads, was a terrible driver, and pretended to know it all.

After about a million detours, we finally reached the place where I hoped all my hard work for the day and the few weeks preceding it would pay off. I told myself not to expect anything because I was so damn much in *love*, after all.

*Wasn't I?*

'Ice cream?' Smriti asked.

'Sure!'

The urge to kill her was now coursing through my veins. I could feel it seeping out of my skin. I had started wondering what options she had if I were to abandon her in a desolate street at 3 a.m. at night in New Delhi, the rape capital of India. It wasn't a particularly clever idea but I did consider it when she looked the other way while I fuelled the car up! It costs money and I was barely above the poverty line. I wished someone would tell her that. It's not that I minded paying, but she could have offered at least.

Well, actually, I did mind paying.

For guys like us, with limited means, dating is like playing Russian roulette. High risk, high gain. If the girl offers to split on a date and it goes well, you're the king. If she doesn't and the date goes bad, you're dead. I was running out of luck.

I wished I hadn't turned down my college senior Nitin's invitation to his birthday treat. But then, girls make the world go round, and I was no different.

My eyes started roving around the complex as we gulped down the slimy, sweet thing she had ordered. It was a two-storeyed building and most people sat outside. It wasn't anything spectacular—in fact, it wasn't even air-conditioned or heated, but then you couldn't expect it to be. It opened primarily for railway passengers and not drunk party revellers. Every weekend it turned into a hot spot for 'bird' watching! Anyone who ran out of money, got thrown out of a club or got too drunk, landed up here. So we would have here a mix of short skirts and long, flowing ones (but mostly short!) bought from anywhere on Janpath (the place where you can bargain till you drop) or some swanky upscale mall in Vasant Kunj.

Delhi girls never dress *conservatively*, making it a pleasure to ogle them. I had no fashion sense and anything that started below the navel and ended above mid-thigh was fine by me. Exposure is *always* in vogue! There is nothing more refreshing than a pair of well-toned, attractive legs. This is not objectifying women; it's just appreciating a certain fact about them a little more than others.

Suddenly, I heard a lot of girls bitching to their boyfriends in tight T-shirts about other girls who wore shorter skirts or heavier make-up. Those girls could have fired up a power station to full capacity. It just worsened my already sky-high testosterone levels. I tried to finish off the ice cream quickly, as it had been a pain watching her chew it down to atomic levels before swallowing.

'Aren't you feeling cold?' I asked, rubbing my hands. Obviously, she wasn't. Girls have an internal heating system that is activated once they put on a short dress or an off-shoulder.

'No. Are you?' she asked.

'Not really, I just thought we could sit in the car; there is too much noise out here,' I said.

'Are you sure?' she asked and smirked at me.

*What is that supposed to mean? Is that a yes? If it is, why doesn't she bloody say so? Can we please cut the crap and make out? At least kiss, damn it! It's been ten months since I have done that!*

I guess she was getting some kind of a sadistic pleasure in teasing me. I think all girls do.

'Yes,' I said.

I started walking towards the parked car, hoping she would follow. For the first time that night, I was being headstrong and manly. I definitely knew what *I* wanted: I was curious to know what it would be like to kiss her. I took the first few steps and paddled my hands around me to hold her by the waist but my hands caught nothing but air. She hadn't followed, and when I looked back, I found her standing near the ice-cream vendor waiting for me to pay the guy. The night just kept getting longer. I paid the guy and asked Smriti, 'Can we go now?'

'Yeah, sure,' she said.

At this point, I was destructively angry but I had to stay focused. As we walked towards the car, I handed over a hundred-rupee note to the moustached security guard. It was a worthwhile investment. I could already feel my hormones kicking into action. I pulled up my jeans and walked swiftly towards the car. The problem with low-waist jeans is that when you walk, it is always as if you have a helmet stuck right between your thighs and if you have mammoth thighs like me, God help you. Yeah, I was a little healthy and majorly detestable.

'Deb, why did you get Vernita's car? The mileage on it sucks, doesn't it?' she asked as she walked ahead of me. I didn't stop her from doing that. Her skirt looked even shorter and more alluring from behind. Yeah, I was being a cheap pervert. But then, every guy goes through this phase!

'My car wasn't serviced,' I said. *It doesn't have tinted glasses.*

She was playing around. She couldn't possibly be concerned with the mileage of the car I drove. If she had, she would have offered to go Dutch, or at least paid for her own ice cream. I might have refused, but she could have offered!

As soon as we settled down in the car, I got the elementary step wrong. However, I didn't blame myself for it. It had been quite some time since I had stared at a real naked girl and I was dying to do it that night. I had started to rub my nose against the nape of her neck, which was meant to send her into the throes of a hormonal overdrive.

'Are you trying to seduce me, Deb?' she asked. I don't think she didn't like it, but I think she still wanted to play hard to get.

'Mmm ... err ... no.'

'Mmm, err, no,' she mocked me and I turned red, only to turn scarlet later. 'You might have had your way with girls in the past, but not this time,' she said.

It was strange because I had *never* had my way with girls in the past. Girls always found me repulsive in that department.

'As in? What do you mean?'

'As in, I will initiate things when I feel like doing so, when I am comfortable with it.' I was embarrassed at my failed attempt. *She was in control?* Something in that tone was incredibly inviting. I wanted her *bad* now. Only I didn't know how to go about it. *Stupid nerd.*

'Okay, whatever you say. I love you,' I said.

'I love you, too,' she replied and I faked a smile, as an airhostess would at ogling old perverts when what she really wants is to have minced by the turbine blades. I sunk back into my seat, wondering if there was any porn left to download. I wished I were in Mumbai or Bangalore. Delhi girls are tough, Shrey had once told me.

'Why do you love me?' she asked. She looked at me as if she was expecting me take out a pen and start making a list on a mile-long piece of toilet paper.

'You are very *different* from others.' That was supposed to include everything on the list.

'How am I different from the other girls you have gone out with?'

I resisted telling her she was *no* different; she asked the *same* questions they had.

'I love you. With the others, it didn't feel the way it feels with you. It wasn't love. Love is what I feel for you, pure and untainted. With you, I feel different, I feel special, wanted. I feel loved and I long to make you feel the same. You make me feel so . . . You *complete* me, Smriti. I love you. I really do.'

I paused and stuttered. It nearly sounded spontaneous!

'How sweet, Deb! I love you too. You are not as bad as my

friends tell me. You are so sweet,' she said and ran her hand over my cheeks. *A little lower, a little lower, just a little lower, damn it!*

We talked about unnecessary things for what seemed like an eon. To be frank, it wasn't entirely boring; she was much more interesting than the average girl. It was just that I wasn't looking for *interesting* conversation—that's what married people do. I was just an average bloke praying to get lucky with his girlfriend. Sex was too far-fetched—Obviously!—but I could have done with a little kissing and little groping. Not too much to ask for, I suppose. Of course, I *loved* her too. True, untainted love.

Somewhere between the interesting conversations, I dropped off with my head resting on her shoulder. It had been a long and expensive day. I slept, wondering if I would feel awake enough the next morning to attend the mechanics of solids class. This date wasn't worth missing it.

Suddenly, I felt something against my cheek, something nice and delightfully wet. Oh, man! She was kissing me. For real! I tried hard to stay still, to see what she would do. I opened one eye and saw a bit of my cheek disappearing inside her mouth and being slathered all over by her tongue. I woke up wondering what I had missed.

'Deb, you look cuter when you are sleeping.'

'I am going right back to sleep, don't you dare stop.'

She started all the nice stuff, crossed one of her legs over mine and sat on my lap until her neck was within licking distance. And then she let go. She kissed me as if it was her last kiss, grabbed my hands and placed them over her breasts as she moaned ecstatically, and ran her hands all over my chest and even lower. It had started to feel real good; I slipped my hand inside her T-shirt, and trailed my fingers up her back to whatever she was wearing inside. I was just about to unhook the joys of being a man, when she stopped me.

'Nuh-huh . . . not that quick, boy,' she said as she pulled my hands out.

'Why not?' I asked, as I pulled my hand out and placed it beneath her skirt and, convinced that she would not notice, moved it up slowly. I aimed for the stars. Clothes can be a pain. Why the hell couldn't we just be dressed like prehistoric cave men with neither clothes nor any source of entertainment other than . . . you know . . . ?

'No, not that fast, Deb. We will save the rest for later. It's not fun doing everything at once.'

'But—' I said dejectedly. I had a major physiological problem in my pants but she was no longer interested.

'I don't feel like doing anything else right now,' she said as she grabbed my hand and pulled it out from its silken abode.

Now what was I to make of it? I had done reasonably well, to think of it. It was officially our first night-out and the fifth date and to have managed all that I had until then was commendable. It came at a price, but who cared? I was no longer angry. *I loved her.*

I took heart from the fact that she had said that we would not do everything at once. That probably meant we *would* do it but not at once.

It was getting easier to love her. She left me with some big mosquito bites on my neck. If mosquitoes ever grew up to the size of dogs, that is. The kisses were great, so I decided I would continue loving her. And I did. After all, it is easier to love a busy, smart girl—who's a good kisser—rather than loving somebody you love. Smriti was turning out to be amazing in all the visual and tangible assets and I loved it.

As I drove home, I tried to think of an explanation for those love bites. Mom would definitely ask about those marks if she saw them. I tried my sister's concealers and they helped a bit. I roamed around in ancient turtlenecks for the next few days.

I was shallow and I knew that. I loved being so and I knew many guys who would have loved to swap places with me.

# 2

'How much did you score?' she asked. The fifth semester results were out. This was January 2007.

'Fifty-two per cent,' I replied.

'That's not bad,' Smriti said.

'It's not bad? My class rank is eighty on hundred. It's not bad, it's terrible. I am done. I'm so screwed this time,' I said.

'You didn't study, so you couldn't have done any better,' she argued.

'Thanks for the support. I could have done without that,' I said.

It's strange how people can't lie when they have to. I knew I hadn't studied, but I could have done without being reminded of that again. But she had always been like this—straightforward and ruthlessly undiplomatic. It was fun when we had just started going out and she would pamper the man in me, saying things like I was the *best guy she had ever kissed* (which is probably the same thing guys she'd dated before me would have heard), but of late she had started saying pretty irritating stuff. Like, '*My friend Virangana . . . her boyfriend is so brilliant that he has got a seven-figure job.*' Or, '*You are not great-looking but yes, I still love you very much.*'

Had I said anything remotely close to what she did, I would have been dead meat. And yes, it had been two months, and things were not the same any more. Relationships deteriorate; mine just did a little faster. Every relationship has an expiry date.

We did a lot of things together but much of it fell short of my expectations. She wasn't as dream-like as I had imagined her to be. She had started acting like a little kid in a big city with no one else but me. We did have numerous night-outs, thanks to Lady Hardinge Medical College's non-existent hostel rules. However, the charm had fizzled and instead my classes became too important to miss. I hated her prolonged kisses that exhausted her beyond twenty orgasms. Yes, we had stamina problems. *From her side.*

'Are we meeting tonight?' she asked.

'Are we? Yes, why not? Let us celebrate; I just blew up my semester exams. I may not get a job after college. That's definitely something to celebrate,' I replied, sarcasm dripping off every word I uttered.

'Deb, we hardly talk for twenty minutes in a day ... can't we meet, at least?'

'Don't be stupid, Smriti. We talk a hell of a lot more than that. And what about the messages I send? The missed calls? We are on the phone the whole day, damn it,' I shouted.

'No, we never are. You never reply to my messages. You have time to talk to Vernita. You have time to reply to my friends' messages. *You* never call; *I* do. You have time for everything in the world, but not for me,' she said. Her voice shook. Her tear glands were on their mark.

'Smriti, I am really pissed off right now and don't need your nonsense. You will *never* understand this. My college marks are important, damn it. I am close to being screwed and all you think about is *yourself*, your dates and your calls and the goddamned messages. I can't believe you would be so selfish. I am hanging up and please don't call back unless I call you,' I said agitatedly and disconnected the call. It is better to shift blame than try to fight it. It also meant a licence not to take her calls for the next few hours.

As expected, my phone kept buzzing with her texts for the

next half hour and she apologized for things she wasn't responsible for. Most of the messages didn't make any sense, but they were long and that is what generally matters. Smriti loved long, never-ending texts and expected them to have the same effect on me. I hardly read those messages.

I knew I was being harsh on Smriti. But something had to be done. I couldn't just walk out of her life, leave her crying and be spat on again. If things were breaking down, she had to take the blame for it too. She had to be bad in some way. The break-up had to result from *mutual* frustration and incompatibility.

It wasn't *my* fault that I didn't find anything interesting in her after all these months. It was a congenital disease. I couldn't help it. For heaven's sake, nothing was changing for the better, it was just becoming worse! I had to talk to her for four hours a day and give her the minutest details of everything I had done in the course of the day. It had started to get on my nerves. She had shut out all her friends and begun devoting every minute to me! Worse, she wanted me to do the same.

She wasn't even sexy any more. Those glistening, marble-white legs now seemed to have stretch marks marring them and her petite breasts seemed to have retreated into her body. I noticed all that. Too bad if nobody else did. And to top it all, she was wrecking my college performance too. The relationship was killing me.

Going on like this was against the very laws of nature. Only the fittest and the *sexiest* survive (don't ask how I did). She was neither. I couldn't have possibly gone against the laws of Darwin. I'm not the church. I'm not even Christian.

'Hey, what's up? How was the result?' said a voice from behind me.

It was Shrey, his imposing six-foot frame dressed in a Manchester United tee (he liked the colour, not the team), faded blue jeans that were soiled to brown now and chappals, not the jazzy ones but the ones meant to be worn strictly within the confines of one's home. Shrey, with his tanned complexion, as he put it, and curly, bushy hair, which according to him had been perennially in vogue since the seventies, was immensely cool. He had gone to the hostel to catch a nap between classes but had not returned for any.

Shrey was the kind of guy who gets on your nerves the first few times you meet because of his theories about life, IQ, education, poverty, progress, engineering, even girl psychology! They are all bullshit. Shrey had stopped caring about his semester marks long ago. To be precise, it was the day we took our first semester exams. The reason? *He had already studied enough.*

That was sad, as he had several high-powered processors embedded inside that noodle-hair-covered head. The big problem with him? He wanted to be everywhere and be everything. To make things worse, he didn't think there was a scintilla of a chance of that not happening.

'Average, I guess,' I said.

'I flunked two examinations. I am yet to check but someone told me that I did,' he said without a touch of sadness or regret. I think he even smiled. I *so* envied him. I would have shat in my pants had I scored like him.

'Marks are material things. They are not something that's going to affect our lives, man. We are meant for bigger things. Are you going somewhere tonight?' he asked. Though a day scholar, he was often mistaken for a hosteller for he spent most of his time flitting from the JCB (Jagdish Chandra Bose) hostel to the BMH (Barah Mihir Hostel) to others, in search of a better bed to crash on or a better computer to crash into. He had flunked two exams and was short on attendance in the current semester, but that would change nothing in his schedule. He would still go out that night.

Not only did he manage to smile in the face of adversity, he had the balls to poke at it with alarming frequency and audacity.

'I'm a little busy tonight,' I said.

'Smriti?'

'I guess. Nothing is sure. I'll surely come if it doesn't work out.'

'C'mon! Now's the time, man! The girls are waiting. You're still on with Smriti? That's great going, man. Is there somebody else, too?'

'It's still *just* her.'

'Okay. We'll go out some other time then. I have to rush now. Vandana is waiting. We're going to the place I told you about with those great kebabs, man! I bet they are the best in Delhi.'

Vandana was his girlfriend of three years whom he loved dearly. But that certainly did not stop him from exploring newer, fresher vistas. He had dated a few girls on the side, too, while he was in a serious relationship with Vandana. It was a simple equation for him—*keep one constant, and vary the others*. Girls were his second love. His first love had always been engineering science, particularly big laboratories and Wikipedia!

'I have been there once, Shrey. It's nothing great,' I said and almost immediately wanted to take back my words.

'Not great? Are you nuts? The softness, the melt-in-the-mouth texture . . . oh man! It is awesome, dude. You have to develop a taste for mutton kebabs and that takes time.'

It had been barely three months since Shrey had gone non-vegetarian, but he thought I, the hard-core non-vegetarian Bengali . . . I needed to *develop* a taste for mutton?

'By the way, Vernita was looking for you,' he said and left for the place he thought had the best kebabs. Poor Vandana, she would have to agree with him too.

Vernita completed the core trio. All three of us were nerdy enough to drag ourselves to a decent engineering college but non-nerdy enough (by choice or by nature) to be suffocated by it. However, it helped that the Delhi College of Engineering wasn't loaded in favour of people who studied until their eyeballs popped out or in. All three of us perennially envied the lives of students in non-professional colleges. The grass is always greener, prettier and hotter on the other side of the fence.

The other side of the fence was Delhi University's North Campus—the place with the highest number of pretty faces per square mile.

Vernita was my only female friend left who didn't mind my presence. Usually, I either ended up dating or disgustingly hitting on my female friends with disastrous resuslts. Vernita and I had come close to doing it once but I realized it was just me! She never had those intentions. It's the same story over and over again. Damn!

Vernita was really short and good-looking. She had a long face with sharp, pointed features accentuated by her creamy white complexion. However, what stood out was her loud and overtly sexy sense of style. She was like those seductresses in animated movies who wore black dresses with *really* long slits.

Let's just say that nature had been very kind to her. The voluptuous Indian curves and gorgeous features that she was endowed with were the reasons why we became friends in the first place. Shrey, for the first few days in college, had stalked her like a maniac. She was too hot to be ignored. Eventually, both of us had stammered and stuttered our way into her life, though she made it clear that neither of us had any chance with her and that she thought we were jerks.

She had a history of boyfriends and a couple of pregnancy scares in the past. I tried to hit on her during first year but she was too smart for my unpolished charms and unflattering looks. It is always easy being the second or the third boyfriend. Making the girl shed her inhibitions the very first time is such a pain! The *It's-okay-everybody-does-it-you're-not-a-slut* routine takes a lot of effort and patience.

Nevertheless, I found her endlessly charming. Vernita had perfected the art of verbal abuse, which I still hadn't. Since I didn't drink, I just had to learn to abuse. Failing at *both* meant that you were socially ill-equipped.

'Hey, going out somewhere, dick?' she asked.

She wore a white Esprit T-shirt that clung to her best assets. A slight rip and the tee would have split all the way down the middle. Her skinny Levi's showed off an ass a million girls would kill for. She hadn't missed going to the gym a single day in the last three years and it showed—her body-fat percentage was abysmally low. I was lucky to see her every day and unlucky to have seen her only with her clothes on. A sight like her was a rare thing in an engineering college such as ours.

'No plans for the day,' I said.

'Why so?'

'My attendance is a little short, so I'll attend classes. I am leaving for Mishra's class. Coming?'

'Obviously. You are not the only one with short attendance here.'

Strangely enough, every year the most worthless kids found their way into the mechanical department, and were tortured endlessly for even the slightest mistake, which they made with gay abandon. We attended all our classes while the students of other hallowed branches—IT, computers and the like—wasted away their time at the nearby coffee shops or on the college lawns. But at the end of four years, they were the ones who lapped up all the high-paying jobs.

It was gut wrenching to see guys who hadn't risked being incinerated in an induction furnace or having a limb sawed off on a lathe machine end up having better lives. All they did day in, day out was sit in front of the computer and write lines of code. No lathes, no welding shops, nothing.

No lecturers, even.

On the other hand, we were blessed with the most frustrated and sadistic lot of teachers, none of whom had completed their PhDs in less than a decade. They were the *dumbest* of the lot. Nevertheless, given their limited intelligence and knowledge, their urge to teach was exemplary. It takes a brave man to pretend he is wise when he is not. The combination of these teachers, the lack of girls (Vernita was the only one in our class!), and an uncertain future made the students of mechanical engineering the most frustrated in the entire college. The heaviest drinkers, smokers and dopers of the lot! And when some of us, defeated by life, go on to become professors, the vicious cycle goes on!

The class went as usual. The frontbenchers jotted everything down, the students in the middle rows pretended to write what the professor said and the backbenchers slept, talked, or texted on their phones.

'Any plans with Smriti tonight?' Vernita asked.

'Not quite. Things have been a little rocky. It's not going too well. We're having some problems.'

'Don't give me that crap.'

'Seriously.'

'I know you better than that, shit face. You are playing, aren't you? It's your bullshit *Let's break up* game again.'

Smriti and Vernita were one-time school buddies but at some point somebody bitched about somebody to somebody, and everybody came to know about it and things fell apart. I never went into the details because I have never completely understood what ticks off women. Both of them tried to make me understand but I never got it. Even the most intelligent men find it hard to understand why girls fight. And I was just a dumb guy.

'No, believe me, I am not. I really want to be with her but things are not going well.'

'Whatever. Don't you hurt the poor girl. I don't think you ever loved her.'

'Of course, I love her,' I protested. 'I won't hurt her.'

'Anyway, how much did you score this time? I got a damned sixty-two. I think all the professors are just biased against me,' she said.

'Sixty-nine per cent,' I said, proudly.

Since Vernita and Smriti weren't friends any longer, I could afford to tell her what I had really scored. Smriti would never know that I had lied about my marks or that I had improved over the last semester, with a good five per cent increase.

'What the fuck? That's five more than what you scored in the last semester. Congratulations, Deb!'

'Yup. Thanks,' I beamed.

'I am sure you study the whole night and don't tell us. You are taking tuitions, aren't you? Such an asshole,' she said and made no attempt whatsoever to hide her displeasure.

# 3

'Whoever goes to a place like that?' I asked, voicing the opinion of Virender and Yogender, who were still swearing at us for dragging them out of their hostel. JCB was the most notorious hostel that year because of these two guys. Every few days, they would catch some innocent guys, make them throw a big booze party on some pretext and turn the washrooms in the hostel into a puke dump.

'It'll be fun, trust me. And we can't let these free passes go waste! You have no idea how rare these are,' Shrey said.

'Shut up, man! Let us go to a coffee shop or watch a movie. Why drive all the way there? We have bloody exams in a few days,' I suggested, not so politely.

'Deb, just because you scored sixty-nine this time doesn't mean you get to do all that exam bullshit in front of us. Are you coming along? Yes or no?' Vernita looked at Viru and Yogi.

They were small-town guys—one from Ludhiana and the other from Jalandhar—and not quite the smoothest, but they complemented each other perfectly. The huge, muscled Virender with his stand-up acts and the thread-thin Yogender with his cutting one-liners did pretty well together. It was hard to imagine them without each other. And just like every other guy I hung around with, they were obsessed with, well, you know! Most of our lives—the engineers', that is—revolved around one focal point: girls.

'Yes, sure,' they echoed. Viru and Yogi usually tagged along with us whenever we went out somewhere.

Arguing with Shrey and Vernita was something they couldn't do. Moreover, they knew as long as Vernita was in the scheme of things, there would be free alcohol which was a change from their Iodex and cough syrup highs. For Vernita, it meant company, as I didn't drink and Shrey had taken to pretending it was cool not to drink since he lost a beer challenge to Vernita way back in first year.

'But guys, seriously! There is nothing out there. It's defunct and nobody goes there these days, definitely not in this weather,' I said but it fell on deaf ears. They had already made up their minds. When Shrey suggested something, everyone assumed it would be something cool to do.

The only incentive of going to an amusement-cum-water park was seeing Vernita in a skimpy bikini. I knew she would not wear anything like that, but the one-in-a-million chance was motivation enough to say yes. Even if she didn't, there was nothing to lose. The *wetter* she was, the *better* she was.

Moreover, amusement parks were places I could actually prove to be a greater *man*. Big rides didn't scare me. As a kid, my sister and my father used to taunt me every time I backed away from the prospect of being flung out to hell from those huge rides! But eventually, I got used to them. Now, it was fun to prod big guys who turned blue and vomitted on scary roller coaster rides.

It was February and it was getting warmer. However, not warm enough to be in Splash, the amusement-cum-water park. But we still went there because Shrey wanted to do something *different*. Normal life is always too boring for him.

We entered the amusement park section and saw that most of the rides were hanging together by a thread of rust. It looked like it had been lying abandoned for a decade. Both Shrey and I—we weighed in the mid eighties—decided against subjecting the already crumbling rides to the unconquerable forces of our mammoth thighs and bulky asses. We chose the water rides instead.

We hired swimming costumes that were supposedly free size but were anything but *freeing*. They almost squeezed my balls into one bigger one. I was getting tired of looking around every time to check if anybody was watching before I could pull out the costume, which kept burying itself deep inside the crevice between the two huge masses of flesh that jutted out from my back. One could have studied human anatomy and the reproductive organs of men by looking at me or Shrey. Yes, it was that tight!

We moved out from our washrooms and what greeted us wasn't actually unexpected but it still left us gaping in shock.

Our *different* day out had empty slides, water with spit and greenish-black algae floating on it, three guys with protruding crotches in undersized costumes and a couple of attendants, woken up from their slumber by the sight of a girl in hot pants and a delightfully tight white shirt that would have turned transparent if she had stepped into the water. An *amazing* thought.

'Now what, guys?' Vernita asked, as she looked around. If we were not to die of pneumonia, then we would certainly die of every water-borne disease known to man.

'Let's look around. There must be a cleaner pool,' Yogi said and left with Viru. The quicker they found one, the sooner we would leave and the earlier we would reach a cheap bar where they could drink themselves silly.

'If you look at it in the broader sense, it's not as bad as it looks. The water below the surface shouldn't be that bad. The algae must be doing a great job of keeping the water clean and healthy. Therefore, if we can just skim the muck off the surface, we have a great day at hand. At the National Physical Laboratory, there is a . . .' Shrey said pulling his swimming trunks down from beneath his crotch.

'Do you even think before you open your mouth or is even that mechanically controlled by some guy in the *National Physical Laboratory*?' Vernita barked at Shrey who had gone into one of his ultra-hi-tech nonsensical talks which we had come to hate.

Meanwhile, all I could look at was the sun glistening off Vernita's legs. I seemed to have a fetish for legs. How could somebody go on with some technological bullshit or look for cleaner water when you had an option of staring at a half-naked girl. It was not something that happened every day! Maybe they weren't just normal. I was *normal*.

'Nice, sexy legs! I could just eat you up. Aren't you just the hottest?'

Vernita stared at me as if she would gobble me up alive. I would have loved that look if it had been in a closed dark room, but not there. *Shit! How could I say that out loud?* I mean everybody knew I was, let us say, a little *overt* with my sexual references and innuendoes, but this was downright ridiculous. *I couldn't have just said that*.

I hadn't.

*He* had.

There he stood, as if mocking Shrey and me. He was a little shorter than Shrey but had a body that was custom-made to turn on women. Huge biscuit-like abs, big cannonball shoulders, rippling muscles and a great tan that would have had Brad Pitt looking for cover. The same costume this time seemed to be made to his specifications. He didn't have an ounce of fat on his body whereas we had oodles of it spilling out from all sides of our trunks.

I wished his sculpted body was the only good thing about his body but it wasn't.

He was a smooth guy from south Delhi and was friends with everybody who mattered. He was Vernita's boyfriend and that's what I hated about him the most. Not that I envied him, as I knew Vernita made for a lousy girlfriend, blaring and knocking the daylights out of him 24/7. She made life tough for her boyfriends when she left no stone unturned to freak the guy out every time her period was late. She *never* trusted condoms. Or self-control. She was one of a kind.

'Hi, baby!' he said as she hugged him in what seemed like

the assembling of a high-precision machine. Each of her curves fit into every muscle on his body as if they were two halves of a beautiful, curvaceous, sensual sculpture. It was so incredibly sexy that we almost started shifting in our places, embarrassed, as if we had been caught watching porn.

Shrey and I had this peculiar habit of finding flaws in perfectly normal guys to feel better about ourselves, often non-existent flaws. Yet, Shrey and I had found nothing wrong in *him*. But we weren't used to regarding anybody as competition and called this the '*nobody-is-a-stud-except-me*' phenomenon. Every guy in Delhi suffers from this. We think we are studs, though we are really not.

It was a good thing that Tanmay was always busy managing college affairs, looking good, sculpting his body or trying to top his exams! The less time he spent with us, the better we felt about ourselves. He was every girl's dream come true—sincere, intelligent, hot and unbelievably soft-spoken.

'Anybody who wants to die today? Pneumonia, cholera, typhoid, tuberculosis? We've found just the place to do that. A cleaner pool,' said Viru, rubbing his hands with obvious delight.

'We can all now die an excruciatingly slow death. The filth in that pool isn't as deadly as this one,' Yogi added with obvious sarcasm. 'Hi, Tanmay!'

'Let's go, honey. It will be fun,' Tanmay prodded Vernita.

'Can't you see the water here? Are you out of your mind? I would rather kill myself than step inside the water,' Vernita shot back.

'The first person who has talked sense today,' Yogender butted in.

'At least let's go and check out the water. The tissues of our bodies are made of cellulose and proteins which actually store sunlight and release its energy according to Planck's law of irradiation where the wavelength is so controlled that maximum heat is released, according to the Dasons' formulae, and our body slowly adapts to the . . .' Shrey started again.

'Jump right in and stay put for an hour or stay shut,' Yogi interrupted thankfully.

'Fucking true, man! Great job, Yogi. Let's see you prove your National Physical Laboratory bullshit right here . . .' said Vernita and winked at Yogi.

'Let's do it then,' Shrey said.

'Let's do it? Are you serious? Are you serious?' Viru exclaimed, as he looked wide-eyed at Shrey.

'Yes, I am damn *serious*.'

'No! Don't bullshit. Three years. Three damn years,' Viru said in a strangely accusing tone.

'*What?*'

'For three years I thought you were this really funny guy who could relate the colour of one's pee to the kind of rum he prefers. Tell me this is the only time you ever talked sense. Tell me all the other times you were just joking!' Virender chuckled.

'Cut it out, guys! This isn't bad . . . one . . . two . . . three . . . just three floating blobs of spit,' I said as I fished out my costume yet again before it was swallowed up by the two humungous blobs of fat.

'Heaven itself!' Yogi smirked.

'See, there is nothing much in this place anyway, so rather than just standing here half-naked, let's all jump in and make something of it, at least,' Tanmay said with a seriousness appropriate only for practical vivas.

The only slide that was working was a 50-foot tall slide that came down vertically. Quite visibly, everybody wet their pants just at the thought of riding that one. I grabbed the opportunity to yet again mock the weak-hearted. After my schooldays had ended, I never missed an opportunity to do that.

'So, are you sure?' Tanmay asked, almost nervously.

*This is new.*

'Of course, I am sure. I have been doing this since I was a kid. I don't know why you guys are so afraid. They are just slides, man,' I said, rubbing it in.

'Okay, see you on the other side.'

As I stepped out onto the ledge, the first doubts crept in. There was no way this was 50 feet. I was floating in the clouds. And all

I could see of the others were their tiny little heads. Nevertheless, egged on by their shouts—and more importantly, by my ego—I lay down on the ledge, one hand stuck to my thighs and the other grabbing hold of the attendant, trying to streamline myself as much as I could. The attendant let go.

*Bucsssshuuuwaaaaaahh!*

I was numbed. The ice-cold water gushed into my nostrils and lungs. It felt like a thousand hands had slapped me on my chest and legs. The impact was terrible. The bump in the slide had unbalanced me and I splashed into the water side-first with my legs and arms wide open. It was surely not the most graceful of dives, and definitely not the kind that I expected from myself. I could already hear their chuckles.

*Make a great appearance out of the water and it will just be fine.*

So I sucked in my paunch and braced myself for a *Casino Royale*-style emergence from the water. I pulled myself up from the pool, helped only by my not-so-muscled arms and felt the water slip down my curves à la Daniel Craig. And seeing the others' eyes stuck on me, it seemed as if I had actually pulled it off. Their eyes were fixed on me as if they were dumbfounded by my stupendously courageous achievement. They followed every step I took as if to register whatever I did, so that they could replicate it when they went in next. Or they were still scared?

'So?' I broke the silence. 'How was it? Pretty great, huh?'

'Hmmm,' said Vernita, looking at me as if to check whether I had managed to come out in one piece. 'Not that impressive! I had expected something ... more. You know. It's just not enough.'

'Not that I am interested, but yes, not impressive enough ... maybe just enough,' said Yogi.

'Yes, but I still want to know, Deb, with something like *that*, how do you get your girls to stick around you? They must be *really* in love with you not to leave you after they see that,' Viru said, with barely concealed laughter.

'It's a miracle, really. I told you guys, something *different*. I told you that Deb has something that we don't,' added Shrey.

'Talent, maybe? Not everybody has it,' I said, still confused about what they were getting at, but I decided to play along. 'I am thankful that I do.'

'Not many need it, but you do need a lot of talent with *that*,' said Tanmay and they started laughing their brains out. Viru nearly fell into the water and as my eyes followed him, that's when I saw *it* floating on the water.

My trunks? *My* swimming trunks? *Oh. Fuck. My trunks!*

All this while, I had been standing stark naked with my stomach pulled in, posed as a playboy bunny, and I had let them make a fool out of me. Not only that, I had joined in too. I will never live this down, I thought as I jumped into the water and with one fluid motion covered what wasn't *impressive* according to their standards. But the laughter didn't stop. Would never stop. This was just that kind of incident that tends to stick for life. It would now and forever be *Deb and the floating trunks*.

As if it wasn't enough to bury my head in the sand and nuke myself into oblivion, I was gripped by the question that would trouble me for a long time to come. *Was I small?* I kept telling myself that size doesn't matter. But then why did Vernita come out with the '*not impressive*' remark? Had she expected *more*? My mind wandered to the time when Vernita got dumped once and went around telling everyone that the guy had a *minuscule* penis. I thought she was being revengeful.

To make things worse, they weren't the least bit interested in the water slides or the water park any more. They now had an issue of national importance to discuss. Very minutely, indeed. How I wished I could go back in time and settle for a coffee rather than the goddamned Splash! Even the Mechanical Department canteen would have been a better option.

'So, Deb, we had fun, right? We got to see your talents. And something more!' said Yogi as he walked out of the washrooms wiping the non-existent water off him. He even smeared moisturizer on his whole fucking body. Oh hell, was I irritated! The damned costume had left an intricate design on my waist but couldn't hold on to me. Damn *Made in China*.

'Deb, it's not that bad, you know. These things can be corrected. Electric impulses in the ultrasonic range can elongate certain tissues in the body if delivered in conjunction with some microwaves. People are known to add a few inches in a matter of months. Don't feel depressed,' Shrey said.

'National Physical Laboratory?' asked Viru.

'Nope! It's all thanks to www.enlarge.com,' Shrey grinned.

'What the hell were you doing at www.enlarge.com?' I asked, trying to shift the focus off me.

'A friend in need is a friend indeed,' Yogi said and they all burst out laughing. It's never easy to be the butt of all jokes and certainly not when it pertains to the most sensitive of areas. Fortunately enough, we left the park soon as there wasn't much to do and the conversation shifted to other things.

'Hey, Tanmay, how're Mom and Dad? Still minting money in the Middle East?' Viru asked as he killed the engine.

The plan to go to a nearby bar had been dropped. The sun had set. The car was parked on a deserted road. The doors flung open. A bottle of rum, roadside chicken, a couple of Cokes, a few cigarettes, a few plastic glasses, car speakers blaring in the moonlight, and the party was complete. Who cared about the ambience!

'They are good there. Mom just got a promotion, so she might just hang around there a little longer than planned. Avantika is there, too. She will be back in a few days,' Tanmay replied.

His parents had been living in Dubai for the last many years and his father had a huge auto-dealerships business there. That explained all the expensive labels on his clothes or maybe they just looked like labels when he wore them.

'So, what's *Avantika* up to these days?' Yogi asked as he rolled another joint.

'Nothing much, doing B.Com. honours at SRCC and preparing for the CAT. She doesn't have too many classes these days now that the semester's almost over, so she took the first flight out. She hadn't seen Mom and Dad for a while,' he said as he stretched out on the car bonnet.

Now that fascinated me—'*she took the first flight out*'. As if it cost pocket change. Whatever happened to booking early and saving money?

However, what fascinated me more was Tanmay's sister. Going by Tanmay's looks and his mom—who, when we had met her on her few visits to Tanmay, looked like his older sister—Avantika must be a definite possessor of some great genes.

'Now that Deb is a little preoccupied with some *small* issues, I thought I would ask something on his behalf,' Yogi said, as he settled before the front tyre and took a long drag. 'Is she single?'

The expected giggles had now started to rankle. I mentally thanked Yogi for doing the needful.

'Yes, kind of. She has a boyfriend she has been trying to get rid of for quite some time now. From the moment she said yes, actually, but it's not working out.'

'So, Deb? Are you interested? Oh, maybe you won't take the chance. Now that we know your *little* secret!' Vernita said, mocking me. She climbed up the bonnet and deposited her body into Tanmay's arms.

'Not interested,' I said, refraining from strangling her.

'Good for you. She has a penchant for beer-swigging, fast-driving, rich assholes, anyway. The kind of guys you wouldn't like to face unless you have a death wish,' Vernita said.

'You have a girlfriend, too, right Deb? Smriti? That cute medical student?' Tanmay asked.

'We are kind of breaking up,' I said as I sat beside Shrey on the road. Such answers were always a reflex action for me. I was always either single or in the process of being so.

There we were, a bunch of aimless kids in the middle of a deserted road, half of us knocked out either outside or inside the car. We were in a premier college that guaranteed a placement, and we cared about nothing else. We had four years at an engineering college to kill. And we were doing it with a vengeance, with a smile and a bottle of rum on our lips.

# 4

*I saw them, my schoolmates, looking for me in my college armed with rulers and stretched, wet, twisted handkerchiefs, smoking like chimneys, one arm around their girlfriends, who found something immensely funny in their boys chasing down a fat, crying Debashish Roy. I stumbled on a step and fell headlong. I looked up at them, and they looked down at me—mocking, laughing at what lay between them.*

I woke up, it was 6 p.m. *No way! Machine design, tomorrow.* I rushed to the bookshop.

Life at DCE had been quite the same for the last three years. We were supposed be studying in a college that oscillated between the seventh and fifteenth rank when it came to countrywide engineering-college rankings, but academics were a joke in our college.

The DCE campus was a huge one, definitely not as big as an Indian Institute of Technology or the Birla Institute of Technology and Science in Pilani, but big enough. Located on the outskirts of Delhi and Haryana, the hostel students had the opportunity of counting *real* cows when going to sleep. However, being close to the Haryana border meant guys could get high like airplanes every night on cheap liquor and weed.

Beyond all the alcohol and the desperation to get laid, it was a college of Indian Institute of Technology rejects, who were just short of genius material when they entered the college. But four years of mind-numbing college had dulled their brains.

'Hi! Which book do we have to study from, Pandey or Lahiri?' I asked Vernita when I called her from the bookshop. I hoped she would say Pandey as I was in no mood to shell out an extra three hundred bucks for a book that would grace my table for less than eight hours. It was March and my sixth semester's mid-term exams had started.

'Lahiri is better. All the *ghissu*s are doing it from that book.'

'But the other one is thinner and cheaper.'

'Yes, I know. That's why the rest of the class is preparing from it.'

'Which book do you have?'

'Both. But I won't prepare from the heavy one, except for a few important topics,' she said

Of course, she had both the books. The seniors were extra generous when it came to Vernita. She had never a bought a book. *Ever*. Her investment in gorgeous bras always paid off in seniors fighting over who would give her their books first.

And Shrey had his friends in IIT, who gave him their books, so I was the only one buying them hours before the exam.

'Okay, I am buying Lahiri. Text me the tentative course,' I said, as I disconnected the call.

There were predominantly three kinds of people in my class. The first kind, the *ghissu*s, attended all the classes, regardless of how dumb the professor was. Their exam preparations began a month before. They created the huge *tentative* course. The next group consisted of the ones who attended classes but never studied. These brainlessly copied what was written on the board just to remain in the good books of the professors! They would generally start studying around ten days before the exams. These guys created the *final* course. They would slash and cut out the useless or tough stuff from the course that was either too hard or had not reared its head in the question papers of the last five years.

You can do without professors. You can do without classes. But life is tough without the previous years' papers.

The final course was finalized the night before the exams and this is what the last group waited for. We belonged to the *last* group. Though the first group people invariably topped, that did not mean the people from the other groups couldn't do so. It always boiled down to the last day. However, it was more likely that someone who had been studying for the last month or ten days would put in more effort than the non-serious ones who bought their books the day before. It was all about the person who ran the last mile faster.

'How much have you done?' I asked Shrey on a conference call.

'I haven't started yet. I was out for a football match, came and slept off.'

'Shrey, are you crazy? Eleven chapters. And its machine design, not some bloody elective,' Vernita barked, as expected. Girls generally panic more in exam-time situations. How often had we seen Vernita begging for an increase in marks even for copying the questions down! She could afford to do that. She was hot and if I were a professor, I would have loved to have Vernita down on her knees, *begging*.

'How much have you done?' Shrey asked, as if it mattered to him.

'Three chapters. I'll sleep for a little now. Wake up at four and do the rest. Besides, the exam is at two in the afternoon. You, Vernita?'

'You have done three? I am still stuck on the second chapter. Okay, bye.'

The conference call ended, in the usual abrupt manner. Shrey showed no signs of concern about whatever had just happened. He would probably play FIFA on his PlayStation for a while. I was happy that I had finished more chapters than Vernita and she, as usual, was panicking. I knew Vernita would crack any question if it came from the portion she had studied. She was way more intelligent than me. I just memorized whatever I couldn't understand and not many things got a coveted place in my minuscule brain.

Shrey did neither. He waited until two hours before the exam and asked people to say out loud whatever they had studied and that's where his preparations ended. It was nothing short of a miracle that he managed to pass in a few subjects.

'Get up, you stinking asshole. It's eight in the morning.'

Vernita had been saying the same thing for the last minute or so and all I was doing was breathing heavily on her. This time, I had to react. And fast. I quickly did my mental calculation and checked if I could still pass with no major glitches if I slept for another half an hour. I couldn't.

'Hmmm . . . I am up.' I wasn't. 'How much have you done?' I croaked.

'I am totally screwed. Just done five chapters. I feel like crashing right now. Wake me in ten minutes. I am leaving the last three chapters. Are you doing them?' she asked.

'Obviously, I am.'

'And keep calling up Shrey, too. He has just done one chapter and is sleeping. Bye.'

Being a day scholar is a tough job. You have nobody to shake you until you wake up, nobody to give you an idea about things to study and nobody to copy *farra*s from. You miss out on exam-time bonding and you miss out on great friendships. But then you have a life outside the four walls of the college and crappy hostel food ceases to be your main concern. I had a *life* outside college. I had been too busy for most of the *could-be-friends* in college.

Coming back to exams, Vernita always relied on *quality* and I on *quantity*. I knew my pea-sized brain wouldn't stand me in good stead if the questions were a little twisted. It happened again as it did on every single exam day: Vernita snoozed through her alarms and I skimmed through the course in a tearing hurry.

Though, I did dutifully take time out to rebuke Smriti for her irresponsible behaviour—calling me up only twice to wake me up when Vernita, who was *just* a friend, had called up some fifteen times. Finally, Smriti was giving me valid reasons to be pissed with her and doubt her commitment to our relationship.

However, there was no trace whatsoever of Shrey, till he finally called to say he had gone for a jog and had left his cell phone at home. It was ten, he had still done just one chapter, which according to him was disconnected from real life machine problems, and hence he left it midway. *Same old story.*

I ended up finishing the course half an hour before time, sulking about the slipshod way I had done the course. *Same old story.*

On the other hand, Vernita's preparations ended as they always did, with a few chapters left out, fifteen minutes into exam time. She was always the last person to move into the exam hall. Once in, she became this goddess of concentration, never looking up for one moment.

Exactly one and half hours into the exam, the inevitable churning started in the restless bowels of the third category of students. That's when these people were most inclined to use the washroom. Going by the time they took to relieve themselves, it seemed as if after all these years they had finally discovered that they had a rectum.

Vernita and I used to do that, too—what was called *Toiletization of Notes*—but we restricted it to desperate situations. For Shrey, it was a way of life.

'You did this question? I did this and seems like nobody else did. I wonder if I did this right,' Vernita said.

'No, I did not,' I said.

This was the time which I never looked forward to—the after-exam time. Vernita was used to cracking the toughest questions in the exam and flaunted the fact all day long or until the time you acknowledged her genius. I doubt whether I had ever scored outside the theory questions in the four years of college. All I did in the exams was look for the *Write-short-notes-on questions*, the *why* and *how* questions and try to fill up pages answering them.

Typically, Shrey did neither. He just created a new answer, a new theory for the age-old concepts based on some experience of his at the National Physical Laboratory. He spent the most part of his time after the exam engrossed in explaining his theories to the dumbest person of the class or a hapless junior or sometimes even the canteen boy. He had a life. Without marks, though.

But his businesspeople parents hardly cared. Neither did he.

Not that my parents were too interested in how I did in my exams. They had bigger troubles. My sister wanted to get married to someone from a different community. My marks could wait. So could the long due appreciation for my hard-earned sixty-nine per cent.

~

'Hurry up! *Orra kintu esshe jaabe je kono shomoy* (They will be here any moment),' Dad shouted as he started stacking at least twenty serving dishes with different food items neatly.

Oh, didn't I tell you? Yes, I am a Bengali. We talk a lot, we shout a lot, we argue a lot and we are a perennially hyper-vocal community.

'They have just left. They will still take two hours to get here,' my sister said irritably.

But dads know it all and dads are always right. My dad, too, like all other dads in the universe and beyond, was just too paranoid about being on time. It was my elder sister's *aashirwaad*. That's the Bengali equivalent of the Punjabi *roka*. Unlike the Punjabis, it's a homebound affair. In Delhi, it was treated as yet another opportunity to flaunt their immensely *hard-earned* money.

Anyway, it was hard for me to imagine Sonali, my sister, getting married. I mean, she still hadn't got out of talking to her imaginary friend and shouting at me in loud guttural Hindi, riling Mom and Dad out of their wits in the process. But I guess those things were not meant to stop, ever.

Also, my sister was twenty-four. That wasn't late for marriage and definitely not late by Bengali standards, but delaying it would mean risking suitable Bengali grooms. Bengali men have these strange tendencies to either fall in love and get married or not get married at all.

Bengalis, as a rule, fall in love way too often. My sister had as well and that too with a Haryanvi Jat, who was by no standards the dream groom my parents had pictured. Not only did his Jat image not go down well with my dad's academic outlook and my mom's kohl-lined eyes and the big, forehead-covering bindi she was partial to, he earned less than my sister—a cardinal sin. Moreover, my other elder sister, Moushmi, had found a husband that every girl in this country dreams of—an Indian-Institute-of-Management-Ahmedabad graduate. They were settled in London and spent their free time sailing in Alaska.

'Advertising?' Dad exclaimed when Sonali put forward the proposal for the first time.

'Why not engineering? Who on earth does advertising?' My exasperated mom said, as if my sister had just decided to marry a leper. Maybe that would have been better.

'Mom, I do. And so did *didi*!'

'Yes, you do. But you are a girl. And I wasn't keen on you doing it either. But Moushmi found someone who doesn't! *Her* husband is from an IIM. What will people say if you get married to a boy in advertising? Why would a sane person ever do advertising? What kind of parents would allow that?'

For my parents, the world was run by four kinds of people—engineers, doctors, lecturers and, lately, MBAs. All other professions ranging from lawyers to IAS officers were for *stupid* people, who either couldn't clear entrance examinations or had the perseverance to stick around for ages till they made it to the civil services list.

'Why not?' my sister shot back.

'How can you even think of marrying someone who earns less than you? There is no money in advertising and neither is it a respectable field to work in. All kinds of strange things go on there.'

'Dad, I work there, and I know better.'

'No, you don't. You were just fooled by this Jat. I am sure he is after our property. You haven't told him about our houses in Vasant Kunj and Gurgaon, have you? I am sure you have.'

'No, Mom, he is richer than our entire extended family combined. He owns a lot of property and farmlands in Gurgaon and money,' I tried to help. 'Ohh! I get it. *You* are after *his* money!'

I regretted it as soon as I had said this. It would have been a great joke; I had just chosen the wrong time to say it. They stared at me, as if I had disrespected Rabindranath Tagore or Sourav Ganguly. Actually, that would have been probably much *worse*.

'So, are you trying to say we will let you marry a good-for-nothing man just because his father is rich? What does his dad do?'

'He worked with the customs department and now he has his own business in import-export,' she said.

*Silly*, I thought, knowing what my parents thought about customs and import-export. Both these professions topped my parents' list of the most hated professions, giving stiff competition to pot-bellied property dealers and auto spare parts suppliers. I just knew it was over for her and the guy. Rich people cannot be just rich. They have to be corrupt too.

'Oh, so now you want to marry the good-for-nothing son of a smuggler who is in advertising?' my mom said and glanced at Dad to take it from there.

'Why would anyone quit a government job and start a business? And where did he get all that money to start his smuggling business? He is a swindler and a smuggler. One raid from the vigilance department and both he and his father will be behind bars,' Dad said.

It had been thirty years since my dad began working in a public-sector undertaking—in short, semi-government—and quite understandably, he saw no reason for someone to quit a low-paying but comfortable government job.

'It's not that. His father had acquired acres of farmland and he sold them off and bought some more and it went on.'

'Okay, so now he is a good-for-nothing son of a smuggler, farmer and a drunkard,' Mom said.

'A drunkard?' Sonali asked dejectedly, not wanting to fight his case any more.

'I am sure he drinks . . . and beats up his wife, too. Would you like to marry someone like that?'

'Mom!'

'*Ar kicchu bolte hobe naa (*No discussions any more). It is decided. You will never talk to that guy again. I will not let an uneducated smuggler marry my daughter,' Dad said.

This, along with similar numerous conversations, catastrophic astrological predictions and examples of how love marriages had failed around them, sounded the death knell for Paresh Ahlawat. My sister finally relented. Slowly, she began to see the upside of getting married the conventional way. She realized that with her cute looks, she was a sought-after commodity in the Bengali marriage scene! That worked better than my parents' incessant hard talk.

What followed was my sister's spree of trying out and rejecting different guys on grounds varying from 'strange teeth' to 'mismatched footwear'. Every possible attribute was scrutinized in excruciating detail. She had some high standards to match up to. She would by no means get someone who was in any way inferior to Moushmi's husband—the suave IIM guy. So it was bye-bye for the strangely named, rich Jat.

*Abhishek weds Sonali*. That sounded nice.

Abhishek was an electronics engineer with a hefty package who lived alone in Delhi. The last part made him extremely desirable in the marriage market. Constant bickering with your in-laws is the last thing you would want after a hard day's work.

Therefore, things fell into place in a jiffy. The guy was a little dumb or that's how I perceived him, as he didn't speak much. But the whole deal was nice overall. Cute, geeky-looking, hardly a problem handling such a wimp, my sister would have thought.

*Trrrrinnnng.* The bell rang.

They had arrived. Hugs, hugs, hugs. Nobody touches feet nowadays; it's considered regressive. And middle class.

'You are looking fabulous, Sonali,' her mom-in-law-to-be said. She was a small dark-complexioned lady with curly hair and the all-pervasive kohl and a huge bindi.

'Thank you!' my sister said and faked a shy expression. That could have very much translated into *Of course I am, I spent twenty minutes on it, and you would have disappointed me had you not said that.*

Suitable pleasantries were exchanged and everybody sat down for the ceremony where the pundit asked everybody to repeat some incomprehensible Sanskrit words over and over again in a sickening tone. It was over in fifteen minutes, giving way to the official photography session in which Sonali and Abhishek posed as a couple who had just found love. As soon as the elders got out of sight to look after the eating arrangements, I pulled out my camera and Sonali brought out her antics, flashing peace signs and what not. Sonali and I loved the look of bewilderment on Abhishek's face. Moushmi wasn't there or she would have added tremendously to the overall craziness quotient. We missed her.

Food was served and it smelled heavenly. Mom was a great cook and eating anywhere else always seemed like an insult to my taste buds and my gastronomic faculties. We had on the table two kinds of paneer, three other vegetarian dishes, two kinds of dal, three kinds of fish and a dish each of chicken and mutton. I was born lucky and destined to be 'healthy'.

Just as we were eating, Abhishek's mother looked at Sonali's hand and made a peculiar semi-angry, semi-shocked face. 'Show me your hand,' she said and almost politely grabbed my sister's hand. 'Isn't that *Asur*?' she asked, looking at her hand.

It turns out there are three *gan*s in Hindu astrology—*Devgan*, *Nargan* and *Asurgan*. Although they are determined by a careful study of horoscopes, a quick estimation can be made by seeing if the little finger is below the topmost line of the adjoining finger. Though not accurate, this is relied upon by many who believe in all this. For our family, it was all French.

'Yes the fingers, it's below the line. It's *Asurgan*. My son is *Devgan*.'

And that meant it was not a suitable match. Out of all possible matches between the *gan*s, *this* combination was not recommended. By some quirk of nature, if the match was still considered, the groom was bound to die.

'But the horoscopes don't show that,' Abhishek's dad added and continued, 'anyway, the finger-checking method is not that accurate, dear.'

'No, it is. It is something that we have followed for years now. Maybe the horoscopes had some flaw in them,' she shot back.

Now that was an outright insult. Was she suggesting we had fudged the horoscope to hook her son? That geeky, dumb guy? I could see the expressions change on everyone's faces.

For the next few seconds all we did was exchange confused glances. Mom was visibly worried, Dad seemed a little confused. Sonali and I looked at each other and tried hard to conceal a smile at whatever was happening around us. I always felt Sonali never took the marriage thing seriously. For her, it was just another day, another joke to smile through.

'We've got to check with the astrologer. Please excuse us,' Abhishek's mom said, tugging at her husband's shirt.

They stood at the other end of the room, talking over the phone in hushed voices. It seemed that the astrologer was assuring them that they had nothing to worry about.

'I am very sorry. My wife made a terrible judgment,' Abhishek's dad said, returning to the table. Mom would have fainted had they taken any longer. Dad was his usual composed self. 'I told you these things are not very accurate.' He looked at his wife.

Somehow, the tension on my mom's face had not eased. Dad didn't flinch. I saw a flash of disappointment on Sonali's face. She had expected more drama and I am sure she'd hoped for it to continue a bit longer. Unfortunately, that was not to be. Abhishek had been quiet all this while. Everything was wrapped up and they left after the gifts were exchanged.

As we sat down after winding up everything, my mom announced, '*Ami eta hote debo naa* (I will not let this happen). I am calling off the wedding.'

That was quite an overtly dramatic statement, considering that nobody except Abhishek's and our immediate families knew about the wedding until then. But then it sounded good and my mom was quite used inducing drama in boring situations! Dad didn't react and I guessed they had already discussed it.

'Does that mean we have to return this?' Sonali said, fiddling with a Mont Blanc set they had gifted her, and then immediately realized that was not the most appropriate thing to say and added, as if she was worried, 'I mean, *why*? What happened?'

'Did you look at the way they behaved? If something happens to the guy tomorrow, they will blame you outright. This won't do. And the guy? He didn't even take the slightest interest. Mamma's boy. That's why he doesn't speak much. His mother must have told him not to. I am sure she will forever bind him to her *pallu*. There is no way this is going ahead. Stop fiddling with that pen! We are giving it back.'

'But it's a Mont Blanc limited India edition! Only two hundred pieces exist.'

'Shut up, and take these glasses away.'

'As you say, but do rethink before giving these back,' she said as we laughed aloud.

I had expected some tension in the house, but there was hardly any. Sonali obviously didn't give a damn about the wedding per se. And I realized Mom and Dad were happier seeing their daughter fool around rather than see her get married off. They were content as they had weaned Sonali off her Jat boyfriend; her wedding could wait for now.

The wedding was called off a week later. All the gifts went back. The Mont Blanc didn't.

We couldn't *find* it.

~

Smriti was sad about the wedding being called off.

Her displeasure at my parents turning down someone from a different community was evident. Though it gave me another chance for banging the phone down on her and be unavailable for a day. She had called my parents *stupidly conservative*; not a very clever thing to do.

'I am sorry about the wedding,' Smriti said dejectedly.

'I am not. Nobody is. It's as if nothing ever happened. Sonali is doing okay.'

'So does that open up any doors for Sonali's boyfriend?'

'No, it doesn't. My parents won't ever allow me or Sonali to marry outside our caste. They are totally against it.'

I had to say that. I had been building up towards the break up for the past few weeks. My allegedly low scores in the examinations, dipping performance at the CAT coaching centre—I had planned to blame *her* for everything. Had those not worked, I intended to exaggerate the resistance my parents put up against Sonali going for a love marriage. I wanted to drive home the fact that we had no future together. And as she would know better, it's always easier to break up sooner than later.

'Smriti, I have to go now. Vernita is trying to call me,' I said, as I looked at my cell phone to swap my call.

1:03:27.

One minute was all I could bear her for. I would have faked a call waiting and put her hold until the time she would have hung up, had Vernita not called. But this time she had.

# 5

'**H**ey, Vernita! Need to show you something. Where are you?' I said, trying hard not to sound excited and give it away. Luckily, she was around. She was always around.

'See you in ten minutes at the Pitampura metro station,' she said.

'Why? Where are you going?'

'Where are *we* going, not where am *I* going. *We* are going to Greater Kailash. I need company. It's a long drive and the traffic is going to be horrible.'

'Fine,' I said and disconnected the line. I put together what I could find easily in my wardrobe and waited for her to reach the metro station. Like every girl, she had the right to be late.

'To his flat?' I asked her, as I got into her car.

Tanmay's sister had just landed and lately Vernita and she had become inseparable bitching partners.

'Naah! Not today. We'll just meet him. I did an assignment for him, so got to drop that, too,' she said.

It was strange to see Vernita behave like a quintessential girlfriend. She always made us believe that she used guys as toilet paper.

'Assignments? I thought all your assignments are done at his place, you know, behind closed doors,' I mocked.

'Shut up, fucker. I don't make out as often as you make it sound. And can you fucking stop saying things like that in the future? I don't like it,' she said.

She didn't sound convincing. She knew her libido and malleable morals were unmatched. I loved her for that. If only she hadn't told me that I was 'too good a friend to sleep with'. Damn, my *good*ness.

'Yes, you are the queen of chastity. You *never* make out. I think you're saving everything for after your wedding. Period.'

We didn't exchange any words for the next few minutes, though both of us knew that our fake anger wouldn't last.

'You wanted to show me something?' she asked what I wanted her to ask.

I wiggled my wrist, weighed down by a shiny glittering object, in front of her.

'What on earth is that? That must be worth a million fucking bucks.'

I liked that. It didn't happen that often. Money was never an issue for her. Her father was the most hardworking man there ever could be. He would be free on days when he worked for eighteen hours and his long hours at a college, bookshop and grocery centre meant a lot of easy money for Vernita.

'I found it in my bag. It's from Mom and Dad, the gift they had promised to get me if I got more than sixty-five per cent. I haven't told them that I found it.'

We drove on and I just kept talking about my newly acquired asset. She was annoyed by the time we reached Greater Kailash. It was the most posh area in Delhi where an average-looking girl would be conspicuous because of her averageness. Skinny jeans, great ass, stilettos, side-brushed hairstyle et al., there was no way anyone could tell one from the other. And you thought people in Chinese movies were indistinguishable.

A house in and around Greater Kailash was worth upwards of three crores, but for Tanmay it wasn't a big deal. He had two, one where he lived with his uncle and the other where he frequently made out with Vernita. I envied his life, and his inheritance.

We finally met him outside his uncle's house. Guys like him never had an off day. Short-cropped hair. Ripped jeans. An expensive-looking light pink shirt, half of which was tucked in while the rest hung out. Carefully done. *Bloody metro sexual.*

'Where is Avantika?' Vernita asked.

'She is coming in a moment. She is unpacking. And she is looking forward to meeting you.'

'Who? Me?' I was taken by surprise.

'Yeah,' he said, as he flicked out his expensively framed spectacles and put them on. Perfect. The humiliation was complete. Now, he looked hot *and* intelligent.

'And why is that? Why is she looking forward to meeting me?'

'I told her that you were this stud who could hook up with any girl,' Tanmay answered.

*Bloody asshole.* I was no stud, not even close. Guys like Tanmay are studs. We're just everyday guys whom girls go out with because they don't have better options. And such descriptions—a *stud who can hook up with anyone*—do nothing other than ensure failure. And *looking forward* sounded more like *Let-me-see-what-he-is-made-of.*

By now, I was already not too keen on meeting Tanmay's sister because of the kind of stories I had heard about her. Avantika had been to rehab for her drugs and alcohol problem but that was more than a year back. This is how Vernita had first described her. I had already started imagining Avantika as a leather-jacketed goth chick with piercings and tattoos crisscrossing her face and body. Not to forget the scary black nail polish on her long-grown nails. Such a girl would kick the daylights out of a nerd like me, I thought.

'Here she comes,' Vernita announced as she spotted Avantika in the distance.

That could have been the last thing I remembered from that day, had I had a weak heart. I passed out for a few seconds for sure. Even skipped a beat or two. Or maybe my heart just stopped beating altogether. I was choking and exploding and imploding, all at the same time. There was a strange churning in my bowels which threatened to consume me. I felt the blood rush down to the

ends of my arteries and burst into a million delightful explosions.
I could feel my brain crashing.

*I am going to die, I am sure.*

She was breathtakingly beautiful. I guess *unrealistically beautiful* was more appropriate! All the things I used to say to score with my ex-girlfriends had just come true. She was a dream. Even better; you couldn't even dream of something so perfect. Plastic surgeons still can't rival god, I thought.

She was indescribable. There is nothing better than a melancholic, beautiful face. The moonlight reflected off her perfectly sculpted face, and that seemed to be the only light illuminating the place. Somebody must have been standing nearby with a blower to ensure her streaked hair covered her face so that she could look even more stunning managing it. She had the eyes of a month-old child, big, limpid, constantly wet and screaming for attention. That perfectly drafted nose, flawless bright pink lips and a milky white complexion would have put Photoshop to shame. Oh hell, she was way out of my league. She was a goddamn goddess. Or was she the *devil*? Either way, she couldn't possibly be human.

I couldn't look beyond her face. Which was strange, as it had never happened before. Things were generally the other way round. But this time cup size didn't make the first impression.

'Hi, Vernita! How are you?' she said or rather sang. Something I would never know. They hugged. Vernita was half a foot shorter than her. Avantika had turned out in a simple dull brown kurta and jeans, without even a hint of make-up. I had definitely passed out, for I couldn't make out anything they talked about. I wasn't seeing right, I wasn't hearing right.

*Maybe I will just wake up in a while.*

'Hi! How are you, Debashish?' she serenaded me with a big golden harp, as I spotted her with a halo and two big white wings fluttering behind her, somewhere up in the clouds. Drugs? Alcohol? Leather? She wouldn't even know all that. However, I spotted remnants of a piercing just above her left eyebrow, and a tattoo peeked out from under her sleeve. A red swastika sign.

*Okay, relax, it's just a dream. It will be over in a while.*

'Hello?' Vernita pinched me and brought me to life.

'Are you all right?' Avantika asked.

'I am okay,' I said in what seemed like my fourth attempt at speaking after the first three ended in the soundless flapping of my tongue.

*Was I all right?* I was sure she was mocking me. Wasn't she aware that half the people she met either slipped into a coma or ended up thinking the meeting never happened, believing it to be a figment of their imagination. I was lucky I was still breathing, damn it.

'You guys talk, we will just take a walk,' Tanmay said, as he and Vernita turned away from us.

*Talk?* I was barely alive. I reminded myself to breathe. I looked at her and smiled stupidly. I wondered if her dog looked cuter than me.

'They look good. Don't they?' she asked.

Look good? *Only you look good! You beautiful angel-faced cherub. Go away! Don't make me fall in love!*

'Yes,' I answered. I tried not to stare into death.

'I didn't quite like Vernita when I first met her, but I kind of like her now. She is good fun. She is a little too brash, isn't she?'

'Yes.' *I like your nose, can I touch it?*

'What do you think? Are they serious?'

'Yes.' *I like your lips, are they for real?*

'Do you ever say anything more than that?'

'Yes.' *I like your eyes, can I lose myself in them?*

Was she kidding? Was I not trying? I could have said a million things, mostly stupid, but my senses had still not recovered from the temporary paralysis she had just subjected me to. I tried hard not to make eye contact and stay alive and there she was mocking me for my dumbness.

*She is here to mock you to death.*

'And why are you constantly looking down? I hope I am not that bad to look at?' she asked. Her voluminous eyelashes fluttered over her big *look-at-me* eyes.

That was it. I was right. She was the devil. She derived sadistic pleasure from pushing people off the edge to an unending pit of inferiority. I was not in any mood to relent and let this drop dead gorgeous witch have her way. I finally looked up.

'No. It's just that I have a slight sprain in my neck,' I said and mentally patted myself, as it happened to be the smartest answer ever under near fatal conditions.

'So tell me, how is Smriti? That's the girl you're dating, right?' she asked.

'She is fine,' I squeaked. *You are the finest. I love the way your hands clutch that handbag. Can I be the handbag? Can you turn me into one?*

'She has exams going on, if I am not wrong?'

'How do you know?' *Silly question. You are obviously a witch. You know everything.*

'A friend. She is studying in the same college as Smriti. Lady Hardinge Medical College. She is in the same year. Being a medical student is tough, she tells me.'

'Okay,' I nodded.

I was getting progressively uninterested in her. I saw no point in talking to her. I could never have her, not even in my wildest dreams. And she wouldn't make a good *friend*. It was hard not to fall in love with her. I knew I had to *not like* her. At least show that I did not like her. I was sure she wouldn't be too impressed with me either. I was just a dumb, average-looking bloke.

Also, *she was a witch.*

'So how is it going with her?'

'Not so fine. I guess we are moving apart,' I said.

She had started to sound more non-witch-like. Maybe she was human after all. Or a goddess.

'And why is that? I have heard she is a nice girl.'

'She says I am a little too distracting for her. That's why. You tell me, how is it going with your boyfriend?' *Can you turn me into your boyfriend? A friend? The fly buzzing across your nose?*

'Who? Shawar? Oh, you wouldn't want to know. I have been begging him to break up with me. But I guess he would have nothing else to do in life if we broke up. For now, he just irritates me,' she said. Her voice had more force and more bass than mine did. Every word seemed measured and rehearsed. Her style was unmatched, sophistication personified. She had the grace of a fifty-year-old sprinkled generously with the naughtiness of a fifteen-year-old.

'So you have started all over again? Give him a break; he is still your boyfriend,' Tanmay said as he approached us. 'I guess you should leave now, it's getting late.'

I had not expected them to return so soon. Maybe they hadn't gone for a long walk. Or maybe Tanmay didn't want me around his gorgeous sister.

'Yes, I guess so. Bye, guys. It was nice to meet you, Debashish. Jai Sri Guru,' she said as we shook hands. She turned around and left, leaving all of us in darkness . . . and I was still in the dream world the touch of her skin had transported me to. Her hand was soft as a little child's. I had never thought a handshake could be so overwhelming.

'What was this Jai Sri Guru thing she said when she left us?' I asked Vernita as we got into the car. I had taken well over fifteen minutes to realize that I had a stupid *take-me-home-I-am-your-puppy* smile on my face. I wiped it off.

'Nothing. Didn't I tell you once about Tanmay's belief in something called the Spirit of Living? Sri Guru heads it. She is quite into all that; it helped her to get out of all the shit she was in. So, did you like her?' she asked as we fastened our seat belts. Vernita wasn't the safest of drivers.

'Nah, not much,' I lied.

'You did *not*?'

'No, I did not!' I lied again.

'*Don't tell me!* Why?'

'She is pretty dumb.' Lying. Again.

'Dumb? Are you out of your *fucking* mind?'

'Anyway, I had expected her to be better-looking than she turned out to be.' And again.

That's it. Now I was certainly on my way to hell. But I couldn't have raved about her when I knew I wouldn't be a patch on the image Tanmay had brainlessly created. I could have boxed Tanmay's teeth in if he hadn't been Avantika's brother . . . and strong.

'That's strange. I haven't seen such a beautiful girl in a long time, Deb. I think she is very good-looking.'

'Anyway, where did she have to go?'

'She had a date.'

'With Shawar? I thought she hated him. That's what she told me.'

'No. With Paritosh. Her ex-boyfriend and Shawar's best friend before they broke up. He is back from the States for a week. Didn't you notice the tears? She *still* loves him. That's the reason why she started dating Shawar in the first place. To make Paritosh jealous. I don't know what Avantika sees in him. She should have been over him by now. The guy's a jerk.'

'Why did he dump her?'

'No idea. Nobody knows. That's the way those rich bastards are. They pamper you and promise you the world and then dump you without a reason.'

Now, Avantika started to sound more human. Somebody had dumped *her*. The guy had to be a freak. Vernita and I talked a lot more about her on the way back. Avantika had wanted to take up engineering but her parents had different plans for her. They wanted her to get married as soon as possible. She had fought her way through the years since she turned eighteen. Through rough relationships, hostile parents, drugs and alcohol. Her parents knew nothing about it. They had gotten used to the snubbing and vice versa.

It was strange to see how little they cared about her. They knew everything that Tanmay did, but, shockingly, they had no idea about Avantika's addiction. She had been a methamphetamine junkie. Ice, as it is popularly known. The first and only time Yogi and Viru used it, the high had lasted twelve hours—more than that of cocaine and LSD combined. They had wisely stayed away from it ever since. The trips often scar users for life.

This was 7 April 2007. The first day I met her.

~

'Don't tell me!' I exclaimed. 'I always knew it was *you*. It had to be *you*. This isn't real. I don't know how to thank you.'

'Yes, it was me,' Smriti murmured.

It couldn't be Smriti. It was a shimmering Tissot watch with a huge blue dial. The watch must have cost her a fortune! I had always wanted one. Or more.

'Do you like it?'

'Do I like it? Are you crazy? I am already in love with it. I've always wanted one of these.'

She hugged me as soon as I said this.

'Aw! You're so cute,' she kissed me. 'Happy six months' anniversary!'

*Six months' anniversary? Wait. What?*

It was the first time I was celebrating such a thing. It was only April and I felt like I had been with her since puberty—the good old days when hormones raged. Things had changed since then. Now even if she dressed up in leather, it would hardly make me unzip. Mannequins aroused me more. She had been around all these months despite the torrid time I gave her. I had ignored her on the grounds of illness/depression/bickering mom/friend troubles . . . the list was endless.

'Same to you. Sorry, I couldn't get you anything,' I said. I thanked god I hadn't. A hundred-rupee coffee mug with her name printed on it wouldn't have appealed to her for sure.

'It's okay; it's not for the anniversary. I just felt like buying it for you because you have been a great boyfriend.'

'And you have been a great girlfriend, the best a guy could ever ask for,' I said. If only I could tell her how much I wanted her hands off me while I was driving. One scratch on the car and Dad would kill me. I wondered if, in such a scenario, I could sell off the watch to get the car repaired and avoid getting beaten up.

'Thanks, there was something you wanted to tell me, Deb. What was it?'

'Did I? I don't think so.'

For the last few days, I had been preparing the ground to tell her that we should end the relationship because it wasn't going anywhere. But the damned watch was too beautiful to go ahead with the plan. What was I supposed to *tell* her? That I really wanted to break up? Tell her that she had been clingy for the last few months and I couldn't take it any more? Breaking up that day would have meant losing the watch. And *that* was unacceptable. I had earned it by being a *great boyfriend*.

'Love you.' She rested her head on my shoulder and snuggled.

'Love you, too,' I reciprocated and steadied the steering wheel. The watch gleamed in the light from the streetlamps.

It was getting scary. I never thought Smriti would ever be like those girlfriends who save for months together to surprise their boyfriends with gifts such as an expensive watch. I loved her, I thought. I could. *I had to*, at least for a while. She wasn't bad.

The watch was beautiful.

~

It was late at night and I had just gone to bed after stressing out on how I could get rid of the girl I had labelled the *best girlfriend ever* when my phone rang. The same ringtone is more annoying when it's a person you don't want a call from.

'Hi, Deb, guess what?' Vernita blared on the phone.

'Not interested. Let me sleep, witch.'

'Yup . . . you got it. I talked to Avantika about you and she isn't *interested*. She found you really dumb . . . and ugly, too, as far as I could make out.'

'Same here. I am not interested in her either. Go tell *her* that.' Click.

I hoped she would not tell her. I was right then: Avantika

didn't like me. I hated Vernita for proving me right. Avantika had seen me exactly as I was—*dumb and ugly*.

I didn't let that bother me as I had my placement interviews coming up and I was not in a position to waste my time on girls I found desperately short on grey matter and the ability to judge great guys. I tried hard but Shrey didn't buy *this* explanation.

I didn't want to talk about it and distract myself from the most important month of our time in engineering college. Placement is the one thing that is always on the minds of engineering students right from the time they enter college to when they leave it.

*What about after college? Where are you placed?*

These questions needed to be answered. The sooner the better. It is why we all took up engineering.

Though, I must mention here, Shrey was more worried about whether there was a better sex life in management schools in India or engineering colleges abroad. He had to make sure he made the *right* decision after college.

# 6

It was May and it was my first on-campus job interview. Four years of hard work or mucking around came down to this very moment. If you clear the interviews to a great paying job, no one cares how badly you might have screwed up your college academics. The tension in the Training and Placement Department was palpable. There was a presentation by the Human Resources Department of the hiring company of which I heard nothing. Nobody asked the question I wanted them to ask—what would the crowd be like? Everyone was busy counting how much they would get to spend, and were trying to find their way out of the winding lanes of Cost-to-Company, which sometimes accounted for the space you occupied in their office. Or the toilet paper you used. Anything to make sure the employees stay poor.

There was a written exam, which people found rather easy. Most hopefuls had their brilliant friends taking the exam on their behalf.

'Best of luck, ass. Do well,' Vernita said.

I texted Smriti saying I was busy in the presentation and would not be available for the next few hours or so. She had forgotten about my interview and I was not going to accept an excuse that we had not talked about *it* in over a month. She had not wished me luck. She was not serious about the relationship. She wasn't serious about my career, my future. I, of course, loved her and she was letting me down repeatedly. Things weren't looking good for our relationship. It couldn't go on like this.

'And we need a treat when you get through!' Shrey added.

'Shrey, I am telling you, there is still time. Why don't you at least try to sit for it? They hire everybody. Couldn't you at least fucking try?' Vernita asked.

For Shrey, it was the best shot at getting hired. With a lowly percentage like his, this was the only company that would take him. But he had a strong reason against trying out for the interview. 'My shirt isn't ironed and I have nothing to wear. If you think they would still take me despite a crumpled shirt, I am ready to give it a shot,' he had smirked. He believed that companies should hire on talent, not marks and crisp white shirts. His laxity and his ideals were not only weird and baseless, but often self-destructive.

'Vernita is right. You should give it a shot. Even if you don't get the job, you can keep it as your back-up plan,' I added.

'I don't want to. It is not about my shirt being unironed. I just don't want to sit for it. I am not interested,' he said. All three of us knew it was about *the formals*. And his silly ideals.

'Whatever, Shrey. I don't know why you act so smart,' Vernita quipped.

'I act smart? Why don't you sit for it, then?' Shrey retorted.

'I have better options. I have a better percentage, and unlike you, I don't have any back papers, get it?'

The HR guy appeared and called out some names for the interview. I was the third person to go in. I was nervous.

'How do you know I don't have any options? You should just shut up about things you don't know,' Shrey said.

'And you want to tell me that you know things? Fifty-two per cent? Eight back papers? You're amongst the lowest scorers in class! That is how you know things?' Vernita asked. You could always count on her being a big mouth.

'Oh, so our college marks tell us how much we know about

things? You know everything about everything? I know enough about the things I should know about. At least I don't go around with guys thinking it is *true* love.'

'Now that's totally off topic,' she protested. 'And my relationships are none of your business, and they are a lot more sorted than yours.'

'Sorted? What about Varun? Did you know he wasn't in love with you while you went around town telling everybody how into him you were?' Shrey asked. He had won round one and was talking nonsense.

'I don't want to talk about it. At least I don't say I love Tanmay and sleep around with others. *You* want to tell me what love is? Go and try to explain that to Vandana. The girl you claim you love but have been cheating on since DAY ONE!' she shouted.

Round two had begun. This was getting ugly.

They were doing a good job of keeping my nervousness at bay. I was called in. They left and I could see them taking different routes out of the T&P Department.

I took my seat and was greeted by a smiling, middle-aged man on the other side of the table. We shook hands. I was already sweating. His bald head shone.

'Let's start?' he asked and I nodded.

'Okay, Debashish, which computer languages do you know?' the interviewer asked. He was still smiling.

'I am afraid none, sir,' I answered, trying to sound confident.

'Why do you then expect an opportunity to work with us? Why should we choose you over the students from the IT department? They are better suited for the job, don't you think?'

'Yes, sir.'

'See, you understand. Then why you?' he leaned over the table and stared at me. I felt like squeezing the biggish blackish mole on his right cheek, which had a few strands of hair jutting out, as if trying to escape the blackness of it. Moles are such fascinatingly disgusting things that you can never take your eyes off them. No matter how hard you tell yourself not to stare at them, you end up doing just that. Especially if they come with hair, like this one did.

'I believe I can learn languages and as long as I have the conviction to learn and the enthusiasm to contribute to the company I admire, I am sure I will prove to be an asset to the company.'

*Was I not dying to work in a company that would require me to sit for fourteen hours a day in front of a blank screen, typing out some brainless codes with another twenty thousand nondescript people with me?*

'But that's nothing different from the other aspirants who have applied. Why should we take you?'

*Because I am an average guy and your company thrives on average people like me? Because your company hires anybody and everybody in sight?*

'Sir, I am hardworking and I am always willing to put in a hundred per cent into everything I do. I have the urge to learn and apply. I will be an asset to any organization I work for.'

'Your exam results don't show that.'

*I know that, you dimwit. It's my résumé. I typed that out.*

'Yes, I know that, sir. However, I wasn't interested in Mechanical. It was a mistake to have taken it up. That's why my grades dipped.'

'Yes, I know. It can be a pain. Mechanical engineering is not a very interesting field, you see. It's a very theoretical field and tends to get very monotonous. It's a languishing field. Don't you think?'

*Screw you.*

'Yes, sir.'

It seemed the only notable thing he did after being born was taking up information technology as a subject. The presumptuousness of IT people never ceased to amaze me.

'See, you understand mechanical engineers in India are no good. What made you take it up?'

'Sir, my dad is a mechanical engineer and is working with Bharat Heavy Electricals Limited.'

'A PSU? All these engineering PSUs are just sick industries with no work culture and absolutely no sense of ambition. Anyway, the IT guys have better percentages than you have, despite IT being a tougher course. It would not be fair choosing you over them. They have worked harder. Don't you think?'

*Oh, wow. You're like Einstein and Sherlock Holmes in one. You know everything!*

'Yes, sir.'

I presumed sitting in the Open Air Theatre—OAT, as it was known—lawns with attractive juniors was what made IT engineering tough. Girls from the junior batches always seem more attractive and vulnerable and sexually active than the girls from the same batch. While people were yet to kiss somebody, our juniors were being featured in grainy MMS videos! We had chosen the wrong decade to be born in. More sex in the latter, no damn IT in the former.

'See, you understand. What makes you think that you are interested in software, Debashish?'

*Because it gets people jobs.*

'Sir, it really intrigues me how certain codes can make things happen,' I said, still not giving up and trying to make something happen.

'It intrigues you and still you didn't make an effort to learn even one language. You know, it's not very easy. In mechanical engineering, things haven't changed in the last two decades or so. But the IT sector has grown. You have to be on your toes constantly to be competitive. You can't just sit and let things happen the way they are. IT and electronics are changing the world. Don't you think?'

*If IT changes the world, why are you still an asshole?*

'Yes, sir.' I would have loved to see his brain splattered against the wall behind him.

'See, you understand that too. People in mechanical engineering and civil engineering really have to start working hard if they want to make an impact. But they make lousy students and that's the root of the problem. Services still constitute fifty-two per cent of the gross domestic product. So we are doing pretty well, unlike you, don't you think?'

I fully agreed to write a program for electronically wiping off Bill Gates' ass each morning because he was busy doing other important things. That's services all right. I wanted to shove it in his face that every developed country had first grown as a manufacturing hub rather than a servicing one, but I let it be.

'Coming back to the question, why didn't you try to learn anything about languages?'

*Are you kidding me? They are the most boring thing ever.*

'Sir, I did not get the time to learn a language.'

'Why? Were you studying for your semester?' he barely suppressed a chuckle. I just got a feeling I was in for some special treatment. He had just laid his hands on a below-average student with no special talent to speak of.

'No, sir, I was involved in extracurricular activities.'

'What kind of extracurricular activities?'

*Oh. Shit.*

'Sir, I have been an active member of the student council and have organized technical and cultural festivals for our college. I have been working with the Society of Automotive Engineers for the last three years . . .'

'Despite having no interest in mechanical?'

*Oh. No.*

'Yes, sir.' This was getting tiring and frustrating. Even staring at the grotesque mole had become boring.

'Okay. But I don't see any certificates for any of them,' the bald guy added gleefully. He would have clapped and done a little jig had he been invisible.

'Sir, I didn't collect the certificates.'

'Why? Because you didn't get the time? Or because you didn't have the interest?' he smiled.

*Will you shut your filthy mouth?*

That was it. I knew he was not going to hire me.

'Debashish? Any answers? See, you have to be a quick thinker to give an answer, but then mechanical . . .'

'No, sir. I think I am not fit for the company nor is the company right for me. Thank you, sir. For the exposure I wanted before I

sit for other *true engineering companies*. It was nice meeting you,'
I said condescendingly and walked off fuming.

It wasn't the wisest thing to do, but it felt so bloody good. It
wasn't until later that I would realize my mistake. Until then, the
huge two-storeyed Mechanical Department canteen beckoned.

*Thanks for the wishes. I had a terrible interview. You obviously
don't care. Please don't call and irritate me right now.*

The text would reach Smriti just as I stepped into the canteen.

'Heard you had a pretty interesting interview?' Shrey said as
soon as he saw me. More than anything, I was surprised by how
fast the news travelled.

Shrey was sprawled on a concrete bench and his mouth was
stuffed with French fries. He was the godfather of the canteen.
Every mechanical student knew him and *the story*. Never did he
spend a single paisa there. He fed off what others ordered.

Shrey had come up with the idea of cutting the water supply
to the Electrical Department canteen in a bid to divert the
crowd to the newer Mechanical Department canteen. It worked
like a dream. College authorities took two months to rectify the
problem, by which time the students had already got used to the
new canteen.

'I don't want to talk about the interview. You tell me, how are
the formalities going?'

'I went to the French embassy yesterday. You have to see it
to believe it. It's heaven. All those girls in short skirts. I wonder
what Paris would be like. I talked to my professor in France. She
sounded quite hot, too. That French accent! Just that accent is
enough to turn me on,' he blabbered.

Heaven for sure. He was soon to be in a place where people
would listen to him and not bludgeon him, for they wouldn't
understand the language he spoke. A place where the people
would be short-skirted university girls speaking in an infinitely
erotic accent. I envied him, even though I knew he had put
many months behind this internship. Something I would have
never managed.

'So your parents are funding your internship?' I asked.

'I am getting a scholarship from the French embassy,' he said.

'What the *hell*? With that percentage of yours? Why? What did you do?'

'I forged the mark sheet. There is this mammoth machine called exxaccopier at the National Laboratory which charges . . .'

'Whatever. What about the signatures?'

'I forged that too. That's what I am telling you. That machine with its meta stable lasers . . .'

'Are you crazy? What if you get caught?'

'I will either be resting in my grave or be too old to be jailed. The forgeries are perfect. So chill.'

'Are you sure?' I asked.

'Yes, I am sure.'

For a few seconds, I wished he would get caught soon. I felt I was missing out on something. French girls in summer dresses and kiss-me accents. I tried not to think about it.

I told myself it was useless to envy him. The Paris internship was just a small piece of the whole career puzzle. With a percentage like his, he would find it difficult to get placed. Or get into a good university for his masters. Moreover, doing a post-graduation in engineering was unthinkable. The very thought of opening the bonnet and looking at an engine made me queasy enough to take a bus back home. But a foreign internship in the midst of French girls would have done no harm whatsoever to my burgeoning health. I couldn't get the thought out of my head.

'What does Vandana have to say about it? Is she cool with it? You're going to be away for two months.'

'She is not someone who reacts easily. Were she to discover I had cancer, the only reaction might be a frown. She is taking it easy,' he said.

'And you? Won't you miss her?'

'Naah, I will concentrate better without her calls and texts. I may get laid, too. Finally, I will be among people who won't go into fits of moral frenzy when it comes to sex. Of all the people of this world, I don't know why Indians are so uptight about sex!

It's not as if we got to a population of a billion people just by holding hands,' he said.

Shrey always acted as if he didn't love her much, since it is cool not to be head over heels in love with somebody. Just because he had a few flings behind Vandana's back didn't mean he wasn't in love with her. Yes, they hadn't slept together yet. He never tried convincing her. *He loved her.* I am convinced Shrey wanted his first time to be with Vandana, and that's why his flings never went beyond certain boundaries. His ideals were perfect even in their imperfections.

'Best of luck, man! But trust me, you will miss her.'

'No, I won't. In fact, I will devote all my time to football and image processing. I have to read a lot too. I will try a little bit of photography, too. It's not a tough thing to do if you ask me. A sunset, a crying child, a poor old woman . . . anything looks good if your camera is good. Take big prints in black and white and you are on your way. And with my modified camera and these focusers brought in direct from Sweden . . .' And it went on. Nothing short of spectacular could ever happen to him, or so he thought.

'So, when are you leaving?' I asked.

'In a month, I guess. Damn! I have to get a paper signed from the principal. You coming?' He got up frantically. I was sure he was late by at least a week.

'Naah! Vernita just messaged. She is coming here.'

'Bye, then. Catch you later. That girl is nuts. And tell her she can sleep with as many guys as she wants to. We don't give a damn.'

He walked off with a wave before I could defend her.

Although they were great friends, Shrey and Vernita avoided each other's company. Shrey always had problems with Vernita's boyfriends, whom she picked up from the strangest of places. House parties. Common friends. Friends of common friends. Even the Internet. Vernita never saw any point in what Shrey had to say and invariably pissed him off. Shrey cared, but Vernita was too blind to see that.

~

The more I wanted to run away from the interview and the incident, the more it caught up with me. People couldn't stop discussing their interviews and their projected chances of getting hired. The entire college seemed to have just one topic to talk about—the results. So when the results came out, the entire batch assembled at the T&P Department to see if they or their friends had made it. I was avoiding going anywhere near the department, but Vernita was consumed with curiosity.

'Why do you want to know?' I asked Vernita, as she pulled me behind her.

'Curiosity's sake. Let's see who amongst us are doomed to a life of codes. Not everybody would have screwed up like you,' she said as we took the long walk towards the T&P Department. We crossed the OAT, which had stood witness to many Engifests, Troikas, INNOVAs and other college festivals, not to mention the innumerable romances that often sprung out of the nothingness that had gripped the college.

Not that I gave two hoots about getting into a mass-recruiter IT company with a sad gender ratio, but I would have loved to be selected. It helped to have a back-up placement as a cushion before you tried out for companies that offered better pay and a better role.

'Hey, Prasad! Did you get through?' Vernita shouted across to someone she barely knew.

'Yes, I did. I am sorry for you, Deb,' he whimpered back.

'Never mind,' I said, as if I hardly cared. 'Prasad? He got through? He can barely talk.'

'It is not about how you speak, Deb,' Vernita shot back.

'Okay, then tell me what he has that I don't?' I sounded like a jealous boyfriend.

'He looks like a geek, not an asshole. He looks serious for the job and you didn't even shave. Look at your hair. Terrible,' Vernita snapped.

'Oh, so now you finally get it. It's not about how you speak. It's about how dumb you look!'

'Whatever. I am glad I didn't sit for it,' she said.

'You would have got through anyway. You're a girl.'

'That's sexist!'

'Sexist? As if you disagree. You know you are overqualified—too good-looking to be rejected.' *You have great breasts, and you look smashing in formals and high heels.*

'Shut up, you chauvinist pig. I have the brains, you dickhead. And I know how not to screw up an interview,' she said.

'Don't give me that crap. Okay, give me the name of one lab assistant who hasn't gone out of his way to help you cheat in practical exams.'

'That's easy . . . I mean, sort of.'

'No, wait, explain this. How have you been consistently outscoring the strongest and the most skilful of guys in the workshop? Don't tell me those manicures give your hands super strength. Or do you manage to do it with your brains? Just accept it. It helps to be a hot girl in an engineering college.'

I knew she wouldn't have a comeback for the workshop retort. She never stuck around the workshop for long. The pervert lab assistants were always too eager to help her out. What did they get out of it? Nobody knew. I would rather see her bend over and sweat it out. At least there would be something to look at while we risked our lives trying to work with molten metal alloys.

'Okay, shut up, sucker. Look, Ayush is coming. Looks like he got through, too.'

'Don't ask him. I can't take it any more.'

'Fine. But I guess he is coming this way. No. He definitely is,' Vernita said.

'Hey, Deb, heard about you. I'm sorry, dude. Never mind. Anyway, I got through. Mohit, too. Bye. Take care, man, and take it easy. Such things happen,' he said and walked off.

'Bloody hell! When was the last time he talked to us? Has he ever talked to us before this? *Sorry, dude?* As if I was dying for the job. Did he just call me *dude*?'

'Shut up, Deb. You don't have to get paranoid about this. Poor guy. He is happy that he got through. That's it,' she said.

'Whatever. Not another one. Don't tell me even he is coming towards us.'

'He didn't even give it, ass. His departmental rank is seventh.'

I hoped he wasn't walking towards us, but given my wretched luck lightning struck me twice that day. Never did the option of killing somebody and rotting behind bars feel so tempting.

Before he could start, I said, 'Hi, Chitiz. I heard everybody except me got through? They are so lucky. I wonder what they did in the interview. Maybe they just knew everything. Or maybe they are just young Einsteins ... and NO, we don't want to know who got through. We just want to keep the suspense alive. Do you mind?' I said.

He was lucky I still hadn't taken my hands out of my pocket.

'Excuse me. I can understand. Sorry to have bothered. Bye.' He walked off visibly perturbed after my uncalled-for rudeness.

*He can understand? What?*

'Whoa! That was mean and totally unnecessary,' Vernita said, as she hopped onto the stairs leading to the T&P department.

'Whatever. But I can do without their sympathy. They don't even know me.'

'There is the list,' Vernita pointed out.

'Ohh! How eager I am to have a look at it. I am not coming. You go and tell me about the lucky people who got through.'

'As you say,' she said and left.

'Vernita. Can we go now?' I shouted across to her.

'Wait,' she said, her facial expressions were changing each passing second. Seemed like more bad news was coming my way.

'So, who are the lucky slackers who got through?'

'You've got to see this,' she said and dragged me towards the list.

'I don't need to see this.'

'Yes, you do, Deb. Just read.'

'What? Ashish, dumbhead; Ayush, dickhead; Ankur, loser ...'

'Deb can you do it a little faster.' She punched me.

'Okay, okay. Ar ... Az ... Ba ... Be ... Ch ... Cu ... Di ... what?'

'At the end of the list, Deb,' she said.

'Yogesh ... Zohrab ... Debashish ... *Debashish?* How is this possible? Okay, wait, what the bloody ...'

I was numb. It was right there for the entire world to see.

Debashish Roy—*barred from all placement activities for the year 2007–08 on account of misbehaviour.*

~

I was crushed.

The higher the ball falls from, the harder it bounces back. I was hit hard for sure. Being barred meant I would be jobless at the end of the academic session! I had almost fainted when I first read it on the board. My head had spun and I felt like my knees would give way.

*This isn't happening.*

I would have to sit at home and watch every one of my fellow students lap up jobs. I would rather die. I was screwed. I had never thought it would come to this. Being debarred from placements is something that happens to others, not us.

I had been a complete ass. I let my mom down, who used to stay up all night to wake me at whatever intervals I asked her to. And Dad, too, who was in tears even after his brilliant son had once again underachieved by not getting through an entrance examination he should have cleared the first time around. I felt worse for them than for myself. They would have nothing to tell people. I would not get placed that year. I would pass out from college without a job in hand. I didn't deserve this. I had never thought one moment that my thoughtlessness would lead to this. I wished I could turn back time and handle it better. Some fights are not worth fighting.

*No, Deb, there are some companies that hold off-campus interviews before the session ends. And, NO, a call centre is not an option.*

I had spent hours with my head buried in my knees by the time Vernita called and broke the string of ridiculous options and way-outs I had come up with.

# 7

As if battling depression over getting barred from college placements wasn't enough, I had to tackle Vernita, who wanted me to come out for the night with Tanmay and Avantika. As a rule, I never won those conversations.

'She is depressed . . . something to do with Paritosh. You've got to do this for me. It's just one night, Deb,' Vernita said.

'I just had the *happiest* moment of my life. I just got barred from placements. And do you know how many people have been barred from placements in the last five years? Just two! That's a reason to celebrate, isn't it? Let's do this! Sorry, Vernita, not coming. Anyway, it is very late and I would rather study for the exams.'

Our sixth semester exams were less than a week away and I had decided to furiously mug every word in my books. My fifth semester marks were the last good thing that had happened and I was dying to feel that way again. Anyway, I knew my life was going just one way—downhill. I needed those marks to get placed in off-campus interviews.

'Please. You will be placed off-campus, Deb. That's not bad,' she pleaded.

'Don't give me that. My profile sucks. And my situation is definitely worse than hers.'

Ordinarily, I would have sold my soul for a night-out with Avantika, but that day was different. Not only was I aware of the fact that I was dumb and ugly, I was barred too . . . and she would know that. She wouldn't want to see a loser like me. Why was Vernita even trying?

'Worse than hers, Deb? Smriti ends up writing your name on a suicide note and dies or you get debarred. What's worse? What would you pick? Tell me?'

'Did Paritosh actually do that? Did he kill himself?'

'Not exactly. He just bashed up three of his classmates in the US with a baseball bat. One of them is dead. He was caught with drugs, bags full of it.'

'Where is he now?'

'Police custody, of course.'

'And?' I asked.

'And what?'

'Where does Avantika come into the picture? The suicide note thing?'

'She was the last person he met in India before he left for the States, after his family and his girlfriend . . . and a few friends.'

'Suicide note?'

'What suicide note?' she asked.

'You said her name was on a suicide note or something,' I grumbled. Vernita had exaggerated again. I wondered how she would describe her own breasts. Hot air balloons?

'I never said that. I just gave an example. There is no suicide note, silly.'

'So what's the big deal then? Why is she depressed? She can just stay in her hostel and relax.'

'Don't you get it? She loved him. Now he is gone. Forever. She tried to get him clean off drugs but she couldn't. She thinks it's her fault. She is blaming herself for everything. Avantika is a little sensitive. I know her. Can't I ask you for this much? You're my best friend, Deb. If you won't help me out, I don't know who else to turn to.'

Her emotional blackmail knew no limits.

I learnt later that Paritosh was a drunkard and had nearly flunked out of school. He loved rock music, as it was hip to do so, drove like crazy and spat blood and bile after crazy night-outs. In short, a despicable, hateful person. And more so for me. He even had half a tattoo on his right hand, half a man, half the pain. Avantika and Paritosh wanted to have the same tattoo, but he had chickened out midway.

'Is there nobody else? Shawar? He should be the one taking care of her, not me. She doesn't even like me. I am dumb and ugly—her words, not mine.'

'Shawar is the last person she would like to meet right now. I am picking you up in twenty minutes. You have to do this. Just this night. For me.'

She disconnected the call before I could put up a cogent argument. More than anything, I dreaded meeting Avantika again. I was not in a mood to deal with a heart that gives up at the sight of her and a rampaging tongue that flaps around wordlessly. It was already eleven thirty and I would have to convince Mom that an important assignment was pending which could not be done sitting at home. Moms always know when you are lying, just that they don't always have proof backing their intuition. Like movie tickets that you forget to throw away. Or parking slips. Or greeting cards.

'Bye, Mom,' I said, finally deciding not to tuck in my shirt.

'Bye-bye. Did they announce the results? The interview?' Mom asked.

'Yes. I wasn't selected. Only five people got through,' I said. *At least fifty people did.*

'Never mind. Sit for others. Anyway these IT companies are biased against mechanical students,' she said. *I was perfect.* I would never put a foot wrong. Her son could do nothing wrong. How could I tell her that I would not be allowed to sit for any other interviews?

I left.

~

'Hi, guys!' I greeted everybody as I entered Tanmay's car.

The best part about his car was the tinted windows that not only did a world of good to Vernita and him, allowing them to fool around in the college parking without raising any eyebrows, they had also helped Shrey and me in our times of need.

'So where are we headed?' I asked, looking at Avantika, before she said anything and cast a spell on me.

She was looking no different that day . . . beautiful. Her eyes barely kept the flood of tears from running down the dried streaks on her cheeks. She was wearing an extremely depressing, dull-blue T-shirt and dark-blue jeans teamed with sneakers. Her social networking profile had pictures of her in spaghettis and skirts with junk jewellery hanging from every part of her, but those days were long gone.

She stared expressionlessly outside the window as if somebody had just sucked the soul out of her. A teardrop caressed her eye for a while, until it could no longer bear her grief and slid down her cheek slowly. The drop was so clear, so radiant, yet so full of crushing sadness. It hung from her cheekbone as if not wanting to leave it. Who would? *What would*, in this case? I caught the ill-fated tear just as it left her face. I held that tear in my hand.

'Now, you may suffer from dehydration if you keep crying for long.' Silly joke, I thought. She looked at me. Sadness never looked so heavenly. I wished she were sadder. *Can I slap you for looking great?*

'Hi, Deb.' She actually talked to me. It may have been out of sympathy. I was dumb *and* ugly, after all.

Somehow, seeing her cry made me feel more comfortable. I had found a chink in her otherwise flawless armour. I had always proved myself to be a good agony aunt. Many of my relationships were rebounds. No girl in her right senses would date me otherwise.

'Hey, you don't have to cry. Look on the bright side. When he comes out of prison, he can sign a book deal and become rich . . . and famous. Oops, he already is.'

'Excuse me?' she said, startled, and her eyebrows made a small hill. She was taken aback and I expected that. I had seen that expression a million times. It is always easier to talk and kid about relationships than actually brood over them and not talk at all. For this very reason, people around me said that I was insensitive whenever I used to make fun of break-ups. But who was to tell them that it was for their own good. Besides, I really was insensitive. I had not been through a break-up, so the whole sense or nonsense surrounding break-ups eluded me.

'Excused. Why are you crying? And just think how proud your grandchildren will be, when they go about telling their friends, *My grandma's ex-boyfriend is one of the looniest criminals in Arkansas.* Now that would be cool.'

*Don't kill it. Don't be over-smart. She already hates you. Chill. Focus.*

'Okay,' she said.

'When did you break up?'

'It's been more than two years. February 2005.' She turned towards the window. We were whizzing past Punjabi Bagh. A string of flyovers on the Ring Road had made the drive red-light free. These flyovers, metros, high-capacity buses made Delhi much more commutable. No longer were the sexier parts of Delhi alienated. Despite the progress, women were still being raped and thrown off moving vehicles on these flyovers.

'Two years? And you are still crazy about him? Look at Vernita; Tanmay is lucky that she is still with him after six months. I think you don't realize that you can get any guy. You just have to point a finger and he will come running after you.'

I couldn't believe I was speaking so much. I think it all came out because of the state that she was in; she wasn't as fatal as she had been the other day. Or I think I was overexcited. A part of me felt like I would pass out.

'I don't need anybody else.'

'You didn't need a cell phone before you started using it. Start using me and you will feel my need,' I said.

*You can't be flirting with her. You are a poor, dumb and ugly guy.*

'I think people who flirt in the first meeting itself are insincere about their feelings,' she said. Quite obviously, I was being unnecessarily oversmart.

'Technically, this is our second meeting. And those who don't flirt and stay shut on their first meeting, you find them *dumb*. Don't you? As for the ugly part, I won't say anything because I am ugly. I will not contest that,' I said as I winked at Vernita.

'I can't believe you told him that, bitch. And you're *not* ugly,' Avantika said as she pinched Vernita.

I was happy and my heart wagged like a cute puppy who's just found the girl who owns it. I had just made the most beautiful girl on earth smile in her saddest moment. She looked ravishing.

'I couldn't help it,' Vernita answered as she looked at me and ground her teeth.

'I didn't mean that. Seriously,' Avantika said apologetically and touched me on my forearm. I felt . . . something.

'Oh! Then what did you mean?' I asked as I leaned into her and fainted. Almost. *Why did I have to look her straight in the eye?*

'I mean. You have to admit. You were acting so dumb that day. You were just average.' She had more authority in her voice than my English teachers after they had spotted a *didn't went* in an essay.

'You could have said *that* instead. I was so hurt. I couldn't sleep for days, you cruel hag,' I said.

'I told her that you were okay. But Vernita wouldn't take it. She wanted me to say that you were dumb. You know how she is,' she said, wiping off her tears.

Wasn't I great? I had just made a girl whose most loved person was going to be dead in a few days, smile. Well not dead, but it sounded more dramatic that way.

'Yes, I know,' I said.

'Anyway, what are you accusing me of? Even you didn't find me attractive. Or rather, you found me dumb. What do you have to say to that, Mr Roy?' she said.

*Didn't that sound straight out of a sex scene from a badly written racy novel? Mr Roy . . . will you marry me, Mr Roy? Will you take out the garbage? Will you . . . Focus! Focus, Deb, focus.*

'Oh that? That was because I knew you wouldn't have kind words for me, so why should I?'

Vernita had been a bitch. But what she had said was actually helping me blow the ice away. I was just plain lucky.

'Okay. So? What were the real words? What did you really think about me?' she asked.

'You were just about average. Nothing great.'

And we all burst out laughing at the pretty average joke, but any joke under those circumstances worked. I felt like a god. A little later, we reached the complex which housed the nightclub we were supposed to go to that night.

'You guys go in, I have to attend this call,' I said as we stepped onto the escalator leading to Hype. It was Smriti.

I waited for Avantika to go past the huge bouncers with bulging striated muscles and through the huge red doors before I answered the phone. She had been off the partying circuit for a year but everyone seemed to know her—the bouncers nodded, the manager had something funny to tell her, and no cover charges. Avantika often scared the shit out of me. She had been the kind of person who made school hell. The guys whom I could never be, and their girls, whom I could never get, both hated me. Avantika was one of them.

Smriti never called when she was back home, in Meerut, during the holidays. So it had to be important, and as expected, I was greeted by a frantic voice.

'What happened? I can't hear you properly,' I responded to her illegible whispers.

'Mom is in the other room. There is something very important I had to tell you. I told them about you. About *us*.'

'Told them what?' I shouted, like moms do on trunk calls.

'*ABOUT YOU*! I told them about you!'

'And? What did you say?' I asked. The last thing you would want involved in a fling*ish* relationship were parents. I freaked out.

'I told them the truth. I love you. I told them we were serious and it is long term,' she said.

'Are you nuts? Why did you have to tell them? Are you out

of your mind? What did you say? What did they say? Man, shit, shit, shit, *shit*. This is horrible!'

'What's wrong with you? You told me that you want it to be long term. So I told them. That's it. Why are you acting up?'

'What did they say? What the fuck do they want right now? Why did you have to tell them? I had said you don't have to tell them anything right now!'

'I was feeling guilty, Deb. I can't keep lying to them any more.'

'What the hell, Smriti! You didn't tell them when you slept with me. Didn't you feel guilty then? Shit, man. This is horrible. What did they say?'

'They want to meet you . . . and your parents. It was tough, but I convinced them, Deb. They are angry, but they still want to meet you,' she said what sounded quite like a death sentence to me.

'Have you lost it? Why do they need to talk to me?'

'. . . to talk about us. My dad is extremely angry with us and what we have. But I told them I loved you and he agreed to meet your parents. It will be all right,' she said meekly.

'What the fuck? About us? Meet my parents? And it will be all right? My parents will burn me at the stake, damn it. They won't tolerate another inter-caste relationship after the one Sonali almost brought home.' I thanked god I hadn't told my parents about the interview. That, along with the news of this affair, would have made things stuffy at my place.

'What am I supposed to do, Deb? I can't do anything. I am doomed either way.'

'I don't know. It's all your fault. Why did you have to act smart and fucking tell them? We could have done that later. I told you so many times not to talk about us to anyone. What got into you?'

'Is it my fault?'

'Yes, it's your fault. It's because of you we are in this mess now. You are . . .'

'It's always my fault. Isn't it? I came after you, didn't I?' she broke down and I hated it. I couldn't bear to see her cry . . . ever. I didn't love her, but hearing her cry now pained me. It also meant she would keep the phone down, not pick up my calls and bitch about how uncaring I was to others. Not acceptable.

'Okay, now don't cry. Your mom will wake up. We will see what we can do. Just tell me what you told your dad. Exact words.'

'They didn't let me speak. They just wanted to meet your parents. I just said that we love each other and you have no problems with our getting married in the future.'

'Okay, go to sleep now. When are they coming to Delhi, if they are?'

'Next week.'

'Okay, sleep now. Goodnight. Love you.'

'Love you, too.'

I cut the line. I was glad she hadn't asked where I was. Not that I would have told her the truth anyway. She hated Vernita and didn't trust me with her. Especially when she knew that I wasn't the most trustworthy of guys.

A million thoughts started running through my mind. I was twenty-one and some old man was coming to meet my dad and propose a match. This was my worst nightmare. Deep inside, I knew it would be *a lot worse* than my worst nightmare. They would accuse me of ruining their daughter's life et cetera, et cetera. Ideally, I would have spent the night sweating it out and thinking about the worst worst-case scenarios, but Avantika was waiting, and I was dying to see her again.

I decided I would deny all allegations of an affair. I made up my mind to tell them that we were just friends and it was Smriti who went crazy after me. *I was innocent.*

'Hey! What's up?' I shouted as the pungent smell of alcohol and smoke wafted inside my nostrils. Hype was a decent place, never too crowded and was open until early morning. It catered to the not-so-affluent but still chic crowd, so it happened to be a good hangout place on a budget.

'Whose call was it?' Vernita shouted back.

'Smriti.'

'Anything worth knowing?' Tanmay asked.

'Nope. It looks like it's going to be a long night,' I remarked as I looked around to see sagging, wobbly breasts and flabby thighs on the dance floor. The younger crowd had decided to stay away that night and we were younger than the average age in that club by at least five years.

'Yes, I guess so,' Vernita said. That was a consolation. Except me, the other three could set the floor on fire within seconds. So, knowing that they wouldn't dance tonight saved me from the embarrassment I invariably faced in nightclubs. Plus, I would get more time to stare wordlessly at Avantika.

'Drinks?' Vernita asked.

'No,' we all echoed.

Vernita was the only one who drank. Tanmay and Avantika were associated with the Spirit of Living, which forbade them to drink. And I never felt like drinking. Ever. The taste just never appealed to me and my highly developed taste buds couldn't take the torture. I had come to despise people who drank. I was often called a wimp for not drinking. I somehow always thought it was the other way around. It was always easy to say yes . . . especially when it was being forced upon you by a bunch of bullies and their giggling bitches. My school days were torturous and I have never been able to move past the memories.

'You don't drink?' Avantika asked. I had heard quite a bit about her wild parties before the Spirit of Living consumed her and her lifestyle changed on its head. The tattoos on her body bore testament to her old life.

'No. What's so surprising . . . that I don't drink? Even Tanmay doesn't.'

'No. But he has his reasons. Guruji forbids people from drinking and we understand why.'

'I have my own reasons.'

'And they would be?' she asked as she rested her chin on her knuckles and leant forward. I don't know whether that is what she intended to do, but I was aroused. My heart rate picked up, my knees started to shake and I was seeing things in double.

'I don't relish the taste. It's just so . . . ugh.'

'It is not about the taste. You can't be such a wuss about it. It is about the feeling. It's about the high,' she said. Words from a veteran, I thought.

'I can do without that feeling or that high. I have seen too many people puke and regret they got drunk the night before. I don't think I need to subject myself to that.'

'People would call you boring. Unadventurous. Not open to experiments.'

'I get my high from other things. Trust me. There are better things to experience.'

'Oh! Now that is interesting . . . and probably a lie.' She rocked back and adjusted a fringe, spiking my heart with her loveliness. She added after a pause, 'Tell me one thing that gives you a better high than alcohol?'

'Umm, sex?'

'Who would have sex with you?' she said and everyone at the table laughed.

'I would agree with that. I am pretty undesirable,' I said and they laughed again.

'Aw! That's sweet,' Avantika purred and touched my cheek. Mental note to self: never wash that cheek.

'Don't underestimate him,' Vernita butted in. 'He is very popular with my girlfriends.' It was a lie, but I didn't mind her projecting me as she did. None of Vernita's friends liked me and, clearly, I wasn't getting laid. Vernita continued, 'But the not-drinking part, I still think you are just a wimp and a loser. You guys want anything?'

'Sweet lime,' Avantika said and continued, 'and Deb, I liked that. It takes courage to refuse.'

*I love you, too. Can I hold your hand? I don't drink.*

'You are a wimp, too,' Vernita butted in.

'Shut up, Vernita. You need to drink because you're boring when you're not drunk,' Avantika said.

'Hahaha! Whatever. Never mind. Deb?'

'Some more of your catfight and a cold coffee,' I added. She cringed at the thought of having a cold coffee in a club. I could tell she was missing Viru and Yogi. They would have got the whole bar to the table.

'I'll come with you,' Tanmay said as he put his arm around Vernita.

'Don't go, I will get them for you,' Avantika said as she started typing out something on her cell phone. Within the next few seconds, I saw the manager rushing towards the bar. The order was on our table in a flash. Avantika was a privileged customer there.

Just as it would happen to any normal person, I fell more in love with her every second that passed. She was lovely and it would have been unfair to god not to appreciate his hard work. It's surprising he hadn't kept Avantika for himself.

We danced a little that night. But to my elation, the music didn't encourage any complex moves that would have brought my disabilities to the fore. All I tried to do was get a little close to her, follow her moves, and catch glimpses of her face hidden beneath her swaying hair, as she kept twisting her neck from one side to the other with every beat. Thankfully, the swaying and shaking became tiring and we walked back to our couches.

'Seems like they have gone to sleep,' I said. Vernita and Tanmay actually had. Vernita was, as usual, drunk on the minute quantities of alcohol she had consumed. Tanmay had passed out from boredom.

'Let's go for a walk. It's getting suffocating here,' Avantika said.

That was the single, most beautiful thing she had said the entire evening. We walked out and sat on the stairs nearby.

'Thank you for coming out today. I feel a lot better,' she said.

'How could I not have come?'

'You're too sweet for your own good, Debashish,' she smiled at me.

'You're too sensitive for your own good. It crushes me to think that you would cry over someone who broke up with you two years ago.'

'I loved him with everything I had. I had come to believe that we would always be together,' she said, her voice cracking. It made me as sad as she was.

'I can never know what you went through, or what you're going through right now, but I know that someone as nice and remarkable as you should never have to cry. I hardly know you, but if I were to see you cry, it would break my heart into a million pieces. I have no idea what kind of a guy your ex-boyfriend was, but he certainly didn't deserve you. You're perfect,' I said and she looked at me with her big puppy eyes. I was worried I had said too much.

'Your girlfriend, Smriti, is a really lucky girl,' she said and put her head on my shoulder.

*Yeah, right.* I didn't say anything to that. A few minutes later, I found her sleeping. That wasn't bad, I thought, as long as I got to touch her and watch her sleep so close to me. She wasn't crying any more. She was sitting on the carpeted part of the stairs, and I was on the concrete. It was uncomfortable as hell, but I didn't want to move and wake her up. I didn't want to lose the moment.

I started to feel like the king who had endured a scorpion bite for years so as not to break a sage's meditation. I could feel my behind tingle from the numbness. To block the feeling out, I looked at her and it was the warmest, fuzziest feeling I had ever felt. Just as I put my arm around her and rested my head on hers, she did the most amazing thing. She snuggled up to me! She purred and put her arms around my waist. It was like jumping into a fountain of warm chocolate, puppies, rainbows, snowflakes and all the good things in the world.

Now, it was definitely *heaven*. I hugged her tighter.

# 8

'*What the hell do you think you are doing?*' Tanmay shouted and I felt shattered to the bone.

'Huh,' I froze. Did he *have to* interrupt?

As we had snuggled, Avantika had begun crying again. With every sob, she clutched my arm tighter, and her nails dug into my arm. I felt sorry for her; a part of me died as I watched her cry. I felt powerless and insignificant. She opened her eyes looked at me and closed them again, and a stream of tears streaked down her cheeks. I bent over and I kissed her tears away. It was surreal. I felt her pain like it was mine. I felt empty and content and sad and happy at the same time.

Seeing her cry pained me and for no reason whatsoever I held myself responsible for it. With those beautiful welled up eyes she fixed her gaze upon me, as if asking me to save her, almost hypnotizing me into kissing her again. I kissed her again, this time on her soft lips, enveloping them, one at a time. She didn't resist this time either. I felt her tears run down her cheeks and wet my hands as I cupped her face. She melted into my arms and I melted into hers and we were one.

Until we were interrupted.

'Let's go,' Tanmay held Avantika by her hand and snatched

her away. 'TO THE PARKING LOT. NOW,' he motioned to
Vernita and left.

Avantika looked back and my heart sank. She made me hers
with that little beautiful moment we shared. Those tears may have
been for somebody else's love but they found me mine.

'*What the hell do you think you were doing?* How could you do
it? Are you bloody crazy?' Vernita shouted and whispered at me
at the same time, not sure whether to be bewildered, shocked or
angry. 'Four months and Shawar didn't even get to hold her hand.
And you? You have a girlfriend, damn it! And you know what
she has been through!'

If she was trying to make me feel guilty about it, she certainly
wasn't succeeding. Not only did I not feel guilty about what I had
done, I had found love, too. Not that I exactly knew what love
is, but it was supposed to be great and this was better than great.
I struggled to understand what I was feeling. Vernita's words
bounced off my ears.

'It just happened. I didn't intend to do it. I am sorry. But it
wasn't just me.'

'It was just you, fucker. She was sad and drunk. And what did
you do? Use her . . .'

'Drunk? She wasn't drunk,' I retorted.

'Yes she was. I had mixed vodka in her lime juice, you bastard.'

'Oh, but—'

No wonder the lime water had tasted funny. I resisted the urge
to tell her that Avantika and I had exchanged our drinks because
she thought the cold coffee was a better option.

Was I going crazy? *Is this what it feels like?* I hardly knew her
but I knew that she would never leave my mind.

Avantika had finally taught me that kissing was more than
the pointless slobbering of tongues.

~

Tanmay dropped Vernita at her place and Avantika at her hostel.
Everybody avoided eye contact during the entire drive. Avantika

was quiet too. She was crying, softly, but not softly enough. I wished I could have wrapped her up in my words and made her feel better. I wished I could touch those lips again and have her clutch my arm.

Nobody exchanged a word.

'Hey, Deb,' Tanmay said as I stepped out of the car. I was feeling good till then. I wasn't scared that Tanmay, twice my size, would beat me to a pulp. I was still stuck in that moment. After Avantika got out, he didn't give me the time to come to the front seat. So we hadn't exchanged a word or looked each other in the eye.

'Yes.' I looked back as he came and stood right in front of me. I sensed a big scene. Maybe a punch in the face and a few kicks on the rib cage. I prepared myself for pain, but it would be a small price to pay.

'Stay away from Vernita and Avantika. You have no idea who you are messing with. Avantika has been through a lot and I can't see her in pain again. She has had her share of guys like you. Do you get it? Think about what you are doing to Smriti. What if I tell her? Leave Avantika alone. For me, for Smriti, for Avantika. Do you get it?' Tanmay said, alternating between being dangerous and soft. His fists were clenched and his eyes bore into mine. He, too, had been a brat once and that was evident. It didn't look like it was the first time Tanmay was asking a guy to lay off his sister.

'I am sorry about what happened. Don't tell Smriti about this. She will be crushed.'

'I won't. Keep in mind what I said.'

He walked away. Smriti would have been broken. I didn't want that to happen, but having said that, I really wasn't sorry about the moment between Avantika and me. The ephemeral kiss wasn't even what I was thinking about when I continually replayed those few minutes in my mind. Instead, it was the cry of help in her eyes and the tears that I had kissed away. I decided I wouldn't tell Smriti anything before I figured out what I felt about Avantika. Was it strong enough to ruin me for all other women?

~

'Why are you crying?' I asked Smriti. She was in Delhi, but fortunately for us, her parents weren't. Tanmay hadn't told Smriti anything as of then.

'Deb, why shouldn't Mahima file a case? The bastard, how can he ask for . . .' Her voice trailed off.

Mahima was her older sister who had got married to a boy from their community in a big, lavish wedding. The marriage ran into problems within the first week itself. Finally, after a year of enduring the physical and mental trauma, Mahima had given up. She was yet to file a police case, but she wanted a divorce and she wanted it quick. Smriti wanted Mahima to file cases on every account possible. Rape. Dowry. Extortion. Attempt to murder. Smriti, as expected, was furious and appalled by what her sister had gone through in the last twelve months.

'Is that why they didn't come?' I asked her. Mahima's husband may have been a bastard, but he had made my life less of a mess. Still, I hoped he would rot in hell.

'Yes. They want me to decide about you. They have no strength left. Mom and Dad spend the entire day with Mahima trying to understand why she didn't tell them before. They are blaming themselves, knowing that they placed their honour before their daughter's well-being. They are gutted.'

'Decide about me?' I knew things would be easy there on. Her parents had bigger issues to take care of. I felt sorry about her parents, but they *were* to blame. They were educated and they still got their daughter married into a family that had no qualms about asking for a dowry in the first phone call itself.

'They want to let me decide whether or not this is a long-term relationship. They want to let me choose whom I spend my life with, unlike Mahima. They don't want to make the same mistake they made with her. Tell me, Deb. I need to tell them in a month. It's either going to be you or it will be up to them.'

'What?' I asked. I wasn't listening to her. All I'd heard was that her parents weren't coming. Now I was more interested in checking out whether Avantika had sent me a text or not. She hadn't. It had been two days and fourteen hours.

'Didn't you get me? They are asking me whether this is serious.'

'As in? Me and you getting married? Are you crazy? My mom would kill me.'

'You don't have to tell her now. By the time I finish my medical studies, you will be twenty-eight. Nobody would care then. You always said we would figure it out later.'

She was right. But I was busy reliving the kiss, Avantika's tears and those precious few minutes we'd shared. *Maybe she doesn't have my number.* But I had seen her online. All social networking sites screamed out my number. She couldn't have missed it. *Does she regret what happened?*

'They would care, Smriti. And eight years is a long time. How am I supposed to commit to you?'

*Yay!* I had a point there, finally.

'At least give me an assurance. At least we can try. If it doesn't work out, I will take the blame.'

'Instead, we can tell them that you have broken up and then if things are good between us in the coming days we will inform them.'

'That can't be done, Deb. They want to know right now. After what happened with Mahima, they are really scared.'

'But ...'

I was interrupted by her little sobs. Crying is acceptable once, twice or at the most thrice; after that, more often than not, it does more harm than good. Tears don't make guys melt, they irritate them.

'You don't love me, do you?' she said. That was it; I had to call Avantika.

'Of course I love you. Let's talk about this later. And do keep me updated about Mahima. If you ever need to talk about her, don't hesitate. I need to go right now. I will give you a call later, okay? Bye,' I disconnected the phone before she could react.

This was the best conversation I had had with Smriti in a while, mostly because I wasn't concentrating on whatever she was trying to put across. I said a little prayer for Mahima.

~

'Hi, Avantika,' I said. My voice quivered and my hands shook. I had finally managed to call her up. It had taken me only a few hours to kiss her, and three days to call her up. Great!

'Hi, Deb,' she said. I wondered if she even remembered what had happened that night. I assumed she had forgotten this as one of her wild nights. It wasn't a thought I wanted to savour.

'Delete this from your call log. Tanmay will kill me if he finds out I called you. He has already threatened me once.'

'Positive,' she said. Her curt replies and uninterested tone scared me. But I hardly cared. I couldn't have let her get away so easily after turning my life upside down. I hadn't been able to think about anything else but her for the last three days and she had to know it.

'I am sorry about that day. Or maybe I am not. It seemed right, didn't it?' I said and bit all my fingernails off. I was confused about what to say because her voice gave away nothing.

'Yes, it seemed right. They still think I drank the lime juice. Why didn't you tell them that it was you?' Her matter-of-fact answers weren't helping. My nail-less fingers had started to hurt.

'I didn't feel like telling them. After all, I wasn't under its effect, I am sure. I didn't have to be drunk to kiss you.'

*It was you, not the bloody drink.*

'It wasn't the drink? You used me! I didn't expect this from you. You filthy man!' she shrieked. And just as I was about to slit my nail-less fingered wrist, she burst out in a guffaw. She laughed.

*Did she just laugh?*

'You nearly had me there,' I said. I didn't quite know what her laughter meant.

'By the way, do you think it is going to work?' she asked.

*What?* Was she talking about *us*? Why? She was even more audacious than I was. I only just kissed her. She couldn't be serious.

'What is going to work?' I countered her question, just to be sure.

'We . . . I mean *us*. Together.'

'Yes . . . I mean I can . . . we can . . . try,' I stuttered.

'You're already scared, Deb,' she said. Her voice was back to where it was at the beginning of the phone call.

'I am not scared; I am just confused about what that day meant.'

'I am sorry, Deb. I don't know what I was thinking. I am such a fool. I know about Smriti I am really sorry. It is just that I am a little disturbed, with this exam tension and . . . Paritosh . . .' her voice trailed off.

'I don't mind you being disturbed,' I tried to be funny.

'Do you mind if we talk later?'

'Why would I mind? I'll wait for your call. Bye.'

And that was our first conversation. I didn't know what to make of it until she called me the very next day. *After* five calls that I made, which she didn't respond to.

'Hi!' she said.

'Hi. Did I bug you with the missed calls?' I asked. Trust me when I say this, but I tried not to call her after the first call went unanswered.

'No, you didn't,' she said. 'In fact, I was quite pleased to see the phone ringing over and over again. I almost answered once.'

'The phone was ringing and you didn't pick it up? Why would you do that?' I asked.

'I have already embarrassed myself enough, Deb,' she said. 'I need to end this. We don't have to talk. It's better for you and it's what Vernita and Tanmay want.'

'And what's better for you? What do you want?'

She laughed and answered, 'It doesn't really matter. I have been at odds all my life. I have never known what I want.'

'I don't know what to say to that.'

'You don't have to say anything. I need to go. I will call you later when I am better,' she said and disconnected the line.

I stared at my phone and wished I had said something that would have made her stay.

# 9

A week had passed since our second phone call and I was slowly losing my mind. I couldn't even bring myself to talk to Smriti for more than a few minutes. Something would trigger me off and I would shout at her or pick an old fight and ask her to leave me alone. I would call Avantika and she would disconnect my call and I would curse myself for doing so. I didn't text her, thinking it would be too desperate. But I was longing to talk to her again. She was like a song you have stuck in your head but you can't remember the words to it and you won't rest until they comes to you. I wasn't depressed; I was angry and irritated that I couldn't drive her out of my mind.

As time passed I was more drawn towards Avantika and I started having dreams about her where she was walking away from me. Post those dreams, I would lie in bed and create my own daydreams where she was walking towards me, telling me how mistaken she had been. And then we'd kiss until her demonic brother appeared.

Finally that day, as I was staring at the cell phone screen, the phone rang. It was Avantika. I braced myself.

'Hi, Avantika. I thought you would never call,' I said.

'I wanted it to be that way, too, but I couldn't help it,' she murmured.

'Why did you want to call me?' I asked. I was relieved that she had called me, but I was also furious that it had taken her so long.

'Did you not want me to call you?' she asked.

'I have stared at the phone endlessly for the past one week. That's all that I have been doing. I don't know who you are, I don't know what you like or what you don't, but I think I am never going to forget you,' I answered.

'Why would you say these things?' she queried.

'I say these things because for the first time I have felt like saying them. Earlier, I used to say them because these were words that needed to be said to appease the person I was with. Now, it has become a pain keeping them inside me. Do you have any idea how many times in the past few days I have thrown myself back to that night? Do you have any idea how many times I have gone back to that moment when you were clutching me and crying? I have tried tirelessly not to think about you, but it just doesn't happen,' I ranted.

She didn't say anything. I felt lighter.

'I wish I could see you right now,' she said.

'You can,' I said and I felt an electric energy running through me. 'Where are you?'

'I'm in the hostel and it's already nine. They won't let me out now,' she said.

'But can I still come to your hostel? Maybe you can sneak out for five minutes? Tell them it's your brother?' I suggested. She said she would try.

I disconnected the line and asked Mom if I could go to Shrey's place for an assignment we had to submit in a few days. She let me go. It was already ten when I boarded the metro and it was deserted. I tried calling her a few times, but the network in the underground sections of the metro was always suspect.

'I am at the Delhi University metro station. Where do I come from here?' I asked.

'Find a rickshaw and ask him to take you to the Kamla Nagar roundabout. Call me once you get there; it's walking distance from there,' she instructed.

'Fine.'

'And Deb?' she said. 'I will just have a few seconds. I have told the warden that you have to collect a pen drive from me and she will be a keeping a watch. I am sorry.'

'A few seconds are enough,' I said and we disconnected the line.

Having found a rickshaw to take me to Kamla Nagar, I realized how scared both of us were. My skin tingled with the possibilities. Just days before, Avantika had been a mirage, an impossibility, and now, I knew I wouldn't rest until I had her. Even as we were getting closer, we were trying to run away.

I let the rickshaw go and called her up again. She gave me the directions to her hostel. It was a two-minute walk and my heart was beating out of my chest by the time I got there. I was sweating from nerves and excitement.

'I can see you,' she said. I looked around to spot her and then I did. She was in a T-shirt that hung loosely over her shoulders and a pair of black shorts that were hardly visible beneath the oversized T-shirt. Her hair was open and in a beautiful mess.

'I'm coming.' I kept holding the phone to my ear, my eyes focused on her, my jaw dropped open.

It took her two minutes. Her warden stood at the door as she walked towards me.

'Hi,' she said and looked straight at me. She handed over a pen drive. 'I'm sorry. Is she watching?'

I nodded.

'I have to go.'

'I wish you could stay.'

She smiled and tried reining in her unruly hair. I wanted to take her home. She was so beautiful I wanted to cry.

Just before she left, she turned and hugged me briefly. I breathed in deeply to absorb the moment. She walked away from me, only to turn back once and smile at me. Her hostel warden closed the door behind her and looked at me suspiciously.

I realized I hadn't disconnected the call. 'Hello? Hello? Are you there?'

'Yes,' she said from the other side.

'I don't know what to say,' I said.

'Are we already running out of things to say?' she asked and chuckled.

'How can someone think of anything to say to you? I get so nervous around you and all I can do is stare at you,' I conceded.

'You're just being sweet,' she said.

'I am not. I can look at your face for hours and still not get enough of you. Can I see you again? I find it hard to believe that this is happening. Can you step out onto the balcony?' I asked.

'Why do you even want to see me like this? I am a mess!' she protested.

'You're perfect.'

'I'm not,' she countered.

'I would know better,' he said. And before I could plead to her again, she appeared on the balcony, moonlight slanting off her face. I found myself short of words again.

'Say something,' she said.

'I don't know what to say. I can just sit here and stare at you for hours,' I said and sat on the pavement next to her building. She was right in front of me, standing on the first-storey balcony. So close, yet so far. 'I wanted to ask you something.'

'Go ahead.'

'I am sure a lot of guys are smitten by you ... don't say they are not. You are, by far, the prettiest girl I have ever seen, so it's obvious that I have lost my mind. But why do you talk to me? And why did that moment happen between us?'

'Can I ask you the last question, too? Why did that moment happen between us?' she asked. She stood there, her gaze on me, and I had no option but to answer her. I wanted to touch her face and know it was for real.

'I felt very sad for your grief and I blamed myself for it. You were with me and you were crying. I felt responsible,' I answered. 'Your turn.'

'For the first time in years, I felt safe,' she said. We didn't say anything for the next few minutes. We kept looking at each other wordlessly. She broke the silence after a few minutes and said, 'I have seen prettier girls than me.'

'I have not and I don't think I want to.'

She laughed and I laughed with her.

*The phone call lasted a full seven hours.* I would blank out in the middle of the conversation and she would ask me to stop staring at her. I would tell her that it wasn't really my fault and she would blush and thank me for being so sweet. And I would tell her I had no idea how people could be anything but sweet to her. We talked till the early morning. She made coffee for herself and threw me a packet of biscuits. I was her puppy after all.

I wanted to know everything about her and though she was annoyed by my questions, she kept answering them. She had lived her life in extremes. She had had her share of alcohol binges and being stoned for days, of reckless boyfriends and countless flings and soured relationships. She hated her parents and her parents weren't very fond of her either. Her parents' whole family's prestige seemed to be wrapped around her getting married young. They never supported her dreams of being anything worthwhile; all they cared about was finding a rich enough businessman for her. Avantika had one aim in life—to be successful on her own some day and run away from her parents. That was the reason she now slogged and took academics very seriously. She was taking the CAT that year but her parents didn't know she had plans to study after her graduation.

Our conversation shifted to our relationships and I realized I didn't want to know anything about the other guys in her life.

She told me that Paritosh dumped her because she refused to have sex with him and I told her I couldn't care less. Every time she counted a guy she had kissed, and she had kissed many, she got me writhing in fits of frenzy that would end up with her trashing the guy as a drunken bastard.

'But why did you kiss him?' I asked agitatedly as I jumped up from the pavement below. I was banging my clenched fist in the air. I already felt cheated.

'Deb? I was stoned. Do you know what that means? I didn't know what was happening.'

'Didn't know what was happening? You could have pulled back. Why continue kissing him?' I asked.

'I didn't know why I did it. I guess you have to be high to experience that!' she chortled. I knew I didn't have to look at her because if I did, I would forget everything.

'You enjoyed it, didn't you?' I said. I was in pain now. I wanted to see if I was any different from the other guys she had kissed.

'What do you want to hear?'

'Something that is not too hard for me to take. Something that makes me feel better.' My heart was sinking. I would have liked a negative answer rather than the choice.

'I didn't remember anything of it the next morning. I am a different person when I am sloshed. And I don't think he was good enough anyway.' She chuckled again.

'Good enough? Who has been good enough for you then?'

'*You!* You wanted me to say that, didn't you?' she chuckled yet again.

'Yes, why not? That is why you didn't call me up? Is that why it took you a week to call me up? Because I was good? Blah,' I said, hoping she would beg to disagree.

'Deb, I had heard a lot about you. I thought it didn't matter to you. And remember, I kissed you when I was sober. That is a first for me, if it means anything to you. And I didn't regret it, unlike the other times. Plus, I had already embarrassed myself enough.'

'It meant a lot to me. I am glad we met that day,' I said, still irritated.

'Does Smriti know anything about me?' she asked, after a few seconds of silence.

'No, and I don't care. If I did, I wouldn't be here at four in the morning, beneath your balcony, talking to you. I like you a lot and her being there doesn't make a difference to me.'

'It does, Deb. She loves you. It doesn't feel right. I already feel I am doing something that I shouldn't. At least tell her.'

'I can't tell her. She won't understand. But I want to know something from you. I know it's a little too premature, but do you think there is any possibility that you might be as smitten some day as I am today? That's all I really care about and I am willing to wait.'

'Some day? Yes. But Smriti loves you *now*. Go back to her,' she said. Her voice sounded as tragic as she looked that day.

'I would rather wait for that *some day*,' I said. We disconnected the call after a little while. It was nearly five and her warden had spotted me loitering outside. She asked me to leave and I did.

I was sleepy but I couldn't get over the night I had spent on the pavement looking at the most stunning girl I had ever seen.

~

That day onwards, we talked for hours on end. The amazingly long phone calls under Avantika's balcony became a routine. The only part that killed me was when I had to leave early in the morning before her warden woke up and the woman woke up really early.

It was almost unbelievable for me to know she wanted to talk to me every day. Delhi University exams were about to begin, but she didn't make me feel so. After the third day, it was assumed I would land up outside her hostel and call her. We had decided we would meet '*in person*' after her exams got over. She told me she wouldn't be able to think about anything else if she were to hug me or get close to me again. So we stuck to the balcony-and-pavement routine. She told me she found it extremely cute that I came to see her every day. How could I have not?

Seeing her every day was incredible. We never told each other that we were in love. She had been dumped for another girl by Paritosh and she didn't want me to do the same to Smriti. I was sure about what I felt, but I didn't know about her.

All that time, we had paid no heed to Tanmay's and Vernita's incessant warnings and frequent checks on us. Tanmay had categorically told me to stay away from his sister, come hell or high water. He never forgot to give me 'the look' whenever he crossed me in college. We both admitted it was fun throwing them off track. *We haven't talked since that day*—that was what I told Vernita whenever she asked me about Avantika.

For Smriti, it was getting tougher. I didn't do well in the sixth semester exams. I kept 'slipping' into extremely bad moods and tempers frequently. I advised Smriti to leave me alone.

But Avantika kept making me feel bad about what I was doing to Smriti. All my efforts in explaining that it was Smriti who wasn't doing much for the relationship fell on deaf ears. Though I admit, I didn't have much to explain.

The wait finally came to an end when Avantika's examinations came to an end and we decided to actually see each other face-to-face without a road or a building separating us. Though I had been seeing her for the last many days, the idea of her walking next to me was unnerving. We were both a little apprehensive because of the number of people who didn't want us to meet.

But the problem was not Smriti; the big stumble was Shawar, her boyfriend. Academic brilliance being the last of his attributes, Shawar was doing a BA (Pass) course in Shivaji College, which barely kept him busy, giving him ample time to surround himself with equally rich, powerful, wasted guys. He slept through the day and partied through the night, and found time to immerse himself in ultra-nasty brawls and fights, some of which even made it to local newspapers.

In spite of him, we decided to go on a night-out. We knew we wouldn't get enough time if she were to sign into her hostel after our little date. She told me we could go over to her place, the place where Tanmay and Vernita used to stay over after their night-outs, after we were done. I had no complaints.

'Where are you?' Shawar asked, as she put him on loudspeaker. It hadn't even been fifteen minutes since we had got together. I was still getting used to her presence when he called.

'Where else? Hostel,' she said as her face contorted with irritation. I could tell from her face she had never liked him.

'Don't fuck with me. I called up at the hostel. You aren't there.'

'Shawar, they can't transfer the call if you call up at ten in the night,' she said as she asked me to go on. The movie was about to start. I wasn't interested in the movie.

'Then show up. I am standing outside your hostel. Come to your balcony. I am not going till you come out.'

Her face contorted until it reached an irresistible degree of cuteness. 'Shawar, I was kidding, I am at my guardians' place. They called me over for dinner.'

'Never mind. I will be there in half an hour. Let's see whether you are there. I am leaving right now.'

'Shawar, don't you dare do that. They won't let you in through the society gate and I don't want you within a mile's radius of the society,' she shrieked.

'They won't let me in? *Me?* They won't let *Shawar* in? I think you're forgetting who I am. Nobody can touch me!' he roared.

'This is the last time we are talking if you come inside the society gate and I mean it,' she shouted, feigning anger.

'This is so fucking great. I thought I should have been angry right now. But just tell me one thing. Why have you been talking to this guy, Debashish, for hours?'

'I don't think I need to tell you that,' she said in the angriest tone possible and still managing to wink at me and bite her lips seductively. God knew what she wanted. She didn't want me to cheat on Smriti—she always tried to brush me off when I would try being naughty over the phone—but she had no problems flirting with me. I knew it was all in good humour but my hormones didn't know that and neither did my heart. As Sean Kingston sang, *Damn all these beautiful girls!*

'Yes you do. When you don't pick up a single call from me for days, you so fucking definitely do. Will you tell me where you are? *Just fucking tell me.*' His anger was palpable.

'Shawar, you swear once more and I will never talk to you. Anyway, I am getting a call. Bye and don't you dare call me. I am going to sleep. Love you,' she switched the call to another call she had to answer.

'Hi, Tanmay . . . yes . . . hostel . . . yes . . . sure . . . bye . . .' she hung up.

'Why did you get so paranoid? I don't think he would have driven down to Greater Kailash just to see you wave from the window,' I said as she rejected another call from Shawar. I didn't think anyone else would love her as much as I did.

'First, he doesn't drive. He has a million friends who for some inexplicable reason tirelessly drive him around the city. Second, he had his friends drive him to Chandigarh once, just to do that.'

'How does he know about me?'

'You? He probably knows about your whole family tree by now. I have some qualified boyfriends, Deb. They know a lot of *right* people. You are a baby, Deb. You have a lot to learn,' she said, as she pulled me into the auditorium. She hated to miss the trailers, as she told me later.

She was the man of the date that night. She decided the places we went to, she knew the people and she knew the routes. Everywhere we went we were given privileged treatment. I loved being taken care of. She had been nocturnal for years now and knew a lot of *people. Everyone* knew her. It's hard to forget a face as beautiful as hers.

'Why don't you just tell him? That you guys are over and you have found me.'

'It wouldn't be too good for your health. He is an uneducated brash bastard. You never know what he might end up doing. He is nuts, Deb.'

I didn't quite like that feeling but I loved the way she trashed her ex-boyfriend. The *other* boyfriend. The one who had all her call details and was waiting to tear me apart.

'So you are officially two-timing me?' I asked her.

'You can say that . . . and you are no different,' she said poking her finger in my cleavage. Yes, I had one.

'Damn! We missed the trailers,' I said. 'Have we started dating?'

She just winked at me and I stood there, frozen and confused. I had fallen in love with that wink too, like I had with every mannerism of hers.

The movie was awful. Probably that's why half the audience ended up watching us instead. Avantika kept showing them her middle finger. Our innocence during the days I talked to her, watched her from a distance went out of the window as soon as she sat next to me in the movie. It wasn't premeditated, and I didn't know we would make out, or even kiss, but we did and we did it with a vengeance. Until now, when I kissed her again, I had no idea I wanted her so badly. Avantika was a great kisser, her tongue worked wonders, and so did my hands. The movie ended a little too soon. Or so we felt. We were embarrassed at how much we clawed and bit into each other during the movie. We were all over each other and it was spectacular.

'Where to?' I asked. I just wanted to make sure. After what happened in the movie hall, just the thought of the two of us in a room sent tingles down my spine. I had to keep reminding myself that it was happening for real.

'I don't think that needs an answer. Let's go.'

She hadn't changed her mind. My face flushed with all the blood from my veins rushing forth. The third and the last click on the door of her house set my pulse racing.

# 10

I was trying not to be nervous, more so because she clearly was not. Her transformation from a tragic beauty to a *dirty–past–devil–may–care* one had been quick, unexpected and thanked for. I didn't know whether I liked the beautiful messy girl on the balcony more, or the girl who just blew me away inside the movie hall.

We entered her place. The lights lit up the room.

And I froze, yet again.

'I knew they would be here! I know this *BASTARD*. I knew they would be here.'

The very next second I was ducking the savage punches Tanmay was throwing at my face. All I could see was Vernita shouting at Avantika across the room.

'*What* did you think, Avantika? *Why?* What were you thinking? What the hell are you doing with him?' Vernita rained a flurry of questions.

I would come to know later that a friend of Shawar had spotted Avantika and me, and Shawar had asked Tanmay to check on Avantika. Vernita and Tanmay were smart enough to put two and two together.

'Didn't I ask you to stay away from him? This guy is a bastard, didn't I tell you that? He is going out with Smriti and still sleeping with you? Why Avantika? Why? What were you thinking? You want to get back to your shitty life? He will do just that—fuck you and leave you. He has done that before and he won't even think twice before he does that to you. And you, asshole,' Tanmay said. He came charging at me and slapped me right out of my senses. He started punching me again. I ducked but he kept going at me until he got a few jabs right in my face. I cut a lip and started to bleed. He backed off seeing that. *Going to the gym helps*, I thought.

'Yogi was right all along. He always said you were a selfish guy. You lied to me? Deb? You are such a bastard. I can't believe it. I warned you a million times not to go near her, didn't I?' Vernita asked.

Vernita was visibly hurt. But I still feel she overreacted. I could have done without her moral lecture. She wasn't a nun herself.

The high-emotion, high-energy drama seemed a little childish for me; it was a small price to pay to be with Avantika. Any price was a price too little. It was just that Avantika was crying now. I didn't quite like that. Moreover, Avantika was old enough to decide whom she slept with, though I knew this wasn't a point I could have raised.

'Avantika, I didn't expect this from you. Tanmay hasn't slept for the last few days. He loves you more than he loves anyone and this is what you do to him? Lie to him? Do you think we are fools? For the last so many days, both your phones were busy. Did you think we didn't know what was going on? Deb, didn't I ask you to leave her alone? Didn't you fucking think what would happen if we got to know about this? Fuck you, Deb, I can't believe you dagged me in the back,' Vernita shouted at me. Every time my phone was busy, she never forgot to ask whom was I talking to. I would take some arbitrary name and hope she would believe it.

'Stabbed,' I corrected Vernita. It wasn't the smartest thing to do but everybody except Avantika did have a smile on their faces for a fleeting second, before Tanmay resumed.

'Vernita, give me your phone. Let's call Smriti. Right now.' He walked up to Vernita and started dialling the number.

'You are not doing that. I will tell her tomorrow,' I said. I could have dumped her any time, but I didn't want to do it like this.

'Why do you think I care, asshole? You didn't care about Vernita. You didn't care about Avantika. Why do you think I would care about your girlfriend?' Tanmay shouted. He spat while he did so.

'Hi Smriti . . . Tanmay here . . . talk to Vernita, she has something to tell you,' Tanmay had called Smriti and put the phone on loudspeaker.

'Hi, Smriti. We came to Tanmay's flat and Deb is here. With Avantika. God knows what's up with these two.'

'*What?*' she said from the other side.

'Yes. He cheated on you. He fucking lied to us and lied to you. Talk to your boyfriend,' she gave the phone to me. I disconnected the line.

'I hope you'll listen to what I am about to say, this time at least. This guy will *destroy* you. I don't want you to be hurt again. It's either him or me. Don't ever talk to me if you intend to see him again. You have the night to decide. It's either him or me,' Tanmay said to Avantika.

'Deb, it's over. You are after all a bastard of a guy. You couldn't even respect my boyfriend's sister,' Vernita said. She was crying too.

They went into Tanmay's dad's bedroom and bolted it. Smriti kept calling me. Finally, I answered her call.

'Why? Deb? Why?' Smriti said as she broke down. *Not again*. 'What do I do now? Why did you do it? Weren't you happy? Why, Deb? Why?'

'I don't know, Smriti. It just happened. I am sorry. You know things weren't right between us. I wanted to love you, but then you were not making it any easier for me. It was not working out and you know that. Things were not the way they were before.'

At this, Avantika came and sat near me and switched on the speaker.

'Don't you love me any more? Please say you do. I will forgive you. Please come back. I am begging you. I will love you. I will never let you down, I promise. Please don't leave me, Deb,' her sobs gave way to full-scale wailing.

'It will be tough, Smriti. I loved you. But I don't know now. We will remain friends. I promise. Our relationship was not working. If we don't break up now, I don't think we can even remain friends,' I said. I felt the guilt seep in. But it wouldn't go deeper; my body had developed enough resistance to fight against these situations. The friendship part had never happened, and I hardly ever cared.

'Don't give me that, Deb. *Avantika?* Why didn't you tell me? Please come back. I need you. You can't leave me like this. I can't believe all this is happening to me. Please come back. You said we would work things out.'

'I can't, Smriti. Please understand. I know I have wronged you, but there is nothing that I can do now.'

'Wronged? You bloody slept with her! Why? Deb, I am willing to wait for you. Tell me how long. When would you feel like continuing it? Give me a time. I will wait, damn it. We will start afresh. Please don't go. Please don't go.'

This went on for hours. She cursed, she cried, she wailed, she begged and she shouted. I contemplated going back to her, but leaving Avantika was not a choice. Eventually, we broke up. She was in tears when we disconnected the line. It wasn't as if I was untouched by her crying. We had been together for more than six months and I cared about her. It may not have been the handsomest of break-ups but maybe it came at the right time. She would now have an answer to her parents' questions. She wasn't bad, I thought. But Avantika was great, sexy, good-looking, smart and I loved her. You don't let go of the person you love easily, do you?

Avantika and I spent the night balled up in an embrace, looking into each other's eyes.

'So, what have you thought?' Avantika said.

'About what?'

'Smriti or me?'

'I have decided. It's over with Smriti.'

'And me? You think you can be with me? Do you even know whether I love you or not? And Tanmay?'

'Yes. It hardly matters to me what Vernita or Tanmay think. As long as you're with me. If you don't love me, that's another matter, but I am ready to wait,' I said.

'I think you should go back. It happened with me once. I can't do this to another girl. It's painful. Believe me. I don't want to be responsible for her pain.'

'It's not *you* who did this. *I* did this. And this had to happen some day. It's good that it happened sooner than later.'

'But . . . I don't know whether I have the strength to get into another relationship. You know what I have been through.'

'I will keep you safe. I know it's too much, too soon, but you can put your trust in me and I will not break it.'

'I was expecting something more,' she said.

'Love you.' For the first time I wasn't getting anything for saying those words. I wasn't unhooking or unzipping in a car with tinted windows. I was longing for her to reciprocate.

'Love you, too. Thanks for everything, Sri Guru,' she said and looked heavenwards and softly cried the night away. All calls from Shawar were dutifully rejected throughout the night. Some sixty-five of them.

I grinned the night away. I was in love! It had (supposedly) happened to me before, but it meant so much more this time.

It was 20 May . . . the day that changed it all.

~

Shrey looked around at the people lugging their suitcases in the trolleys outside the Indira Gandhi International Airport. It was roughly a two-month long trip to Paris and he was just carrying a single backpack.

'Take care, Shrey.' We hugged. I didn't want him to go. Vernita wouldn't be talking to me ever again and I would have no one to kill time with. I hated goodbyes and this was one very discomforting one. 'Get me something from France.'

'I will try. Actually, I am on a strict budget. But I will try and steal the university hard disks for you. Bye,' he said as he disappeared behind the clearance gates. He wouldn't be back before the seventh semester. Long time. Two damned months.

~

After any of my relationships ended, I kicked myself for getting into it in the first place. I felt bad for the girl and made up my mind to never repeat such a thing. But then within a few days or months things were back to square one. The girl I had dumped would be smiling and I would be robbed of the guilt.

Smriti was dumped. Though I couldn't say I loved her, it still wasn't very easy for me. For no fault of hers, I had given her a torrid time. Not only had I broken up with her, it was a terrible break-up. I had cheated on her. She wasn't actually going through a great phase and ditching her wasn't very sensitive of me. I cursed myself for it but I couldn't help it. I hadn't intended to cheat on her.

In fact, all this time I had wanted *her* to break up with me. For the break-up to be a *mutual* decision. I hated to think of her crying.

Over the next few days, I couldn't keep Smriti's wails out of my mind, often pulling back from the brink of shedding a few tears myself. She was the only girl who had considered me a good boyfriend even after what I had done to her. I missed her. I missed her bugging calls. I missed her irritating messages. I missed being with her. I missed her imperfections.

But I was with Avantika now. I loved her. I loved her 'perfectness' more. *And I was sure this time.*

I was in a relationship. I was committed—not just in words, but in my actions too. But the most glaring fact of all was that I *accepted* this gleefully. This automatically meant I was unavailable, but it hardly mattered. I was neither single nor in any mood to be so. I still loved tinted car windows, empty movie halls and the like, but now the phone calls meant more than anything else. The short sweet messages meant more. Holding hands meant more than a lot of other things I had craved for in my previous relationships.

Though it would have been a little strange for the people who saw us together. I am sure about what they had to say—'*Shit man, that girl is actually with that guy.'* Or *'Damn man, the girl has shitty taste in men.'*

I was way too ugly to be with her.

~

'Hi, Avantika. Where are you?'

'I am on my way. Where will you pick me up from? I am about to reach Kashmere Gate,' she said.

Even though I had to eventually reach where she already was, we still met midway and travelled the remaining distance again. It gave us more time together; I hated every moment not spent with her.

I had come to be very dependent on Avantika. With no Shrey and Vernita around, there was no one else I could talk to. Not that I even wanted to. Yogi and Viru had gone back to their hometowns and I found no sense in spending money on STD calls to discuss why girls from Punjab have better breasts.

Where people were scrambling for internships that would see them through to great jobs, I spent my days with Avantika, trying not to think about the fact that I would not get any. I was faking my internship. Mom and Dad occasionally asked me where I intended to apply for a job when the seventh semester started. I could do nothing but avoid their eyes, brimming with expectations and enthusiasm.

Avantika saw me through all my mood swings and there were many. Sad, for I had lost one of my friends ... agitated, because another was away in France ... jealous, for people were gearing up for their job interviews ... angry, because I was letting my parents down ... and worthless, as I was letting *myself* down.

'Hi, Avantika, what a surprise! It's been so long.' We hugged as we met. Tanmay wasn't talking to her any more. But she said he would be okay and the bigger problem was his ego and not me.

'True. It's been eighteen hours, I suppose, since we last met. Very long. We should meet more often!' She smiled.

'Where to?' I asked.

'North Campus, where else? Oh, wait! Take the Civil Lines route. There is a deserted place there. It's called Bhoot Bangla. We used to go there often. It's sealed now. It will be fun.'

'As you say, baby.' I always hated using terms of endearment, but things had changed now. And this was one of them.

'So where is it? There?'

Driving had become insanely tough now. She used to look at me while I drove and it was hard not to look back at her.

We reached where she wanted us to. It did look like a haunted place. It was a modestly big clock tower surrounded by overgrown trees from an adjacent park. I remembered spotting it once from the metro. Big thing jutting out from a vegetated area reminded me of only one thing. Ugh.

We climbed the fence and reached the main tower. It was locked. I was not a National Geographic lover and never did want to spread my arms and swirl around a mountain edge and try to fly. But the place was beautiful. And so was she.

'So this is it?' I asked.

'Yup.'

'I see.'

'What?' she asked.

'I see that I see nothing. I see that there is no one around. Which means that no matter what we do here, no one is going to notice!'

That was enough encouragement for our frenzied hormones. We lunged at each other and within seconds, we were all over each other, searching for things inside each other's T-shirts. She hadn't quite left her wild streak at the Spirit of Living conventions. We were very much in love but who says you can't be *in lust* too?

'Hey there!' a big voice boomed behind us.

'Oh! Fuck!' I whispered as we separated and pulled down our shirts.

He was a huge guy. Or a small guy with a huge paunch. He was the most dreaded creature under the circumstances—dishevelled sparse hair, untrimmed moustache, red-stained and decayed teeth, and a pumpkin-sized face—the Delhi Police!

The only thing worse than being caught pants down by your parents is to be caught by the cops.

Not that it was within their right to do anything about it, but they always played the *we-will-tell-your-parents* card. Traffic policemen were getting richer by the day thanks to the exorbitant fines, so the others type of cops didn't quite relish being left behind. It became expensive to get caught.

'Sir, we are sorry.' I almost broke down and bent down to catch hold of his feet. I pulled back just in time. Overacting wasn't cool. As I was getting up, Avantika put her hand in my back pocket.

'Sorry? What the hell do you think you are doing here? What if somebody puts a knife through you here? Who will save you then? There is nobody within a mile from here,' he shouted.

'Sorry, sir.'

'Give your names and your addresses,' he said as he came closer and sprayed bits of the betel he was chewing on me. He was still a metre away from me, the closest his paunch would allow him to come. 'I will have to inform your parents about this.'

*Aww! C'mon! At least say something new!*

'Sorry, sir. We will never do it again,' Avantika said apologetically. *We will never get caught again.* She was a natural, finding time to blow kisses and winking at me in between. Not to mention sticking her hand down my pocket and squeezing my butt again.

'No, nothing will do. You will have to come to the police station with me. Give me your names. Right now,' he said and whipped out his notepad. He was taking it too far. He went through the full motion of writing down our names and addresses, not even bothering to look up our identity cards even once. It was a sham.

'Sir, we are sorry. Can't we just settle the matter here?' she said in a *cut-the-crap-and-get-to-the-point* fashion, bent backwards and placed her hands on her waist. His big moustached face lit up. I was sure we were the first ones to get caught today.

'No, that won't do. Give me your names. Right now. You can't be let off easily,' he said, trying to make it sound like a big offence.

'Sir . . . we told you we are sorry. Let's forget it, sir. I am sure *something* can be done,' she said.

'I know how you kids behave. Your parents should be told about this. Let your parents come here and then we will decide.'

'Please don't do that, sir. Let us settle things between us. Why drag parents into this? Sorry, sir,' she said. She was the *man* again. I would have sobbed my way out of that, with the same result. The act was over and it was time for some money to exchange hands.

'Okay, if you promise that you will never do such a thing ever again, then I will leave you.'

*Oh. You fucking saint!*

'We promise, sir,' we echoed. We were being preached at by someone who had unlawfully caught us and would unlawfully accept a bribe. *Sweet*.

'Where is your car?' he asked.

'There.' I was thankful the game was cut short by Avantika. It was getting boring and the stench of his sweat was getting unbearable.

'Let's go,' he said and asked me to follow. Avantika followed us. 'How long have you two been doing this?' he asked, as he climbed into the car, which seemed too small for his two-hundred-pound frame.

'I . . .'

'Anyway, how much do you have? Take out your wallet.' He was getting impatient with the preaching.

'Sir, not much. Plus, we are students, sir, and we don't have much. It's the end of the month . . .' I said, as I brought out my wallet.

'Show that to me.' He snatched it from me. As expected, there were just a hundred bucks in there. I was shocked and impressed. *Good job done, Avantika.*

Avantika was not squeezing my butt earlier. She was squeezing out the wallet from my back pocket and all the money in it!

'Sir, I need to go back home. I need fifty bucks for that,' I said.

His face shrank to the size of a raisin. The ethics of bribery guided them not to take money from a female accomplice. I was sure he wouldn't ask her for money.

'I will leave you this time. But watch out. Next time, I will inform your parents. You are lucky that I didn't do that this time.' He took the fifty bucks and left, disappointed and nearly empty-handed.

'Not a bad deal, eh?' I said.

'Nope. You owe me a treat. I just saved you a thousand bucks.'

Avantika was intelligent and experienced and it showed. I hoped her experience was a traffic violation incident and not kissing her ex-boyfriends in public.

We kissed again. And the world stopped to matter.

~

The two months went past in a flash. We met every single day, every single night during those two months. We crashed farmhouse parties, weddings, even stayed locked up in her college classroom for a night, as it was her fantasy to make out on the professor's table. I loved the way our night-outs ended, especially when they ended at her place. Most of the times it used to be a bubble bath, after which we would wrap ourselves in a single white towel, her head on my chest. We would kiss and I would feel the wetness of her hair on my face and it felt like heaven. Our life was a montage from a cheesy romantic movie.

Night-outs were about much more than groping. Much more. They were not a pretext to make out. They were a necessity—the only way we could have spent more time together.

We dodged Shawar and his friends a million times during those days. A lot of them hung around the places we did. Avantika obviously couldn't tell Shawar about me. Tanmay had not said anything but by now Shawar had guessed that it was not sisterly love that I had for Avantika. The last time she talked about a break-up, Shawar spent three days drinking and asking about me and cursing me. So, dumping him for another guy meant two of us going down. Shawar and me.

*He will hunt you down and kill you . . . not beat you up, but kill you for real. Trust me, he can do that,* Avantika once told me.

# 11

I had never been a morning person. I hated mornings. I hated the chirping birds, I hated the milkman, I hated the morning shower, and I hated alarm clocks with a vengeance. It only took Avantika to change all that. She would give me a time when I would wake her up. Usually it was two hours too early for me, but I wouldn't miss her early morning voice for anything in the world. That day, I wanted to see her. It was the first day of the two-month-long vacation and she was staying in the hostel. Since she was one of the few girls who had stayed back, I had figured she could do with some company.

'Hi baby, what time is it?' Avantika asked in a low, husky groggy tone.

'Seven fifty. We still have ten minutes.' I had changed my number again, to the one that had reduced call rates up to eight in the morning. Invariably, I woke up minutes before 8 a.m. for those precious few minutes of dirt-cheap ecstasy. It is amazing how love changes one's biological clock.

'What's up, Deb?'

'Nothing, the *doodhwala* did not come today. So, I'm coming back from the grocery store. I got three litres of double-toned milk, want some?' I lied.

'Why didn't you call me when you woke up?' she asked. With others, it was always an accusing cross-question. *Why didn't you call me? Where were you? What were you doing? What was so important that you couldn't take out a single minute for me?* With her, it was just a question. The details of place, time, nature of work were secondary.

'Nothing, was in a bit of a rush,' I said. I had reached her hostel. 'I will call you in a while.'

'Okay, bye. Miss you.' I disconnected the line because I didn't want to get caught. She always saw through my lies. I drove around and parked the car nearby. I called her again.

'Hi, Deb.'

'Hi! What's up?' I asked. Just then, an ambulance passed by me, with its siren on full blast. Damn.

'Hey! What is that siren behind you? I can hear the same here. Are you here? Outside my hostel? You are here, right?'

'Oho! That's so unfair! I wanted to surprise you and the freaking siren . . . Yes, I am outside and I waiting,' I conceded.

'I will be there in ten minutes. I am still in my pyjamas.'

'Shut up and get out. Nobody is around, and I love you in your pyjamas.'

'But . . .'

'You have two minutes. Quick!' I disconnected the line and waited for her.

She came running out of her hostel door, a big smile on her face, and hugged the life out of me. Even with her ruffled hair, crumpled T-shirt and the pink pyjamas, she looked adorable. I stood there imagining what it would be like to watch her sleep every morning.

'Such a surprise, Deb! Thanks for coming. I missed you.'

'The pleasure is all mine. Can we sit in the car?' I asked her in anticipation.

'Yes, sure.' Bang. She closed the car door. A little harder and it would have fallen off. But then, you always have poor quality mechanical engineers to blame it on.

'Your car smells great! New freshener?' she laughed out.

'No,' I said as I adjusted the rear view mirror. 'Look,' I pointed out to the mirror.

'OH MY GOD! Deb!' she shrieked covering her mouth with both her hands, her eyes quivering and looking at me. Hundreds of yellow and red petals were strewn all over the back seat, covering every inch of it, and a huge pink card screaming in bold red letters: *Love you, Avantika.* My experience with gifts and surprises was minimal and I had no idea what would make Avantika happy. Still, I wanted to do something for her, something that communicated to her beyond my usual words. Cards and flowers were clichéd, but that's all I could think of.

Her welled-up eyes told me that she appreciated my effort. She read the card, on which I had written everything I felt about her, and she was immediately in tears. She lunged at me and hugged me.

'Love you, Deb, I love you so much. This is the sweetest thing anyone has ever done for me.'

'Oh, c'mon. Your ex-boyfriends must have gifted you things much better than this,' I said, trying to fish for compliments.

'It's not about what they gifted me or what you did. It's the intention behind it. And these,' she pointed to the card, 'are words I will never forget. That's all that matters. Your words are all I need.'

I blushed. We spent the rest of the day driving around in the car. She didn't want to leave the setting. The good part done, I later had to do an even better job of cleaning the car before I handed it over to Dad. It helped that Avantika had stuffed a lot of the petals into her nightsuit pockets, fists and armpits before leaving. I loved her. Our love was flowering.

As I drove back home, my surprise felt silly but I was glad she liked it. It was cheesy, but it worked. I couldn't stop smiling for the entire day. My mom was sure something was up. Moms always know.

The next two months were a repeat of that day. I would wake up early and take the metro to her hostel while she would wait in her pyjamas for me. We would go out for long walks, share a coffee at the nearby coffee shop and she would go back to her hostel. We never ran out of things to say. No matter how much you trust someone, there are things you always hide from them. Sometimes it's out of the fear of judgement, sometimes it's because you're ashamed of those things. It takes courage to admit to stuff in front of someone when you haven't accepted them yourself. Avantika gave me that courage. I didn't think twice before telling her all my shameful secrets, all my desires, and my ambitions. She never judged me.

'No one's perfect,' she would whisper into my ears and hold my hand.

I would whisper back, 'You're perfect.'

She would smile and lay all my fears to rest.

~

Just as Avantika's vacation ended, Shrey's vacation came to an end too. He was back from Paris and I wanted to hear all his exotic stories. He used to send me pictures on mail, but he said he would give me all the gossip once he was back in India.

'Hey! Welcome back,' I said as I hugged him. I looked around for some gifts that he may have got for us but I couldn't see anything. Thank god I hadn't planned a 'Welcome Back' party for him. But at least he was footing the bill for that day's lunch.

'Before anything, give me the filthiest Hindi abuses you have ever heard of. It's been a while since I have heard any of that. Missed them a lot, man. French people are always so nice to you that sometimes you want to kill yourself.'

'I am sorry. But with my impaired vocabulary, I don't think I can be of any help. Why don't you call up Vernita instead, *bhenchod*?' I said.

He hadn't changed. I dreaded that a Paris-returned Shrey might have an accent and an air of sophistication about him but, thankfully, nothing had changed.

'Oh yes, I am meeting her tomorrow. But tell me. Is there something wrong between Vernita and you? I heard something but I didn't want to interfere. You know how we end up fighting every time I try to talk sense into her.'

'It's just a little fight. It will be okay in a while,' I said, not wanting to go into all the details.

'Whatever. Are Yogi and Viru coming over?'

'They should be here any moment. Rohit is coming with them too. Oh, they are already here.' They barged in through the door. Their enthusiasm was unbelievable. Even I wasn't as happy to see him as they were and I was his best friend.

'Dude! So tell us. How many girls did you sleep with? Do all women have anti-gravity boobs there? Was your professor as hot as she sounded over the phone? Did you make a girlfriend?' Viru asked, pinning him.

'That's more questions than he would have been asked in his research in France,' Yogi quipped.

'Ha!' Shrey smirked.

Damn! It looked like he had had loads of fun.

'So, how was it?' I asked.

'It was fun. I just hope I don't end up with a couple of white kids claiming to be my sons if I ever visit that place again. The worst girls out there would make the best here seem like baby elephants. Even the older ones. They are just so young and so fit,' Shrey said and licked his fingers.

'Did you sleep with older ones, too?' Viru asked as he drank his beer.

'No,' Shrey shrugged.

'Why? Never mind, tell me more.'

'My professor, she wore hot pants on holidays. She is fifty, beat that. I started going to the gym just so I could see her.'

'Did you sleep with her?' Viru asked. His curiosity made me uncomfortable. Shrey's sexual escapades didn't excite me either. If anything, I was a little jealous. I reminded myself of Avantika and calmed down. He wasn't as lucky as I was.

'No,' Shrey said. I was relieved.

'*Why* not? Why the hell not?' Viru was getting restless.

'Why the hell not? I respected her, dude. She is the first

person in the world to have successfully digitalized the entire electrochemical broaching process. Even at the National Physical Laboratories . . .'

'What? Is that your reason?' Yogi mocked.

'Not acceptable, man,' I added.

I loved that he had not slept with the supposedly stunning professor. Maybe his Paris trip wasn't as much fun as it had seemed in the pictures. Besides, I was still dating the hottest girl ever. Yeah, we are men—we are shallow and silly.

'That and the fact that her sister wouldn't have liked it,' Shrey smirked.

'What . . . what do you mean?' I gasped. There came the challenge.

'Obviously he means that he slept with her. Didn't you?' Viru answered quite intelligently.

I needed something to eat. Or beer. French girls would have done best, but . . . *Avantika! You have Avantika*. I calmed down.

'Yes. I did,' Shrey said, his chin pointing up. He smiled like he owned the world. *I am dating a goddamned goddess*, I told myself to calm down. I wanted to shout that out but I ate my words and my parantha.

'What was it like? Man, did you make a video? Don't tell me all you got us are these stupid Eiffel Tower pictures,' Viru added.

The video, apart from the obvious viewing pleasure would have also meant free membership of the greatest Indian porn site— www.debonairblog.com. Like every hosteller, DCE hostellers, too, had just four avenues for time pass—porn, movies, sex talk and alcohol. A few of them had a fifth—a girlfriend.

'Obviously, no videos.' He held his head so high he might have touched the ceiling any moment. I hoped the fan would come in between and cut it clean off his neck. I was glad there was no proof of his sexual conquests. It would have been disturbing.

'Tell me. Is it as easy to hook up as they show in movies and other sitcoms?' Viru asked.

'Pretty much. You just have to look out for the drunken girls, approach them with an English-to-French dictionary and boom

. . . you find yourself in their flats and apartments and houses,' Shrey said.

'Is it that easy?' Viru asked. A few cars could have passed through his gaping mouth. He had probably started fantasizing about having a drunken French girl on his knees. I know *I* had.

'So how many girls did you sleep with?' I asked, hoping the number wouldn't be mind-boggling. I also reminded myself of how much I loved Avantika.

'Six. Beat that.'

I could not. Not even close. For the past few years, people who knew me bashed me for being a male slut even when I was not. Shrey was the slut!

'Six? Man, you are lucky,' Yogi shrieked. He was yet to see a topless girl off-screen.

'But what about Vandana?' Rohit said. He had been quiet all this time, wringing his face to signify different degrees of disgust.

'What about her? She is good,' Shrey said.

'No, I mean, have you told her that you have slept with someone else?'

'Are you nuts? Obviously not.'

'No?' Rohit asked, and his face contorted beyond recognition. He was still going around with his school sweetheart and had accepted every other girl as his sister. Since he was from the IT department, he never realized what the scarcity of girls felt like.

'But I think you really should. It's not right what you did to her. Anyway, you guys carry on. I better leave now. Bye.' He got up and left unceremoniously. Maybe, he found us repulsive and immoral.

'Deb, I heard you have started going around with Avantika. How is it going?' Shrey asked.

'Did you sleep with her?' Viru added. 'I have heard she is hot as hell.'

'It's going fine. And some things are personal,' I said. I really wanted to tell them how we were making out in a graveyard parking lot when the freaky-looking guard freaked the shit out of us. But yes, Avantika and I had not yet slept together and I didn't feel the need to ask her about it. It would happen when it would happen. I wasn't too concerned.

'French girls may be hotter. They may have figures one would die for. They may even be better at blowjobs, but I still long to do it with an Indian girl. Deb, you are a lucky dog. I would love to swap places with you,' Shrey said.

*Yeah, right.*

'But why is that?' I asked. No matter what he did in France, I would have never given up the time I had spent with Avantika for the time he had spent in France.

'I don't know. There is a sense of achievement when you run around after someone and finally get her,' Shrey said. 'French girls are easy.'

'But what about the frustration when you run after someone and you get nothing but disappointment and when you are alone at night staring at porn. I wish Indian girls were as easy,' Viru said and looked at me.

'I understand your pain.'

'Of course you don't. You just slept with six French women! Anyway, how *is* Vandana? Did she miss you? Of course, *you* didn't miss her,' Viru asked Shrey.

'I hope she did. I did,' he said wistfully. I had told him he would.

Viru and Yogi left after a little while. Shrey told me he hadn't slept with anyone in France. He said he just couldn't muster up the courage to cheat on Vandana any more. He said he had lied to the other guys because he didn't want to disappoint them.

'So, you really missed her a lot?' I asked him.

'Not a single day went by when I didn't think of her,' he said. It was nice to see Shrey, always too cocky, having a vulnerable moment. I liked this Shrey better, better than the one who claimed to have slept with six French women.

He dropped me home and left to see Vandana.

~

Shawar was becoming a menace now. Avantika told me that he was tracking me but she said there was nothing to worry about as long as both of us were careful. Night-outs became a little tricky when Shawar started calling Avantika's roommates every day to check on her.

As if that wasn't enough, he even called on my landline once to ask where I was. My parents obviously told him what they knew—that I was in the hostel, studying. But Mom never forgot to ask why a drunken-sounding guy was interested in knowing my whereabouts. I lied; whether she believed it or not, I would never know.

A few rebukes from Avantika stopped him from calling, but then he started calling me. He was just barely polite in the first call. After that, he had just one question to ask—*What is going on between you and Avantika?* Often laced with the filthiest Hindi expletives.

He was a year or two younger but he made me piss in my pants. I was clearly instructed by Avantika to call her if I were to spot a few suspicious-looking guys hanging around big cars and puffing on cigarettes, beer bottles in hand.

*They could be them. Be careful, Deb.*

# 12

'Are you jealous that Shrey had a wonderful trip?' Avantika asked.

'Certainly not! A paid foreign internship, replete with sex? Why should I be jealous? Naah!' I said sarcastically. I didn't tell her about Shrey's weak moment. He wouldn't have liked that.

'I cannot say that I am particularly sad for you. Though I can make it up to you in ways you have only imagined,' she said. Most of the times this was an empty promise, but the sheer sexiness with which it was delivered made me go bonkers with passion.

'Oh, yeah? Now, I would love to see how you do that. Three chocolate-syrup fantasies are already pending if I remember correctly.'

'Oh, yes I do, baby! All of them together. Wouldn't you just love that?' she said in a low husky voice.

'Yes, I would, but shut up right now. I am in no position to talk dirty.' I was dead tired. Mom and Dad weren't asleep yet. It was a bad time for phone sex and I knew why she had chosen it. She loved to arouse me at times, and in certain places, when I would be absolutely helpless.

'You want me to shut up? But I was just about to unzip your pants and go down and—'

'Will you please *stop*? I've got to study!' I shouted non-angrily. This had to work; she could screw me over the phone, but she would never screw my studies.

'You have to study? Ha! DCEites study? Don't give me that.'

'Why? I do study. I know I am intelligent enough not to study. But then . . .'

'Yeah, yeah. Whatever! But seriously, go and study. There is not much time left for the CAT.'

'As if you study the entire night every day,' I shot back.

'I won't get through, anyway. But you can. Go, study.' Her words of encouragement always worked for me. Deep inside, there was still a nerd in me who wanted to score the highest marks and be patted on the back by teachers and peers alike.

'Okay. Will think about that. What are you doing tomorrow? I mean can we go to your place?' I said. I couldn't get the dirty talk out of my head.

'Ohooo! So now you want to make out suddenly? What happened to the studious Deb? I am sorry, but I am a little busy tomorrow.'

'Don't play with me. Tell me, I'm serious. If not your place, can we go watch a really bad movie?'

I was already a little turned on and felt she was toying with me.

'I am serious. I am going to my rehabilitation centre. Something to do with SOL.'

'What exactly?'

'You will not understand. Go and study.'

'I don't feel like studying. Even if I get through the written examination, there is no way I can clear the interviews.'

'And why do you say that?' she asked irritably.

'Why? There is nothing in my profile, Avantika! Four years of college and I have practically done nothing! No certificates. No extracurricular activities. No recommendations. They won't just take me because of my score. They need people with hobbies and shit like that.'

'You have been part of those societies and stuff, won't that help?'

'Obviously not. Everyone can see through it. Even the guy from that software firm knew I was bluffing.'

'Then do something. Pick up something. Anything. Say you love cooking. And that you can cook anything under the sun and mug up recipes. What say? That's a good enough hobby?'

'Crap, they will ask me to go and be a cook. And cooking? I would need something that can act as a pretext for bad academic scores. Cooking doesn't quite fit in.'

'Writing? Say, blogging? That would be cool. You can say that you weren't ever keen on engineering, so you spent a lot of time writing on your blog,' she said.

I wasn't very interested. I couldn't see how it could have enhanced my unimpressive profile.

'What exactly is a blog? What exactly do I do?' I asked, completing a mere formality.

'Nothing, just a free website, a log of whatever happens to you or around you. You can write about anything under the sun. A photographer friend of mine has a photo blog. He uploads all his pictures over there. So people go there, read the stuff, see the stuff and comment on how they like it. In short it is networking, but through written stuff or photographs or videos. Even Amitabh Bachchan and Aamir Khan have blogs.'

'But no one is going to read my blog, Avantika.'

'Oh, c'mon! Blogs written by normal everyday people have millions of followers. I am not saying you will get to that, but there is no harm in giving it a shot,' she argued.

'Whatever. I will think about it. Can we go on a night-out tomorrow? I really want to see you.'

'I will be too tired tomorrow, Deb. Later, I promise, baby,' she said.

'Okay, but I won't take no for an answer the next time round. I swear.'

'Sure, tell me one thing. How's D.E. Shaw as a company?' she asked.

'D.E. Shaw? I would give an arm to work for them. They literally bathe you in money. It's a huge package! And I have heard they send their employees to the US within the first week of employment. They are pampered like anything. I think it came in sixth in the list of the best companies to work with last year.'

'But isn't it software? I thought you weren't interested in software, especially after that day.'

'That's because I don't like working. I will flush toilets if you pay me that much. A fully paid trip to the US? Who's going to give that up?'

'Shut up, Deb, it doesn't work that way. It's about interest. Like I am desperate to have a career in finance, there must be something in your mind?' she asked forcefully. She was lying. I knew she would accept anything that would pay her well enough to run away from her family. Lately, her uncles' marriage-related jabs at her were getting unbearable for her.

'Nothing. I am not desperate to have a career in anything! Okay, if I give you a choice between McKinsey & Company and Dena Bank, consultants and finance, where would you go?'

I knew I had her. McKinsey paid three times as much as Dena Bank, and all its employees were placed in metros, unlike Dena Bank. For fresh graduates it's all about the bottom line. Almost no one is looking for job satisfaction or a work–life balance. It's simple, fire the Human Resources Department, pump the money into benefits for the newly hired and watch young talented kids flock at your company doorstep. But nobody listens.

'I don't know what I will do. Tanmay just called, Vernita got through D.E. Shaw. The interviews were held today,' she said.

'What? What?' I spluttered. The same flapping of tongue struck again.

'Yes. She is through. They are probably sending her to Mumbai. They are yet to give her the location.'

'I cannot believe this. That bitch—' I went supersonic.

'Don't swear.'

'Why shouldn't I? Why shouldn't I? That slut has a lower percentage than me, and doesn't know a thing about software. Why do you think she got through?' I was still way above the audible range; I was expecting hyenas outside my window. This was unbelievable.

'It's not her fault if the interviewers liked her.'

'Don't give me that. You know she didn't deserve it! Why is every average being around me suddenly transforming into a genius? People are going to France on internships, someone's suddenly a software genius, and I am stuck here talking to you. *Great!*'

'What do you mean you're stuck here talking to me?' Avantika said.

'I am just angry. THIS IS SO NOT FAIR! She's such a slut!' I bellowed.

'Calm down, Deb,' she said. 'And don't call her a slut.'

'I am sorry, Avantika. I didn't mean to say that.'

'Better. Now tell me. Who is more important? The girl who is crazily in love with you or the job at D.E. Shaw?'

'Silly question. You . . . of course.' Though it would have been better if I had the job to go along with it. We always did the *who-is-more-important* thing every time one of us was depressed. It had started out as a joke but soon we realized it was effective, and we started using it more often.

'Keep studying, Deb. There will be scores of off-campus interviews. I am sure you will crack one of them,' she said.

'We will see.'

'You need to put in some effort. Things won't just happen to you. I am not criticizing you, I am just saying things will happen. You just need to be patient and work towards it. You will never get the pants ironed if you don't take them off,' she said.

'Maybe. Anyway, I don't need to work. You will do that. I will be home taking care of our kids,' I said.

'Is it, Deb? We are getting married? I am thankful you told me that.'

'Obviously we are! You know I am not into short-term relationships. When have I ever been in a short-term relationship?' I joked.

'Yes, I know. You have had just ten long-term relationships until now. Haven't you?' she mocked.

'No, baby, but seriously, this time it is long-term.'

'Long-term till you get bored of me,' she complained.

'I will never get bored of you. You are the only girl I have ever loved. I just lusted after the rest of them.'

'That's not very nice to hear. And you don't lust after me? I am not good enough for you? Or were they better?' she let out a wholehearted laugh.

'You are the best. You are a porn star strapped in Avantika's body! Okay? You turned down tomorrows' plan, not me! If it were up to me, I would have you naked and locked up. On that note, is there is no way I can see you tomorrow?'

'I wish I could have, but I can't. Is that why you are upset with me? I knew it all along! You're incredibly horny, Deb.' She laughed out again.

'Shut up. Any guy with a girlfriend as attractive as you are would be as horny as I am! I love you, and you're my little porn star. By the way, I have decided the names of our kids too. We will have around seven of them, five girls and two boys and hopefully no hermaphrodites—' I was interrupted.

'You can keep all that nonsense to yourself and study. Don't make a long face when others beat you in the placements scene. I am serious, Deb. Go study.'

'Okay. I will.'

I didn't like people beating me but even then, I wasn't doing anything to change that. Trying to change it also meant poking at the beehive—failure. Failing when you don't put in an effort always hurts less.

*Even if you win the rat race, you still end up being a rat . . . okay, maybe a rich fat rat.*

Avantika always made sure I never lost hope.

But I was gutted that day. After Vernita and I had drifted apart, I always looked at her in contempt. If given a choice to kill six people on earth, I would pump all six bullets into her. She, too, left no stone unturned to make sure my life was hell. Her constant bitching about me to our classmates and common friends didn't do any good to our soured relationship either. Since she was a girl, a girl most people liked, people believed her easily. I tried to give back in equal measure. We were becoming obsessed with screwing each other over. She always had the upper hand.

Shawar was not making my life easier either. He called me up numerous times from different numbers, but I never picked up his calls. Avantika asked me to get myself a private number, the kind where you can bar your incoming calls, but it was too much of an effort and I wasn't connected enough to get one.

~

'The hair is *fine* and you look great. Trust me,' I reassured Avantika for the millionth time as she brushed her hair again and tucked in stray strands of hair behind her year. McKinsey & Company was on campus for their interviews. Obviously, she was quite nervous. This was her shot to run away from a potential uneducated businessman husband and she was determined to give it everything she had.

The placement season had started at SRCC and, shockingly, the line-up of hiring companies was better than what was scheduled for DCE that year. It hadn't even had a placement cell till a few years back! I was disappointed at their blistering progress, as my college wasn't making any.

College life had treated Avantika well. Especially after she kicked her drug habit and got clean. It did not have a hostel, though she lived in one a few kilometres away from her college. It was a hostel for rich kids and everything was taken care of. That was in stark contrast to the DCE hostels where students used a bedsheet until it turned grey and went without food for days on end. DCE hostellers could be ideal candidates for any *Man vs. Wild* episode because their bodies were used to eating and digesting horrible food at the hostel mess.

Her hostel, though, was perfect. Situated bang in the centre of Delhi University, she never ran out of places to hang out. Tom Uncle's Maggie Joint was where Avantika and I spent most of our daytime dates. We loved going there. Sharing hot swirling noodles with Avantika under the open sky was one of my favourite things those days. I am not sure she liked it as much. The joint was bang opposite Miranda House, the college with notoriously smart, pretty women. Avantika never liked the girls from Miranda House, Jesus & Mary, and Lady Shri Ram College. They were potential threats.

'Will I make it?' she asked nervously.

'You will make it. How can they not take you? Look at you! You're cuter than a mash-up between a little child and a cute puppy.'

'That's not qualification enough, I guess,' she argued.

'Don't ask me, then. I am the barred one.' I couldn't help being sarcastic. I used to get pissed off and lose my mind whenever our conversations hovered around placements. Even Yogi and Viru had managed decent jobs. The companies didn't offer great salaries, but any company was good enough for them, given the huge number of papers they had failed, the state of their intestines and their smoke-battered lungs.

Avantika would soon join their league and that wouldn't be comforting either. She was my girlfriend and she wouldn't judge, but I didn't want to be the only loser around. Shrey would be in the same league as mine, jobless and clueless, only he didn't care. It would be a long time before I could start applying for off-campus placement interviews and I wasn't too hopeful about that either.

'Oh. Never mind. You will get a better job than all of us,' Avantika said as she checked out her pointy-black-witch shoes. She stood as tall as I was. She would look great in those. Just those. I often wondered if it was just me who thought dirty all the time.

'I'll have a better job than you? Yeah, right. That's easy for you to say. You will be employed in a matter of minutes.'

'Oh, shut up. You are a blogger now. No one knows, your blog may become famous and all, you might end up richer than all of us.'

Avantika had created a blog on her mail account and invited me to write on it. She pestered me to keep writing and uploading stuff on it regularly.

'Yes, how can I forget that? The blog, which I stopped writing after the first few blog posts. The same one you trashed!'

'I didn't trash it. I just said I felt that it was a little boring and dragged in parts,' she laughed out.

'Dragged? I wrote about my school life, damn it. I thought it was heart-wrenching and honest. Was that a drag for you?'

'I am not sure what I have to say now,' she said, biting her nails and yet winking at me.

'Whatever you say, I got about forty-five comments on that post!'

'Whatever, Deb! All your stupid comments are filling my mail box up. And I don't really like it when you write about your crushes on your blog. I hated that blog post where you ranted about Surabhi, the girl you had an immense crush on. Even that silly blog post had like twenty comments.'

The blog had her mail ID on it. All the comments reached her ID, not mine, but I never had the drive or interest to change it. And I didn't know how to.

'Avantika.' The placement coordinator shouted her name and called her in.

'Best of luck.'

'Thank you,' she said and rushed in, brushing her hair again. She looked fabulous.

I prayed for her to do well. I knew she would get the job and felt a little sad about it. I felt left out. Avantika, Tanmay and Vernita were busy making something out of themselves while my future kept looking bleaker. I pushed out those negative thoughts and concentrated on the more important things in life. I looked around to see everyone dressed to entice, in short black skirts, stockings and stilettos. It helped calm my nerves.

I loved coming to SRCC. Avantika and I had spent a lot of time in its libraries, front lawns, Irfan's and the cooperative store. I had more attendance at her college than mine. More people knew me here. I missed my own college fest but never missed hers—Crossroads. Avantika got me passes to every fest in Delhi University, a lot of those out of bounds for DCE students given their history of getting into drunken brawls and getting the police involved. For a college full of nerds, we were surprisingly belligerent and short-tempered.

Her interview lasted only fifteen minutes.

'Hey, how did it go?' I hugged her as she came out of the room.

'It went fine. What did you do all this time?' she asked. I knew her interview had gone great. Had it not, she would have cried her way out. She was unbelievably child-like when it came to anything about her career. Even a bad rap at coaching classes would drive her to tears.

'Nothing, just some bird watching. It's not as if you are the only good-looking girl in SRCC.' I winked at her. You would be surprised at how strikingly beautiful most of the girls studying at SRCC were. Most of them were stinking rich and dolled up every day before coming to college.

'Bird watching, eh? That's not very exciting to hear,' she said, making a fake sad face.

'You tell me. What did they ask you?'

'The usual. They got stuck to Spirit of Living. The guy himself is a part of it, so it was pretty easy! Plus, I think they liked me. Now would you call me a slut too?' she winked at me.

'Obviously not. But that doesn't make Vernita a *non*-slut,' I said while looking at a girl who just stepped out of a car.

'Who are you looking at?' she asked, turning in the direction I was staring.

'She is hot, isn't she?' I pointed out to the girl. She was dressed impeccably in a knee-length skirt, half of her face was covered with humungous shades, her hair was done up, and she walked quite comfortably in her bright red stilettos. I think it was a Mercedes or an Audi she stepped out of. All big cars are the same to me: big cages of metal I would never be able to afford.

'That's our senior. She works at Deloitte. Had a super-rich boyfriend, took her to Goa and stuff, so out of your league.'

'What do you mean? You had a super-rich boyfriend and I ended up dating you.'

'She *wants* her boyfriends to be super rich. Not a miser like you. Get the difference?' she said, tapping my head.

'I am not a miser. You never let me spend. Not my fault that you know everybody around. And certainly not my fault that my father doesn't have huge cash reserves that I can indiscriminately spend on my girlfriends.'

'I know it's not your fault,' she said. I knew she didn't mean to hurt me. I was a poor kid by her standards. Some of her friends never even dated someone who didn't have a car of his own.

'Then I guess you should go to your senior's ex-boyfriend. Maybe he will take you to Goa and dump you. Won't you be so happy?' I said irritably.

'Aww, I am sorry. I love you and you know that. There is nothing that could change that, Deb. I am addicted to you. I have dated rich guys before and they are jerks, trust me on that. Moreover I like doing the little things that I do with you. I don't wish to go to Goa or some fancy dinner place; I just want to sit at a roadside joint and listen to all the nice things you always have to say about me,' she said while pulling my cheeks and thus putting things back in order.

'You have some really hot girls in your college.'

'If you say anything good about the other girls in my college one more time, I am not going to talk to you. Ever. Again.'

'Okay, fine,' I said and we laughed out.

'But you do have a point, Deb. I never noticed that,' she said.

'But then I didn't expect the girls at DCE to be like the one that just passed us by.'

'Let's just say all engineers are terrible-looking. I think that's a fair enough generalization,' she winked at me.

'Oh, that's not totally correct. There is a reason for it. The rich kids take commerce and humanities. The poorer ones take up engineering. That explains the good-looking-bad-looking phenomenon. Makes sense?'

'No, it doesn't. I don't get the *poorer ones take up engineering* crap,' she said, stationing both her fists on her waist, visibly pissed off.

'It's quite simple. The rich kids tend to take up commerce and humanities because they have a lessened sense of responsibility. Career isn't the be-all and end-all of everything for them. So they take up something that allows them to have more fun and eventually, in most cases, join their father's businesses or get married.'

'Lessened responsibility? People around here have an equally bright career as you, Deb.'

'But this wasn't the case five years back when you actually took up commerce. It's just been two years since the placement cell started in your college. There were no companies that were hiring commerce graduates five years ago. You only had a career if you had an engineering degree.'

'You do have a point there. But I still don't agree with your rich is equal to good-looking funda.'

'That's an easier one to grasp. If you are rich, you have access to better clothes, better accessories, better shoes, better places, so you learn more and you implement more. Most people here may not be inherently beautiful. But they dress smart, bathe in expensive creams and you have a legion of girls who look as if they just stepped out of the cinema screen.'

It was obvious logic. Also, the richer the girls get, the sexier they are. The sexier they are, the better guys they get, who invariably are more desirable and attractive. Better guys who are better in bed lead to superior craving. Once they have already tried it, they are more liberated and assertive about their needs. More assertive is what is often wrongly labelled as being horny. Just because a girl knows what she wants doesn't make her horny or lustful or vile. If it were the case, the entire male species is vile.

Anyway, what we just derived is that rich is sexy, but what matters is that *rich is invariably lusty* too. You never say, *poor horny* housewives; it's always *rich horny* housewives!

'Okay, I lose, but that doesn't mean you are right,' she said, easing up.

'The list is out.' The placement coordinator shouted out.

'Please, please, please, please go and see. I can't,' she clung to my arm and squeezed the place to pulp where I would have had biceps and triceps if I ever went to the gym and worked out.

'As you say.' I loved the jostling and pushing around. I was the only guy in the crowd shoving around in a sea of great-smelling women.

Why was I not surprised? Predictably, her name was the first on the list! I was incredibly happy and sad at the same time. And then I was just happy.

'Have I been selected?' she said as she tried to look for a smile on my smug face.

'Yes, you have!' I shouted and we hugged furiously. They had selected just three out of the eighty students they had interviewed. The one I sat in took fifty students out of the hundred they had interviewed and I still didn't figure in their list. *Opposites* attract! She was immensely intelligent while I was a smelling turd of stupidity.

'Thanks, Sri Guru,' she whispered.

'What? *I* was the one who was praying for you and your Sri Guru gets the credit. I don't know how you can believe in hideously bearded, stupid god-men.'

'Hey, don't you dare say anything about Sri Guru. If you don't like him, keep that to yourself. He is family for me. It's because of him that I am what I am right now. I don't want to get into this discussion again. You won't understand what I have been through, so you have no right to say anything about him.'

'Okay, I'm sorry.' I wasn't. 'Anyway, the basic point is, I need a treat now that you're going to be a big investment banker. And you need to tell me how an investment banker is different from a cashier at the bank I go to. It's all the same to me!'

'That's not funny, Deb.'

'Aw.' I hugged her, but seriously, I had no idea what an investment banker does. All I knew was that they wear expensive suits and shoes, drive big cars, and take home a fat paycheque.

I was very happy for her, even though I felt like a complete loser. I had spent a year at home trying to get through an engineering entrance exam, spent four years in engineering and there she was, a commerce graduate, *just* a commerce graduate, who would end up having a better career than I would. I hated to be envious and not give credit for what she had achieved because after all, getting into SRCC was almost as tough as getting into DCE.

'Hi, Shawar,' Avantika said as we were leaving college and looking for a rickshaw to Kamla Nagar, a market where the entire Delhi University used to hang out.

Just as we left her college, her phone rang. It was Shawar and she took the call and put it on loudspeaker.

'Hi, Avantika. I heard you got through with that interview you had today. Who are you with right now? Debashish? Stay there. I want to meet you and him. After all, there are too many things I have to congratulate you on.'

She looked at me almost pitifully as I wet my pants. We both knew what *meeting* me meant. The last time he *met* a guy, the guy ended up in a hospital bed with six stitches, a broken jaw and a couple of broken ribs. I was a big guy but I wasn't a fighter. I have tried to stay out of scuffles after one of my adversaries left me with a chipped tooth. I had not thrown a punch in fifteen years.

'Shawar, he has to rush. I am sorry he can't stay.'

'Why not? Give the phone to him. I need to talk to that bastard.' He didn't sound friendly to say the least.

'He is drunk,' Avantika whispered in my ear.

'Hey, dude. Where do you have to go? Too busy to meet me, eh?' Shawar said.

'Yes, kind of. I have an exam tomorrow and I have to study for it.'

'Ohh, do you? Both of you think I am a fool, don't you?' he bellowed.

'No seriously, I do have to leave. I can't meet you right now.'

'Just wanted you to know that I called Vernita up and she told me everything about the two of you. And you don't have an exam. That means you have a choice. Either you meet me right now or I will see you at your place. It doesn't seem too appropriate that

I beat you up in front of your parents. The *choice* is yours to make. I am reaching Delhi University in ten minutes.'

He disconnected the line. I wish I could *choose* to be invisible.

'Damn, I am so dead. Will he actually beat me up? What did Vernita tell him?' I was petrified.

'I don't think he will let you off easily. Let him come, I will try to talk to him. And I agree. Vernita *is* a slut, after all.'

'What do you think he will do? Is he big?'

'He is half your size. He's really short.' She punched me.

'Is that supposed to be a joke? I haven't fought since forever and I know I suck at it.'

'No, seriously, he is half your size, but he won't be coming alone. He will come with his hooligan friends for sure and they love getting into fights.'

'Thanks for the consolation. Can't we do something? Go some place. The police? Some *hawaldar*? What do you say?'

'The last guy who tried to do something ended up in bed for four months. Calm down. It's just a street fight. You will be okay.'

'Calm down? You're not getting your ass kicked, I am! Yes, sure. Street fights? That's pretty okay, too. Don't you know that's what I do for a living?' I started walking around in circles, wondering how fast I could run ... *could I possibly tire him out?*

It was too late for that, the Chicken McGrills and the chicken buckets had taken their toll on my body. Damn McDonalds and KFC! I had always assumed I would die of obesity, not of a smashed head.

'You want to call the cops? Go ahead. But what will you tell your parents? And yes, he owns the Shababs' chain of restaurants. That incidentally makes him rich and powerful beyond your imagination. He can bribe the whole police department, for god's sake. Just calm down. Let me handle him when he comes here.'

'Fuck, fuck, fuck, fuck. Fuck man, I will so kill Vernita if I survive this.'

'Deb? Can't you get some guy to side with you? They won't have to fight, just keep Shawar's guys from fighting. They might not get into a fight if they foresee it getting out of hand,' she said.

I knew I couldn't get anybody to fight for me. I didn't have any friends who would be willing to fight on my side and I couldn't involve Shrey in it. I was still on talking terms with girls I had dated or flirted with, but I was sure they would fight on Shawar's side and not mine. Wouldn't they just love to see my face smashed against a pavement.

'No, I don't think I can get anyone.'

'What about Viru? Yogi?'

'I don't think so. They will take an hour to reach and I can't drag them into this. They are hardly friends.'

'Shit!' she said, covering her mouth.

'I am officially dead. Is that what you are trying to say?'

'Not exactly. He loves me. That might save you . . . if anything can.'

'You know what? I hate your guts so much right now. How can you be so chilled out? Your boyfriend's going to be stripped and beaten up and you are just standing there, looking sexy. I hate you with everything I have got.'

'I love you, baby. Here they come, I guess,' she said pointing to the red light. Two massive cars screeched to a halt near us. The cars were new but marred with hideous modifications and gross stickers that screamed '*Drink beer, fuck fear*'. I couldn't do any of that. I wondered how many people were inside the two cars.

A door opened. And a dark complexioned midget popped out.

Shawar was barely five-foot-three, two inches shorter than Avantika and a good seven inches shorter than me. He had strange curly hair and bloodshot eyes. It was a funny sight watching him take big strides like a hard-core villain from a low budget south Indian movie. He was in a black shirt, sleeves rolled up, and desperately tried to look menacing. Incidentally, the dog he almost tripped over looked more threatening.

He walked up to me and stopped inches away from me. He was so short that he could have had a whiff at my armpits without bending. I wish he had. My greatest weapon, that is, if he didn't allow me to place my butt on his face and I had a faint feeling that he wouldn't. His teeth were decayed, as Avantika had told me. Too much methamphetamine and gutka does that to you. His skin had red sores all over it. The drugs leave you with an itching sensation. Avantika had survived all that, and I shudder to this day thinking about what would have happened to her if it were not for the Spirit of Living and Sri Guru. Maybe she was right when she said I wouldn't understand what she had gone through and what Sri Guru meant to her.

'Let's go,' he grabbed at my hand. It wasn't funny any more.

'No . . . no . . . I can't come . . .' I struggled for words as I fixed my eyes on the bald patches between his curly hair. He would be bald in a few years. Smoking makes you lose hair, and also makes you impotent. I was about to be thrashed by a half-man who was puny and looked ridiculous.

'What makes you think you are in any position to decide, *chutiye*?'

'He is not going anywhere, Shawar,' Avantika said as she freed me from his puny hands.

'Avantika, I am not talking to you,' he said as he grabbed my hand again.

'C . . . c . . . can't we j . . . u . . . s . . . t . . . just talk here?' I stammered. I was glad there was nobody around to see the terrified woman in me. There was usually a crowd around in my school days, mocking my helplessness.

'We fucking can't. There are certain things we need to settle. You bloody screwed my happiness. I will now do the same to you. You are not getting away with this.'

'What did I do?' I squeaked.

'What did you do? Do you even know who I am? Do you? You bloody took my girl away from me, that's what you did, asshole. Get it. I will destroy your whole life. Can you do something about it? Go ahead. Try it.'

'Shawar, mind your language!' Avantika shouted.

'Avantika, I love you. I am not doing anything to you. But stay out of this; it's between the two of us.' He looked at her. His shoulders drooped and he seemed to melt and sublimate. He reminded me of myself when I first met Avantika. I prayed to god to turn me into a girl then. You can't be beaten up and you can choose when you want to have sex.

'He is my friend. There is nothing between the two of you. Whatever happens will happen here, right now. In front of me.'

'Yes, in front of her,' I said.

I repeated it again. He looked at me. I knew I had said something outrageously cowardly, but I didn't care if it saved my ass. I was surprised I didn't hide behind Avantika and stick a thumb up my mouth.

'He is a friend? Vernita bloody told me everything. She hates him. And you? What are you looking at, *bhenchod*? Vernita told me where you are and asked me to bash you up from her side too. This is what his friends think about him. And you left me for him? Why?'

'Vernita is not a friend,' I said. I was hurt. I hated her too. But I didn't want her to be hurt. Deep down she was still a friend. Suddenly, I was angry and I thought about taking Shawar on and beating him to a pulp. Only a little bit though. Maybe in a video game.

'Shut up, you asshole. Come with me.' He started dragging me towards the car.

'SHAWAR!' Avantika shouted. 'What do you think of yourself? It's not his fault. Leave him.' The mere decibel-level of her voice shook him enough to let go of me. I thanked her. She continued, 'I love him. And you can do nothing about it. You do anything to him and everything will be over between us. I never loved you. I loved Paritosh. I dated you because I wanted to hurt him. Who do you think you are? You thought we could be together? My foot! I could have bloody stoned myself to death and you would have hardly cared. Shawar, was there a single time when you showed a little bit of care? Once, when you asked me not to drink? Or smoke? Fuck you, Shawar. I love him. You do anything to him, I will *destroy* you. You know I can. Love is not stalking someone, Shawar. Love is what Deb has for me. I was wrong with Paritosh. I was wrong with you. I have finally got it right. Touch him and you are not getting away with it. I will so *ruin* you. I so will. You have a choice.'

My jaw, literally, hit the ground. I stood there frozen and scared, even though the words weren't directed at me. She said she used to be a rude bitch before she joined Spirit of Living and I never believed that. Now I did. She could have blown apart a building, shattered glass and ended a war with that outburst. Shawar was just a rich powerful guy. And he was crying.

'Deb, can you leave us alone for a second?' Avantika asked me. Shawar had slumped onto the pavement, his head buried in his palms as he sobbed.

'Sure,' I winked at her, but she didn't respond as I would have liked her to.

It was a lovely sight to see him cry. Shawar stayed on the pavement and continued weeping for quite some time. *Who's the little girl now?* Avantika was sitting right beside him. They talked for twenty minutes and Shawar left in his hideous car, not once looking at me. I had emerged victorious.

'Thank you, Avantika.' I hugged her. 'You beat the shit out of him. That was great!'

'You found it funny? I had to hurt the poor guy,' she said and looked away.

'I am sorry,' I said.

'Don't be. I loved it too. I think he deserved it,' she winked and hugged me again.

'Oh, love you.'

'You know what? He expected you to get some guys with you. He was somewhat disappointed. And yes, there were cops, too, in the car. Just in case. Who knew my new boyfriend would be such a wimp?'

'A sexy wimp?' I asked, trying to gain at least somewhere.

'Yes, a *very* sexy wimp. Thanks, Sri Guru,' she whispered and I suppressed an urge to ridicule her. I always wondered, would these god-men, evoke the same saintly sentiments if they had to shave off their beards?

Shawar had wasted a lot of our time. It meant Avantika had to go back to her hostel sooner.

'I think we will have to settle for Tom Uncle's Maggi, then,' I said.

'I was thinking about a night-out,' Avantika said and winked at me.

# 13

'Now, that was a close shave,' Shrey said, as he put the form in the envelope. I had just done narrating the incident with Shawar.

'Yup, nearly had my face boxed in,' I said, as I darkened the bubbles in the form. Despite being a technophile, he, too, was taking the CAT, the management test that decides the fate of many. Around 2.32 lakh students took the exam every year.

'How do you rate our chances?' Shrey asked me.

'I can't really say. It all depends on that day.'

'Yup, that's true. But you have been studying for it. You will obviously do much better than I will.' He hadn't joined a coaching institute while Avantika and I had. We had scored better than him in the mock examinations and he was pissed about it.

'CAT isn't about how much you prepare. Maths and data interpretation are purely IQ based and there is nothing much you can do about English if it isn't above average by now. They can't teach you how to read, damn it.'

'Whatever. What happened to Shawar? Any further news?' Shrey asked to change the topic. We had had numerous arguments on whether coaching institutes helped or not. He had attended mock classes at different centres in Delhi and didn't feel challenged enough. I am sure he meant: *there weren't enough pretty girls*.

'I heard he was planning to ask his long-time friend Purvi out, the one he puts up a lot of pictures of.'

'Do you think he has slept with her?' Viru butted in as he wrapped up the form, too.

'I think so. I mean it's highly likely. They get sloshed all the time. It's possible that they have done it. Anyway, Purvi had had scores of boyfriends, so it's inevitable. But then again, Shawar is amazingly repulsive. He has red-stained teeth! How can anyone kiss him? But I don't know, Avantika says she thinks they are sleeping around.'

'If he's that ugly then I don't think he is sleeping around with her. Because if he was, he wouldn't want to ask her out. Why get into a relationship when you can get everything without getting into one?' Shrey debated.

'It's not as if it would be totally guilt-free sex. Maybe Purvi goes on a guilt trip and gives him a hard time every time they hook up?'

'Maybe Shawar wants something more than a hook-up. Maybe he wants a real relationship. Not everyone is like you, Shrey. Or you, Deb. People want meaningful relationships, too,' Viru said in all seriousness.

'Excuse me? I am in a meaningful relationship!' I protested.

'Fuck that! Did you just hear what Viru said? I can't believe we are taking relationship advice from him!' Shrey said and all of us doubled up in laughter. The only girls Viru ever talked to were the ones on the metro counters. The only one he had an affair with was in customer care. It had lasted fifteen minutes.

In the world of engineers, where there are no major hetero-groups, we never treated any girl we met as a friend. Everyone was a prospect. *Every* girl was an *opportunity*. Vernita had been one, too. Meaningful relationships, being friends with a girl, being best friends with a girl who's dating someone else—these were things that meant little to engineering students like us. On the evolutionary chart of dating, engineers represented gorillas.

As for Shawar, his male ego had taken a huge blow. Everyone in his circle knew that Avantika had dumped him for another guy. He had to do something to redeem himself. Purvi was his shot at redemption. Everything was okay as long as he kept his hands off me, which he did.

The last two months before the CAT went exactly as I had not planned. Shrey and I had planned to study together but our study sessions, more often than not, ended up as movie/TV series-watching sessions. The lesser time you have, the greater is the urge to splurge time on things that don't matter. Occasionally, we switched our phones and PCs off, ready to bring the world down to our feet, but that never lasted beyond an hour. Avantika, meanwhile, worked hard and the results showed. She even threatened to match our scores occasionally. A job had already ensured freedom from her parents, but clearing the CAT would mean doing it in a spectacular fashion. Her parents didn't know she was preparing for the CAT.

'Hey, Avantika! All set for tomorrow?'

'All set? I am so nervous I think I will pass out.'

'Nervous? Chill! Just go out there and try to attempt the easier questions and you will be through. You have worked hard for this.'

'Easy for you to say that. You have been the one topping all the mock exams. Not me,' she argued.

'All that doesn't matter tomorrow. It's what you do in those two hours that matters.' I had been doing really well in the mock examinations and people had started to expect big things from me. Though I showed I was irritated by their constant *you–will–get–through* thing, I liked it.

'Anyway, I just hope Sri Guru helps us in the examination.'

'Helps *you*. I had better rely on *myself*.'

'Whatever. I am going to sleep now. My centre is two hours away and I have to get up early. Bye. Goodnight. Love you,' she said.

'Love you, too. Bye. You will do great.'

I disconnected the line and promptly went to sleep. Sri Guru didn't help me the next day and the exam went horribly. And once

I started screwing up the paper, I started picturing all my fellow classmates (a few of them from school, too) laughing at me, as if saying, '*You couldn't do this, you are such a fool.*' And laughing the hardest amongst them was Vernita. I screwed the exam big time.

Avantika didn't answer my calls for the rest of the day. I assumed she had screwed it up, too. Shamefully enough, I was happy about that. I spent the day writing about my CAT debacle on my blog. My fictional make-out escapades were a huge hit among visitors to my blog and people had started expecting frequent updates. It is a perverted world, I tell you. I knew many people would start turning up at the secluded, deserted places I had mentioned in my blogs. I used to exaggerate and blow things out of proportion in my blogs and a lot of people tended to believe everything I wrote.

Writing the blog was better because I didn't want to call up Shrey and listen to him speculate about the cut-offs and his chances. And he did better than me, so I tried to stay away from him. There was no way I could have got through any of the IIMs.

Bad news travels fast and people didn't fail to bring it to my notice that Vernita had indeed done well in the exam. So consequently, I started trashing the exam itself and began to harbour dreams of making it to Stanford a few years down the line, after I had the requisite work experience. But all of this was just an escapist route and didn't keep me from making my mind up to take the CAT the next year.

I spent the entire month of December trying not to bump into my classmates who had calculated their scores and fancied their chances at getting interview calls from at least one of the IIMs. I took a few other exams and screwed them up too. I was getting good at it.

The only worthwhile thing I did during December was going out with Avantika every night. We ate out and partied like never before. My dancing skills now extended beyond stomping cockroaches! It felt good when people started treating me as one of the regulars. With Avantika, we always managed to get huge discounts on our bills and it was something that kept us going.

Somewhere between the partying out and the eating, the eighth semester started. It was the last semester, and I knew attendance and marks would cease to matter. Now, all I needed was a job and I got my first opportunity within the first few weeks of the eighth semester.

'Hey Deb! I have good news for you,' Avantika said.

'What?'

'Eighth semester, baby! I thought you would be now eligible for some off-campus interviews and I forwarded your résumé to Lehman Brothers. They are a big investment bank and they are holding interviews. You have got a call.'

'No shit!' This had been the second most exciting news I had heard. First was that nobody who was close to me got any calls from any of the good management institutes. In fact, I had done better than most people around.

'Yes, shit! Before I forget, they are paying exactly thirty per cent more than the company you were willing to give an arm for—D.E. Shaw. Like that? I told you Sri Guru is great. Isn't he?'

'Excuse me. *You* are great. Not Sri Guru. Anyway, when is the interview?'

'It's tomorrow. Don't you dare screw this one up.'

'I won't. Will you be coming? And message me the place.'

'Will do that. And no, I won't be coming. Sri Guru is reaching New Delhi tomorrow and I am going for his convention. He won't be returning to India before March. I know you won't listen, but you should attend this once. Anyway, I will mail you your CV. I made some changes to suit their needs. Do check.'

It was one of the many times that she had put Sri Guru and Spirit of Living before me in her list of priorities. I hated it when she did that, but then she had made it very clear that it was because of her Guru that she wasn't a wreck any more. We had had many arguments on this, which I invariably lost, convincingly. Just because no one could win an argument against her.

'Perfect. I *so* love you!'

'I love you too. Check your mail. I have sent you a document which explains all the basics of finance. I don't think they will delve too much into that, but it doesn't hurt to prepare. And best of luck. Do well.'

'I will try.'

'It would be so great if you get through this. You will be a rich guy and you could fly down to Bangalore any time you want to! What say?'

'That is so true. By the way, have you tried getting your posting shifted to Delhi?'

'No, I haven't, Deb. I see no point in that. There is no tangible growth in the Delhi office. And anyway, we can meet whenever we want to. We have great paymasters, or we *will* have, won't we?'

'Ohh . . . that means I am not important? Only your growth is?' I said in a baby voice. I hated to think that she was leaving Delhi in a few months. I hated to be an impediment in her career plans but then, it was hard to let her go. This was the first time I had shown my disapproval of her leaving for Bangalore.

'Of course you're important, but then . . .'her voice trailed off. I wished I had been a little serious in my displeasure at her going away.

'It's okay, Avantika, I understand.'

'Okay, Deb, I will try. I surely will. I will talk to the HR department tomorrow. First, say you will never let me go, only then will I try.'

'Of course, I will never let you go. You are my baby, how can I let you go? You're supposed to be mine and I will see to it that it never changes.'

'I won't go. You are so sweet, Deb. I don't know what I would do without you,' she said. 'I will talk to the main office tomorrow. Or after my exams are done. I love you more than you do.'

'Thank you. Love you. I will call you in a while.' I was ecstatic and hopeful.

The next day, I dressed up the best I could and went for my interview. As it was an investment bank that paid a ridiculous package, the turnout was huge. Most of the guys seemed excessively smart for me . . . and knowledgeable. I was still the best dressed one. My fat thighs were skilfully hidden behind the slick suit that Avantika had chosen and had got me at a huge discount.

Somebody once told me that investment bankers are so busy during their seventy-hour work weeks that they often end up sleeping with their colleagues. It was always good for an investment bank if the applicants were people you could fancy in times of distress and frustration. I wished to gain a few points there. Avantika had done a good job on my CV. There were projects on terms I hadn't heard about before. But she had given me a half an hour class about the projects and had said it was enough.

'Are you there?' Avantika asked. It was the twentieth time she had called me that day. The previous ones were to check whether I had gotten up, bathed, brushed etcetera. She really wanted me to clear the interview. I hadn't bathed though. But my CV was spectacular.

'It's been an hour. The list was out just a few moments ago. I am the fourth to be interviewed.'

'You are the fourth? Just one before Vernita? Cool.'

'Vernita?'

*What?*

'Yes, she is taking the interview, too. Tanmay just told me that she is fifth on the list.'

'How on earth did she come to know about the interview?'

'I told Tanmay about the off-campus interview. He had seen your résumé on the computer. He may even have flicked through it,' she said. For the first time I felt like slapping her somewhere other than her ass. She might have just helped the person I hated the most get a job that I wanted!

'What the . . . ? Why didn't you hide it? Are *all you girls* like this? First there was Smriti, who couldn't hide a relationship and now it's you? You are all the *same*, aren't you? I didn't even tell Shrey about the interview and you slipped this to Tanmay? I cannot believe you did this. Couldn't you just have lied to him about this?'

'Deb, I didn't want to lie to him. I did that before and I regret it. I was not going to do that again.'

I have never understood why people make a big deal about lying. It doesn't even figure in the seven deadly sins!

'Have you completely lost it? It was a different matter. It was about a goddamn relationship. This is about my life, *my career*, which you just royally screwed up.'

'Excuse me, Deb, *goddamn relationship*? I got you this interview, damn it. Now I am sorry I did.'

'Hey, hey, hey! You didn't do me a great favour doing that. Tanmay did that for Vernita, too, didn't he? Anybody would have. But they wouldn't have told the world to ruin his or her chances. You did that. Thank you for that.'

'Deb, I am sorry.' She broke down. 'I'm really sorry. But did you ever think why *I* didn't apply for it? It was something I always wanted to do. Finance. I never wanted the job at Mckinsey as much as I wanted this. But I thought . . . I am sorry.'

*Click*. She disconnected the call. I looked around to see everybody staring at me.

Then on, I spotted Vernita everywhere in the hall, almost like you start to spot a word you just looked up in the dictionary everywhere around you. I couldn't talk to anybody around me as I had just established myself as a swearing, shouting bastard. In short, a typical *Delhi* guy.

'Debashish Roy,' the HR person called out. 'You are next.'

History repeated itself. I messed up the interview once again, thanks to the brilliant distraction Avantika had just created. I knew the answers, but just couldn't mouth them. Or that's what I would like to think now. I stammered, blabbered and stuttered, and I was kicked out. Vernita cleared the interview. Avantika was to blame.

~

I spent the rest of the afternoon in a shitty mood. I had planned to curl up in my bed, watch television and cry for the rest of the night when my phone rang. It was Shrey and I first hesitated to take his call, but then I thought I could use the distraction.

'Deb? Can you come to my place? Right now,' he said. It had to be one of the two reasons he usually called over for. It was either a new movie he had got hold of or he had come up with some robotic bullshit of his. He usually had to lie for the latter.

'Shrey, I am not exactly in the mood. I had a long day. That bitch Vernita got through another interview and I screwed up again. I don't think I will ever be employed.'

'We have broken up,' he said, sounding as if he had been asked to stop going to NPL.

*I have to go. This is serious.* I disconnected the call and headed to his place. His mother told me he was upstairs.

'What happened?' I asked and switched on the lights of his room.

His eyes were bloodshot. He had been crying before I reached. I had seen quite a few girls do that and used to think that I would never see a guy do the same. 'She found someone else at work,' he said. He announced the news as if she had died.

Vandana had been working at an analytic firm known for its vibrant work environment. A *vibrant work environment* generally means a healthy gender ratio and a great sex life. That's how we interpret it.

'Who?' I asked. I was somewhat bewildered. I had never thought Shrey would go to the extent of crying for her. That's something girls are best and prolific at. I thought Shrey would take the break-up offered to him on a silver platter and move on.

'It's some guy she met in the office. She said they became close during the two months I was away.'

'But did she give you a reason?'

'She says she can't rely on me any more. He apparently has a great career in front of him. She has even met his parents. It's over between the two of us. I should never have gone to Paris,' he murmured.

'Are these guys getting married or something?' I asked. I had always been a gossipmonger. So was Avantika. And she would kill me if I didn't give her all the details. I knew he loved Vandana, but I also knew he would get over it and find someone else to run after in a few days.

'Not right now, but they have plans to get married eventually. That's why she met his parents,' he said.

'How old is this guy?' I continued with my research. 'And how the hell does he have a better future than you? You're like this technology genius!'

'I don't know. He has just done English honours or something and claims to earn a lot. He's just twenty-four,' he said as he located that guy on a popular social networking site.

'Damn! He looks thirty. Or probably even more . . . and is awesomely bad-looking. How can anybody possibly like him?'

I wasn't trying to soothe him. The guy, Suhel, really looked like a monster. With big fat lips jutting out of a square face. He'd put up some stupid snaps taken in front of the Petronas Towers with some Thai people, flashing his big hideous smile. Such a wannabe. His jeans looked straight out of the eighties and his jumper sweater was in sync with his monstrous face.

The *nobody-is-a-stud-except-us* formula worked again. We found something wrong with a perfectly normal guy, again. Apart from his previously established grotesque looks. Besides, what was I supposed to tell Shrey? *I think he is a perfectly normal guy who deserves Vandana?* Of course not.

'Anyway, what do you plan to do now?' I asked him. We had proved that Shrey was phenomenally better than the guy and Vandana had got a raw deal. It was her loss.

'Nothing. I will wait for her to come back, beg me to take her back and dump her once we get back together. Meanwhile, I am talking to your ex-girlfriend, Smriti. She is not as boring as you claimed she was. Oh, by the way, she has some nasty things to say about you. And she told me that you were a horrible kisser.'

*Smriti?* I thought she wanted somebody to get married to! With Shrey, all she would get was painful love bites and rejection. I didn't know how to react. Not because it was Shrey, my best friend, but because like all men, I, too, was foolishly territorial about my ex-girlfriends. It didn't matter whether I was over her or not, she wasn't supposed to see other men, especially my friends. Maybe she was doing it just to get back at me.

'I don't want to know about anything that happens between the two of you. I can do without the explicit details. Anyway, best of luck with her. Hope it works out.'

'I hope, too, man. I thought Vandana would write the patent application for the aggregate assembling robotic arm I had designed . . .'

'Don't start all over again. I am too tired of techno-crap.' I was feeling way too sleepy. It had been a long day, and a very frustrating one.

'Sorry, Deb. How is your blog going? Any fresh readers?'

'Pretty bad. Had a fight with Avantika regarding the blog a few days back.'

'Why?' he asked as he started checking out girls in Suhel's list of friends. I saw him put in the search bar, 'Bannerjee' and 'female'. Was he looking for Suhel's sister? He was crazy.

'Nothing. She didn't like certain parts where I had written some good things about Surabhi.'

'Surabhi? The hotel management girl you used to hit on? She had the longest legs in the world! You never dated her, did you?'

'Not even close. She always behaved like I was invisible. Anyway, I wrote a whole paragraph about how stunning she was and people liked the blog post. She hated it though and swore she wouldn't read it again.'

'So are you still going to write for the blog?'

'As long as you give me such interesting stuff to write about.' I was already asleep, only my lips weren't.

'That sounds good,' he said. 'Make Suhel look really bad if you write about my break-up.'

'Done deal,' I said and flopped on his bed. I didn't know when I drifted off.

~

Shrey loved Vandana. Shrey hadn't been perfectly loyal to Vandana but she knew nothing about it. And after the way Shrey treated her, she wouldn't even believe it if somebody told her. For the first time, by his own admission, something bad had happened to him. He wasn't anticipating the break-up.

Post break-up, Shrey never lost an opportunity to hit on whosoever he thought deserved him. But he never forgot to slow down his bike whenever we passed Hindu College, Vandana's college, on our trips to Kamla Nagar. He would stare at it until it went out of sight. And then he'd spend the next few seconds with his head tilted upwards to keep the tears in check. It was only after parking the bike at a suitable distance from where I got down, that he would take his helmet off. Then he would take a moment in the washroom and come out, eyes red from 'Delhi's dust', amongst other things.

It was only after Shrey was dumped that I realized why it's the friends of girls who have been dumped by heartless boys who are the most agitated lot. If I were to lay my hands on Suhel, I would have cut his guts out and hung him with them.

# 14

'Hi, Deb! Why aren't you picking up your phone?' Avantika asked, her voice frantic.

'You had called before?' I asked and checked my phone. There were eighteen missed calls and about twenty messages. She would never call me so many times unless it was important.

'Are you still angry about the interview?' she asked.

'Not at all. I was at Shrey's place, came back tired, and drifted off. Though, I am still a little low because apart from a silly job at a software firm, I have nothing to rely on.'

'Software firm? I didn't know you sat for any other off-campus interviews?'

'No, I didn't.'

'But you just said you had a job?'

'I lied to my parents that I do. What was I supposed to do? Everybody knows the placement season is over. My relatives kept asking my parents about my placement and I had to give them something to say.'

'But why didn't you tell me before? Now?'

'I didn't know what to tell you. And yes, my father still isn't happy about it. He says he expected better from me.'

College was about to end and every conversation I got into

with my dad, started with the topic of placements. People around my dad, with kids in inferior colleges, had jobs. So, lying that companies weren't recruiting this year wasn't an option. I gave them different reasons, every time they asked me.

*I am not interested in technical jobs. And non-technical companies aren't recruiting these days.*

*I am concentrating on taking the CAT again. Jobs come and go, education stays.*

'But what are you going to do now?' Avantika asked, worried.

'Wait for other off-campus interviews, what else? Just like you said. Anyway, why were you calling? Eighteen missed calls? What's wrong? Don't you know I can't remain angry with you for long no matter how badly you screw me?' I laughed. She didn't. Something was certainly wrong.

'Shawar is in jail,' she said and paused. She added, 'He ran over a few people. Purvi is critically injured too. God knows why he attempted to drive. I am so scared for him.'

She went on to tell me more about the accident that had taken place the previous night near the Dhaula Kuan flyover. Shawar was drunk and trying to drive when he rammed into a police barricade and a couple of other cars. It was a mess, she told me. Crushed steel and blood.

I sinfully loved these incidents. Being an awfully slow driver, I always hid behind the pretext of road safety. And these incidents just made my point stronger. There is no point in driving fast.

'Am I to take this as bad news or what? Because I am happy he's off my trail now. Maybe he deserved it for all the shit he gives to other people.'

'Are you crazy? You are so insensitive. He was a friend, Deb. I am feeling bad about this. I met him today. He is in a terrible condition, and the bleeding hasn't stopped yet. I could barely look at him. He is battered, has multiple fractures in his right leg, got his face smashed in and has a broken wrist. They might have to amputate his leg, if the bleeding doesn't stop and the infection spreads. He is on a ventilator for now. I am so scared for him.'

'He will be okay.'

'I just hope so. I don't know why these things are happening around me? First, it was Paritosh. Now it's him.'

'It's just with your ex-boyfriends. Oh yes, that reminds me. Vandana dumped Shrey. She started going out with somebody while Shrey was still in Paris and says it's serious. Shrey looked crushed, man. I don't know why! I never expected this from him. I wonder ... what would it be like if you dump me for someone else?'

'I won't,' she said.

'Avantika, I am sorry for your friend.'

'It's okay. I know you don't like him. I will catch you later. I have to study. Law tomorrow and I am so disturbed right now. I can't get Shawar's image out of my mind. It scares me a lot.'

Avantika's internal examinations were on and generally, she left no stone unturned to maximize her score. She hardly slept on the nights before her exams.

'I am going to sleep. Catch you tomorrow after the exam,' I said as I hugged the bolster tight, the one Avantika had gifted me. I had a hard time explaining to my mom why my *guy* friends had gifted me a *bolster*.

'Catch me tomorrow before the exam. Be at North Campus, eight thirty sharp. Be there or I will think you don't love me. I am serious,' she chuckled. I heard a few girls laugh behind her.

'But why?'

'I will tell you tomorrow. Bye for now.'

'Don't act childish, tell me now. Right now or I won't come.'

'You will come. Bye, bye, bye. I am switching off my phone and studying. Be there. Please, please, please.' Click.

I had a faint idea of why they were calling me there.

I went back to contemplate whether I should wait for some time or go and talk to Dad at once. I was waiting to get through some management college but since that hadn't happened, I was in deep shit. There were no off-campus interviews in sight and as per some seniors, there weren't going to be many. Not talking now could mean disaster. However, the company I was supposedly *selected* in had joining dates in August, leaving me with loads of time to find a job. Offer letters were still due, so Dad wouldn't know.

Avantika had promised to get me a job in a broking firm at a decent salary if I ended up with none by September. That promise was what kept me sane. But there was no final word on it.

I just had to talk to Dad and tell him what had transpired. He had to know the truth. I had lied enough.

~

I turned up at SRCC at 8.30 sharp to see three girls wrapped in dull shawls. Their heads were wrapped around in scarves. They walked towards me with bundles of handwritten notes tucked in their armpits.

'Hi, Deb,' Avantika said, 'this is Yamini and this is Radhika.' She pointed to her friends. They both looked kind of alike, their faces white in the cold and their lips pink and chapped. Yamini was skinnier and taller though.

'Hi. So why have I been called early in the morning when I could still have easily been in my blanket?' I asked as they handed over the handwritten notes to me. Their forearms were covered with little sentences written in black ink.

'See, it's extremely simple. These are the papers we have got Xeroxed. The questions are going to be asked from these sections only. All you need to do is dictate these answers to us over the phone. All four of us will be on conference. We have written the keywords to the answers to every question. Yamini will tell you the keywords and once you find the keywords, you have to start dictating. Be slow, but not painfully slow. Get it?' Avantika laid out the entire plan. It was indeed quite simple. They had tucked in earphones behind layers of hair and scarves, so they wouldn't get caught. I had seen people try this successfully in movies.

'You're sure the questions are going to be asked from these notes? And what if somebody drops out of the conference? Will you be able to call me back?'

'That is our problem. You just keep on dictating,' Radhika said, as if she was paying me to do so.

'Deb, Radhika has talked to Murari Sir. He has confirmed the sections,' Avantika added.

The best thing about SRCC or Delhi University in general was that if you are cute and your professor is a guy/man/oldie, you can easily have the question paper in your hands a day before the examination. It wasn't the first time that I had heard from Avantika that she knew the questions. But these stunts were reserved for internal examinations only, where there was less at stake.

'Okay, I'll do that,' I said.

'Great then. We will leave now. Call me up and let us arrange the conference call,' Avantika said.

'All right,' I said.

They left and we set up the conference call as soon as they entered the examination hall. The exam started and Yamini started reading out the keywords.

'Memorandum of association . . . Conditions . . . Companies Act . . . Annual general meetings,' Yamini whooshed into the microphone. 'Quick.'

'According to section 173, a company and every officer who makes default in holding AGM is liable to a fine which may extend to rupees five hundred and then there is something like a three *W*s.'

'What?' Avantika shouted in whispers. I heard somebody shouting the words *stop talking* in the background.

'It is like three *W*s and followed by t? e? d?. Make it look like three *W*s. Write what I tell you to. Make three *W*-looking things and t . . . e . . . d . . . then . . .'

This went on for an hour or so before Yamini told me that all the questions were taken care of. I waited for them outside their class. The three of them were amongst the first few to leave the examination hall.

'Thanks, Deb,' Yamini said, came forward and hugged me.

'Yeah, thanks Deb. You saved the day for us,' said Radhika as she hugged me, too, a little too hard, a little too long. All three of them had got rid of the shawls and the scarves and looked prettier. Winter adds colour to a girl's cheeks.

'Pleasure is all mine,' I said.

'Can we go now, Deb?' Avantika said.

'Yes, sure. Are you guys coming along? Lunch at Noodle House?' I asked Yamini and Radhika.

'Ohh! You guys going to Kamla Nagar? Great, I have to get the books for the next exam. I can come along. Radhika, are you coming?' Yamini asked Radhika and she nodded in affirmation.

'Actually, we are going to Connaught Place. You guys carry on. We'll catch you later,' Avantika said and ground her teeth at me.

'Okay, never mind. Bye then. Bye, Deb. Catch you later. And now that you know what to do, I may need your services more often. Avantika is new to this while I do this in every examination. The external examinations are in a few days and I will make sure you are here,' she laughed and hugged me again.

Avantika and I walked away from them and started walking towards the metro station. I didn't know we had plans to go to Connaught Place that day.

'Deb, who is it?' Avantika asked, as soon as my cell beeped.

'It is Yamini. A *thank you* picture message. Cute, eh?' I said before she snatched the phone from me.

'Such a pile on. And why have you stored her number, Deb?' she asked, not quite impressed.

'I stored it just in case I had to call her if she happened to drop out of the conference call. At least she thanked me! You forgot to do that,' I said. I could see that Avantika didn't like the ongoing argument. I did. It was nice to see her get possessive about me.

'Shut up. So, I can delete it now, right?' she asked and didn't wait for my answer.

'Why are you getting so worked up? I would not even look twice at her.'

'Cut the crap, Deb. I saw you staring at her.'

'Firstly, I wasn't. And secondly, even if I was, I am not going to start going out with her. And what is the big deal? You point out cute girls to me all the time.'

'Deb, I know her. She is a *slut*. She sticks to guys. And you hugged her, damn it. Not once, but twice!' she went red in the face and slightly wet in her eyes.

'Aww . . . Avantika, I love you. *She* hugged me, *I* didn't do it. And it was just a hug,' I said as I put my hand across her neck and pulled her close. It was quite an embarrassing thing to do on the streets of Delhi University.

'You are not replying to that message,' she said, as she broke free from my hold.

'I won't, baby. But you have to admit, there is something about me.' I winked at her.

'There is nothing about you; she even flirted with Shawar once. She is a slut and that is about it.'

'Whatever. But she is hot . . . you have to admit that at least.'

'Hot, my foot! Just because I don't throw myself at every guy I meet doesn't make them hot,' she stomped down her point. I had never seen her so full of spite. But I had to agree, Avantika could beat them to a pulp if there was a comparison.

'I know that, baby, you are the best,' I said and blew a kiss at her.

'I better be.'

We walked for a while before she asked in a very meek tone, 'Deb, are you sure you want to be with me?'

'You're the only one I have ever wanted to be with,' I chuckled.

'How do you always manage to say the right things?' she asked and held my hand as we started to walk towards the metro. 'By the way, what are you wearing on your farewell?' Avantika asked me.

'There are still a lot of weeks left. I am sure you will find something in which I don't look like a waiter or a chauffeur.'

'Don't put yourself down. I find you pretty good-looking!' she protested.

'Yeah, right. I look like your house servant,' I retorted. She rolled her eyes. I hugged her.

Yamini didn't call me and gave her external examinations without my help.

~

Finally, I had got my words in order. I was ready to talk to my dad, and I did. I had braced up for his anger. I was ready to face it and bear the consequences of my actions and my foolishness. I felt heroic when I walked up to him to tell him that I was barred from placement activities. It ended in such an anti-climax.

All the preparation I had done the day before to tell Dad the truth about everything went waste. All that came out of my mouth was, 'Dad, I really want to work in BHEL.'

Everyone was right. I was such a wimp.

I knew I could get a job at BHEL. But I couldn't admit that I had failed in getting placed and it was my last resort. My last college exams had ended and I was running out of time. Mckinsey & Company had already couriered their offer letter to Avantika asking her to join in just over two months.

'Why?' he said, putting the vegetables in my bag. It was a Wednesday. Every week on Wednesday, Dad, Mom and I went for an outing to the weekly vegetable market, where I acted as an unwilling porter. I underwent the whole ordeal week after week, year after year with my head bowed down, lest anybody from college spotted me. Even if somebody did, both of us would be so embarrassed that we'd smile and pretend it never happened.

The clangour of the market was impossible to bear with aunties and vendors matching pitch to pitch. That's what middle-class families do. They do not dress up like light bulbs and scheme and talk to themselves to bring the whole clan down. *Damn those soap operas.*

'I want to work in the mechanical industry before I go for an MBA later,' I said, pushing a beggar child aside. They sell irritation, not sympathy.

'Why? What happened to your software dreams?' I knew the sarcasm would start flowing. 'Or those KPOs, analytical firms and investment banks? No longer interested in working for them? Your non-technical jobs?'

'Kids don't know what they want to do. This is the problem with the whole generation,' Mom said. Her voice was already squeaky with all that bargaining with the vendors, which wouldn't amount to more than a few rupees saved. Maybe it just satisfied their egos. Probably gave them a topic to talk about in their next kitty party.

'I know, Mom. I want to work in BHEL and then go to ISB or something. I have it planned out.' I hadn't. I was just looking for some security before I started going for other off-campus interviews. I was just as clueless and aimless as the moths buzzing around the halogen bulbs those vendors used.

'Please talk to Mr Malhotra and try to get him in,' Mom said.

'I will do that. Which department do you want to work in?' Dad asked. I could sense he had just won a moral war against the present generation. His rotting company still had young takers.

'Piping,' I said. It was the only department I knew of, besides the one Dad worked in. My dad's department was not an option. His perfectionist attitude made me feel nervous as shit. Despite being a government employee, he worked like a maniac.

My father nodded approvingly. I got my first job. The interview was shorter than expected. The conversation ended. Thank God for the rogue vegetable vendors who then had to be accused rightfully or wrongfully of faulty weights/pesticides/exorbitant prices.

At the end of the day, I, too, ended like them, the rich bastards. I had a job I had not earned. I was nothing without the job Dad got me. Dad probably knew I had failed in getting placed beyond a silly IT job. What he would not know was that I had failed to get placed *anywhere*. But whatever it was, I knew he would never pick that topic up. I was a hero for him and he would never make me feel otherwise, no matter how many times I faltered.

He loved his work. It was a government job, and he never slipped up. But now, everybody would have something to level against him.

*You know, Mr Roy? Yes, the one from the planning department. He got his son in. Heard he is from DCE. Must have failed or something. People like him are spoiling this office by getting everybody they know inside it.*

An office he had upheld over anything else. For thirty-two years. Dad would feel all that, but I would never get to know. He loved me. I loved him, too. I felt bad about that, but I didn't have a choice. He deserved a better son.

Once I got home, I called up Avantika to give her the good news.

'I got the job. Aren't you so proud of me? Now we can go shopping for the farewell night.'

'So you did finally talk to your dad about it,' Avantika said, clearly unimpressed.

'Yes, I did. I told him I really wanted to work in BHEL. And that's it. I got the job. Ha! I didn't screw this one up,' I said sarcastically. I wasn't happy, but I was relieved.

'That's not *talking* to your dad. That's *lying* to your dad. You will be in big trouble one of these days.'

'I won't. Guess what? Mom, Dad and Sonali are shifting to Hyderabad for a couple of years. They just told me about it. Mom wasn't too keen about it but Sonali convinced them that it was the right thing to do.'

'You didn't know about it? They didn't tell you?'

'It wasn't confirmed. But now, they are surely going.'

'So you're going to stay alone in Delhi? Where? How will you manage everything?' she asked, concerned.

'I will find a way! I will get a chance to live alone. Won't that be the best thing ever?'

'I don't think you're mature enough to live alone,' she argued.

'Oh, c'mon! I will manage. Did the HR department reply to your mail regarding the shifting of your posting from Bangalore to Delhi? Imagine, if they agree to it, you can come over and stay any time you want!'

'This just makes me sadder. I don't think they will agree to it,' she conceded. 'But I will come every second weekend if I get the time and stay at your place!'

'That would be so much fun! But I still wish you didn't have to go to Bangalore. If only my parents had told me they were shifting to Hyderabad, you could have sent the relocation mail earlier.'

'Aw, don't be sad now.'

'I am not sad. I'm just thinking how great it would have been if you could have shifted to my flat,' I said wistfully.

'Okay, get over it now. Do you want me to choose your suit for the farewell night?'

'That goes without saying,' I said. We talked for a while and discussed the things we would have done together if she could have moved in. Having talked almost the entire night, we were tired and we drifted off, our phones still glued to our ears.

The next day, she met me and we scoured every possible suit shop to find a suit for me. Avantika wasn't in the best of moods that day. What had happened to Shawar still haunted her. After we bought my suit, she took me to his hospital room, guarded by police officers on both sides. My heart sank as soon as I set my eyes on him. The battered image of Shawar seared my mind. His condition was pitiable. He was extensively bandaged and every bit of white was soaked with blood. He had still not regained consciousness and was on the ventilator. I could not help but notice that he had lost his right leg. I held on to Avantika, who almost fainted. I felt sorry for him. It was a terrible sight. We did not exchange a word for the rest of the day.

She told me that she needed to see Sri Guru at the soonest. I didn't object but I wish I had because what Sri Guru would tell her would ruin my life.

# 15

It was our farewell night and the four of us were cramped in the minuscule JCB 208 hostel room, trying to look our best for the day. Our best was other people's average.

'That's so cool. You have so much to write about in your blog. The Shawar incident and then the cheating one,' Viru said as he adjusted his tie. It didn't do him any good. He just ended up looking like a low-budget movie star in his skin-hugging suit.

'I am not writing controversial stuff any more. Radhika got to know about the shit I wrote about her. She cannot do anything about it. But Shawar will kill me this time if I write anything about him. And Avantika will do the same if I write anything about Yamini. But Yamini was a stunner, man!'

I had started liking blogging. It was a vent and it had an audience. We all want to be noticed, don't we? But I was taking liberties and not everyone thought I was funny. In fact, some people wrote me long emails telling me I was downright offensive.

'C'mon, how will he get to know?' Yogi said. He looked far better than Viru. But in isolation, the sherwani on his scrawny frame looked more like a huge rugged invisible cloak. But he looked good in the snaps we took and at the end of the day that is what mattered. Ten years down the line, we would only have pictures to remember this day. Or even the next day, when the pictures go up on Facebook or other social networking sites.

'For your extremely kind information, my blog has some fifty dedicated readers. And I know there is one who knows Shawar through someone. Though it is slightly farfetched, why take the risk? I have been almost dead once and it was not nice.'

'Who reads your blog?' Shrey asked.

'Gitanjali, one of my most regular readers.' I said.

'Who is Gitanjali now? Deb, tell me just one thing, where do all these girls keep coming from in your life? It is almost unrealistic! Is that all you do? Look out for girls?' Yogi asked.

'Oh, shut up. I am just lucky and she is just a reader,' I said.

'Is she hot, then?' Shrey asked.

'*Naah*, not quite. But she is well read. So her opinion counts.'

Gitanjali was intelligent but looked just about okay. But then, I had started comparing everyone to Avantika so it wasn't really fair.

'Leave all that, yaar. I don't want well-read women in my life. It's better to date dumb women

who believe whatever you have to say. Can I meet Yamini sometime? Accidental meeting types?' Shrey asked me.

'No chance. Avantika wouldn't let me within miles of Yamini's reach. You can talk to Avantika, though.'

'Fine, I will,' Shrey said and the four of us hung around for a little more time in the hostel room. We didn't want to be the first ones to be out there eating.

~

The farewell crowd was great on the eyes. It left me wondering that if these girls could actually look so good, why didn't they do it every day? For those few hours, I was proud of the gorgeous girls in my college. All the girls looked desirable in the backless blouses they wore, and I don't know what they wore beneath it, but I sure spent a lot of time staring at all the wrong places.

The evening, on the other hand, wasn't anything spectacular. After the dancing and the nickname session got over, people pounced on the food. It always tastes better when there is no bill following it. Meanwhile, Yogi and Viru, drunk as shit, found it difficult to stand straight. However, they danced with the college dogs with unmatched finesse and grace.

'Hey, *Messenger*! Where are you going?' a voice called out from behind as I walked away from the main stage. *Messenger* was the name given to me by our juniors in the part where every senior was given a nickname. They chose *Messenger*, lame as it was, because I was always caught texting somebody or the other. *Very* creative indeed. I didn't blame them, though. I was a nondescript senior and no one really knew about my existence.

'Huh . . . ? Nowhere. All this noise just got to me. Going for a walk,' I said. I was running away from the food. I had no intentions to overeat that night. Especially not after the major trouble I had fitting into the suit I had bought myself barely a month back. Moreover, free food wasn't a rarity now. *Thanks*, Avantika.

'Can I join you? If you don't mind?' Vernita asked. She bent down to unstrap her stilettos and handed them over to me. They were heavy and pointy. I hadn't yet said yes. Vernita looked radiant in her peacock blue glittery sari wrapped tightly around her, accentuating her fabulous behind and baring her midriff right down to her navel. An equally glittery blouse, held in place only by threads, and an equally glittery gold bag completed the picture.

'Of course, you can join me.'

We walked next to each other in silence. Five minutes passed by and neither of us had said a word. Finally, she broke the awkward silence.

'See, Deb. Now that this is the last day in college, I thought let's end it on a good note. We may not end up being good friends after we move out of college but at least let's be friends for this last day,' she said.

'Sure.'

I shot discreet glances at her massive cleavage even though I didn't want to. I hadn't had the opportunity to do that in a long time. It had been months since we had talked to each other. And we had been hurting each other in some way or the other. She had sold me out to Shawar. And I hadn't been all that innocent either. But I was happy that we were finally talking, even if it was for one last day.

'Now tell me, you were the asshole who told Sethi Sir that I missed the practical for a date, right? Don't lie. I knew it was you, bastard,' she said, laughing. 'You nearly got me a back paper that day. I will never forgive you for that. It was so embarrassing.'

'Okay! *Did I?* And what did you do? Shawar almost killed me that day!'

'Don't tell me. Could he do that?' she giggled.

'A lot more than that! But he is behind bars for good.'

'Tanmay told me that he'll be out in days. He is very connected, no?'

'Even I thought so. But he had hit an MLA's car on the way. The MLA's son was injured too, so it may be a little tough. Rich people. Big egos.'

'Okay. Isn't it good?' she said.

'What? Shawar?' I asked.

'The *walk*, stupid.'

'Yup.' It was. It was a beautiful night. No stars or anything, but the long road from the hostel to the campus, which had witnessed four years of great memories, made it beautiful. Not that we couldn't come back and experience it again. But it wouldn't be the same. We would no longer be a part of the road, or the buildings or the college. It just wouldn't be the same.

I wasn't in love with my college. My four years had been eventful, but the college had nothing to do with it. I hadn't made many friends, as I thought the students weren't my type. I was too busy pursuing and going out with girls, most of whom I found intolerable. When I saw huge groups of guy buddies, I used to feel a little jealous. I wanted to be a part of a huge group of guys who run amok and find trouble. But I was not comfortable in large boisterous groups after a few unpleasant experiences in school.

But I would still miss college. It was still the place I first held hands with a girl, first kissed, and first finished in the last ten in class rankings. College was the place where I made my transition from a fat nerd to a semi-fat, non-nerd. It was much better than the torturous time in school, where I was a bloated bag of people's jibes.

When I passed out of the twelfth, I never thought I would get over the bullying I was subjected to during my school days. I was broken and ashamed of myself. But the four years of college had changed that. I had redeemed myself even though the irreparable damage caused still bore tell-tale signs on my personality. It was a small victory over those who had mocked me at school, but it was a significant one. In my times of self-doubt, a remnant of years of ridicule, Avantika used to joke, 'They aren't dating the prettiest girl ever, you are. Feel proud of what you are. You're special.' I would smile and brush it away and never tell her how much her words meant to me.

'Vernita, I am sorry, I lied. But I really didn't think you guys would make such a big issue out of it ... and it seems pretty stupid now that Avantika and I are happy with each other.'

'Deb, let's not debate that. It was a big issue. For Tanmay, it was. You were bloody fucking his sister when you already had a girlfriend. For me, I was upset that you lied to me. You could have at least tried to make me understand,' Vernita argued.

'I am sorry for that. But I just didn't know what I was doing. We couldn't have met had we told you. I am sorry, anyway. But I missed you and hated you. You didn't even bother to contact me—' I was interrupted by a screeching Vernita.

'I didn't bother? *I*? Even today *I* bothered, not *you*. All this time, I have been bothering, Deb. I know everything you do, everywhere you go. I had to listen to Shrey's NPL bullshit just to know how you were doing. And you? Was it so easy to walk off with her? Just one night and you killed our friendship? Three years, damn it! How could you do it? Did it ever occur to you what I was going through? I love you, Deb. I always have.' She broke down into little sobs. For the first time in four years, I saw her crying. It was unreal and sweet at the same time.

'WH . . . what?' I asked, as we sat down on the pavement.

'Deb, don't read too much into it.'

'But what did you mean when you said you *loved* me?'

'I had this huge crush on you in the first year.' She sniffed and coughed and tried to stop crying. 'And don't look at me that way. I am not crying any more, dick.'

'Sorry. Go on,' I said.

Quite frankly, I felt like the handsomest guy in the world. I knew I wasn't even in the vicinity of handsomeness, but there had to be a reason for all the luck I had had, with the stunning women in my life. And I chose this one: *I must be handsome.* It made perfect sense.

'I mean, I had boyfriends, boyfriends who are far better-looking and more accomplished than you. But I always wondered what it would be like to date you. I mean, you're smart and funny. I just used to think we should be together.'

*Funny* and *smart*, I noted those down.

'But why didn't you ever tell me that?' I asked. I was sure I would have said yes, at least my hormones would have made me do so. You have to imagine the most popular girl in college asking out the ugly outcaste—that's what represented the two of us in college.

'Why didn't I ask you? Can you remember a single day you hadn't trashed me for something or the other? I was always a loud, brash girl for you. You never treated me like you would treat somebody you would like to date. I didn't want to be one of the girlfriends you used to have during those days. It was hard. You would have probably laughed at me then and walked off to sleep with somebody else.'

Laughed at her? Not in my wildest dreams. I would have stared at her in disbelief and shock. And I would have locked us inside Tanmay's car, the one with the tinted windows.

'Excuse me, what do you mean I would have gone and slept with someone else? I have just kissed four girls in my entire life. I wish you had tried!'

'Poor you ... just four?' She took out a small mirror and started setting her smudged kajal right.

'Whatever. I am not as bad as you make me out to be. So, do you still, you know?' I asked.

'Obviously not! That was just an emotional outbreak. I love Tanmay quite a lot now.'

'Do you? I thought you just had to go on with him till the time Avantika and I broke up,' I said.

'Why so?'

'*This guy will just fuck you and leave you.* Remember that? It would have been a little hypocritical then if you guys broke up before we did.'

'Yes, maybe. But I love this guy. I met his parents at the Spirit of Living convention. They kind of like me, too. Saw Avantika, too, though she wasn't looking very happy. Are things all right between the two of you?'

'Things are perfect.'

*Avantika? Sad? She always is, whenever she is with her parents.*

'She is beautiful. You are a lucky bitch. You are not planning to dump her, are you?'

'Not in the next hundred years, I suppose.'

'She is lucky too,' she said. 'I am glad you finally found someone you can be in a *relationship* with and not with someone who was willing to just get intimate with you.'

'Don't make me feel bad about the choices I have made in the past, Vernita.'

'Fine, fine. We should leave now. Tanmay will be really mad if he sees me with you,' she said.

'Where is he?' I asked. 'I haven't seen him all night.'

'He is busy getting photographed with all the girls he can get a hold of. Bullshit,' she snapped. She was right. I remembered him being surrounded by a group of girls, all wanting to have him in their albums. Big deal, I am not photogenic, he is. I am not a Greek god, he is.

'He is lucky, but I am luckier. The most smashing of all girls is with me tonight, not him.'

'Don't flatter me,' she laughed. 'See, you're funny and smart. You always have the right things to say. Though I am not impressed. Keep those words for your girlfriend.'

'Whatever. Let's go,' I said and we both laughed.

'Yup. Wait. There is something I always wanted to do,' she said and turned towards me. All of a sudden, she grabbed hold of my tie and pulled me close till I could smell the perfume off her neck. She held me there briefly and breathed heavily. Then, she forced her lips onto mine—her lips, wet and soft like candy—and kissed me deep, holding me close against her. My pulse shot through the roof; her body felt better against mine than it looked. Her tongue explored and played with me, her teeth bit at my lips and she breathed into me. Already panting, she pulled my head back and dug her teeth into my neck. Then she started to suck on it. I placed my hand on her exposed waist and clawed in to keep from moaning. Just as I started cursing myself on missing out on four years of fabulous kissing under the moonlight, she pulled back and started to walk away from me. I stood there, panting and trying to make sense out of it, and struggled to string my words to say something.

'So ... any last words?' I shouted as she walked a few yards away.

She looked back and adjusted the tufts of hair falling on her eyes and shouted, 'Now I know why Avantika is crazy about you. And the other girls. I hope now you feel that I was girlfriend material after all.' She smiled and walked away.

*Did that mean I was a great kisser?* Obviously! And the other girls? There were just four whom I had kissed and none of them had said I was any good.

Anyway, great kiss, though!

Life's about the small victories and the small battles you win every day. On the farewell night, the most stunning of all girls kissed me. Life isn't all that bad.

~

Vernita was right. Avantika was sad at the Spirit of Living meeting nd she didn't tell me why clearly. Probably it was because her application to change her posting to Delhi had been rejected and she had to shift to Bangalore in a little over two months. I was equally depressed but I knew we would stick it out. Our sadness wasn't borne out of the fear that our relationship would crumble down in due time, but it was because it was hard for us to imagine spending days on end without seeing each other. We didn't have much time left together.

I had started counting time backwards. As we approached the date and she had to leave for Bangalore, she started to slip in and out of depression. We spent those two months trying to spend every possible minute with each other, spending hours at coffee shops till the waiters politely asked us to leave.

We held hands till they became sweaty, we kissed each other till it became embarrassing, we said we loved each other till we got tired and then we said it a few more times. We never got enough of each other. We started to plan ways we could meet each other, compare the merits of Google Talk and Skype, among other things.

With every passing day, I saw Avantika become sadder. Sometimes, she just cried all night and didn't answer any of my calls. All that made me equally sad because I wasn't able to make a difference.

Though, even in Bangalore, she would only be a call and a flight away from me. But not meeting her thrice in a week was a depressing thought. I started to look for jobs in Bangalore, but no one was hiring. I would have flushed toilets for a living but all I got were IT job openings.

I had already started missing her and every time I said anything like that to Avantika, she sobbed like a little child.

She was a little child, my baby, my sweet little baby. *Tattooed* little baby!

The crying and the depression took a toll of her face. It was always dry and tired and devastatingly tragic. It took me to the time when we first met. She was sad then. She was beautiful then. She was beautiful now. She would always be beautiful to me. She may be ninety, her face may be riddled with wrinkles, she might lose all her teeth, her gums may bleed, she may miss a few limbs . . but she would always be my little child. I would still kiss those hollow cheeks, still hold her wrinkled hands and still say that I loved her. Because I didn't know what to do if not love her.

She was the only girl I had ever loved and it had taken eight years since I hit puberty to find her. I was going to keep her for the next eighty.

# 16

Days flew by and the time for Avantika to leave for Bangalore came near. It wasn't until fifteen days before she left that I finally realized why Avantika had acted strangely over the last two months. I had assumed it was because she didn't want to leave Delhi, but there was a lot more going on in her mind than just that. I hadn't braced myself for it, and I certainly didn't see it coming.

'Deb, I need to tell you something,' Avantika said. She didn't sound great. I knew that tone. I could sense the despondence in her voice. It was there every time she talked about her family or her ex-boyfriends. Things that troubled her. I wondered what it was this time.

'What?' I asked.

'We need to break up.'

'WHAT?' I asked just to make sure I had heard right.

'We need to break up. We need to end this. I don't think you will understand this but you have to try. I am sorry, Deb. I am really sorry,' she said, almost breaking down.

'Is this some kind of a joke?'

'No, it's not. I swear on Tanmay, it's not,' she said. She couldn't be joking. She never swore without a reason.

'But—'

I was speechless. It felt like somebody had driven a ram though my chest. I started feeling dizzy. For a moment, I wished she were joking. I began to lose my footing and everything Avantika and I had shared flashed in front of my eyes. Just like life does when one is about to die. I felt my heart beat out of my chest. My stomach churned and I could taste bile at the back of my throat. I could feel myself getting sick.

'Deb, just listen. Please, do this for me and don't ask for explanations. I don't have any. You have given me the most wonderful relationship of my life. And I love you and will keep doing that. But we have to end this. Had there been a choice, I would have made it, but there is none.'

'Is it your parents? Please tell me?' I begged. 'I will talk to them. I will talk to mine. We will figure this out.' I paced around the room, slapping my forehead and trying not to cry and smash the phone against the wall.

'It's not about them,' she argued. I could feel her voice steeling up. The moment of vulnerability had passed and I knew I wouldn't get past her now.

'But . . . ? What? Why? What? *What?*'

I was in tears. I wasn't sobbing softly. I was shouting and I was wailing. Like someone had died. It felt like I had died. I loved her. Avantika was all I had, and I had never thought beyond her in all those days I was with her. My days started with her and ended with her. She filled everything in between. I had come to believe she would always be around. I had accepted her as a part of me, a part of my existence.

She waited for me to stop crying.

'It's not in my hands, Deb. I wish it were but it's not. This is what Sri Guru wants and I can't go against that. It's best for the both of us.'

'Sri Guru? Your Sri Guru? Did he ask you to do this? I can't believe this, Avantika! Are you out of your mind? You are breaking up with me because that stupid Sri Guru asked you to? You can't be serious!'

'Deb! Deb, you can say anything to me, but please not a thing against Sri Guru. He didn't ask me to break up.'

'Then what? Did he want you to abandon the world and become a sanyasi? Or did he find someone for you? Huh? How can you be so irrational? I still can't believe this is happening. Of all people, I didn't expect this from you.' It still sounded like an extended joke and she would crack up any moment. She didn't. I didn't know whether I should cry, or feel ridiculous.

'No, Deb. Will you please listen? I have been somewhat disturbed with what happened to Paritosh and Shawar. It happened so suddenly. So I talked to Sri Guru about it and . . .'

'Great! And he loaded it with astrological bullshit about you and that you are responsible for it. Hasn't he? Tell me, Avantika? You never loved me, did you? Why? All you care about is your Sri Guru. He tells you to leave me, you do that. Tomorrow he will tell you to go fuck somebody, you will do that. What are you? It's like I don't even know you,' I shouted at her. I heard Mom and Dad stop talking in the other room. They were then trying to listen in. I knew Mom would come into my room eventually to ask for something she didn't need.

'Deb, will you listen, for god's sake?'

'No, I won't listen to you! You can go tell your Sri Guru to fuck off. Do that! That money-sucking swine who lives off stupid, innocent people like you. Why can't you see it? He is fooling you and everybody around you. How is this so hard to understand?'

'Enough!'

'What enough? He is a bastard and nothing is going to change that,' I bellowed.

'Don't call me unless I tell you to. I am hanging up. I can't be the reason for your pain. I can't see you suffer because of me. Check your inbox and you will know. Bye, Deb. I love you. I always will. It may hurt you for a while, but it is for your own good.'

'Avantika, listen. You cannot leave me just like that. Not for that piece of shit.'

'Deb, I don't think there is anything to argue in this. It's about my faith. Go, check your mail. It is not easy for me to do this. Bye.'

She hung up and she it seemed as if she hadn't shed a single tear. I checked my mail after I handed over the paper puncher Mom asked for. She asked me if everything was okay and I nodded. I told her something went in my eye and she asked if I needed an eye drop. I shook my head and she left my room.

After I read the message, I was sure about two things.

First, I would definitely kill all god-men before anybody, if I ever got the chance. And second, that this was the silliest break-up ever. I always thought Avantika was wild, not stupid and irrational. There is a fine line, a line that everyone who goes to religious *satsang*s, *jagaran*s and pilgrimages invariably crosses. There is no god, or god-men, who can be against two people being together.

The message read:

*Sri Guru: 'It's you who is responsible for all the trials and tribulations that people around you go through. You determine the happiness or the sorrow that they experience. You have to make their lives worthwhile. It's you who define their lives. What fate they have is of your giving. It's you, only you who can make or break their lives. Child, if you think that somebody is suffering around you, it is only you who can set it right. You are the one responsible. It is because of you that they suffer. It is because of you that they don't.'*

*Deb, I am not strong. After what happened to Shawar and Paritosh, I am scared. I won't be able to carry on if something ever happens to you. You were barred from your placements a few days after you met me, you screwed your CAT examination and maybe it was all because of me. I am not sure, Deb. I'm scared after seeing Shawar in the condition that he is in right now. I don't know, Deb. I cannot take it. I would rather be away from you and see you safe and happy. Your life was perfect before I came along and spoiled everything. It's best that we don't talk.*

*Sorry, Deb. I love you.*

*Avantika.*

Now what was that supposed to mean? If Paritosh and Shawar did something stupid, it did not mean *Avantika* was at fault! If she couldn't get Paritosh off drugs, how was she responsible? If Shawar was a drunkard, it was not because of Avantika. And even if it was, it did not mean I would end up in the same situation.

I couldn't believe she could be so dumb! How could she not see the lack of logic behind this? I knew she loved and respected Sri Guru more than anybody else, but this was downright stupid. And he had not asked Avantika to leave me! I texted her and vented what I felt about her and her Guru. She didn't reply. I called her incessantly from my cell phone and my landline. She didn't answer any of my calls. I mailed her and she ignored my emails. I left messages with her roommates and friends but there was no response.

How could she move on? How could she not respond to anything? How could she not see that I was wrecked?

The next day, I called her from a PCO and broke down into little sobs as soon she said *Hello*. I knew she was in pain, but she had her reasons to end this relationship. I had none. I wanted this relationship. It was the only thing I had. That relationship was the only thing that kept me going those days. It defined my days.

Two days later, she finally answered my call. I begged her to meet me, make me understand what her fears were, but she refused. She told me that I wouldn't understand. She told me that if I had been through the things she had been through, I would understand what her Guru meant to her. She told me that I should respect myself and not call her. While I was on my knees, she kept driving me to the ground, telling me that I would get over it. Relationships end, people break up all the time, she argued. How could I have told her that it wasn't just a relationship for me? How could I have told her that I wouldn't live to see another day?

I wandered around North Campus every day, hoping to catch a glimpse of her but she had moved out from her hostel. Isha, her roommate, told me that she hadn't spoken about me since the break-up. I asked her if she ever saw Avantika crying and she shook her head. How could she not even cry? She had cried for two years when Paritosh left her. Was I that insignificant in her life? Could she move on that easily?

It was hard for me to stay home. Everything reminded me of her. Every day I took the metro to North Campus and walked around aimlessly to block her out of my head. I would come back home, exhausted and teary-eyed, and go to sleep. Weeks went by and I kept pining for her. My calls and texts still went unanswered.

It had been days since I had slept, eaten, breathed or smiled to my heart's content. I needed her. One touch, one hug was all I wanted. I badly wanted to see her, hold her hand again, capture in my mind what it felt like, and kiss her to know that she still cared. I wanted to ask her how she was doing and see her break down in my arms. I wanted her to tell me that she was crushed and I was all she could think about. Her regret, tears and disappointment would be my consolation. I felt cheated. Like I had died and no one even cried.

Had I died?

~

More days passed and I continued to spiral down into depression. My parents thought it was because they were moving to Hyderabad and I would miss them. My mom would sit next to me and ask me if I needed her to stay back. I refused.

All their bags were packed and the boxes were sealed a week before they had to leave. It felt like I was being abandoned. They asked me a million times if I was okay and whether Sonali or Mom needed to stay back. I vehemently refused and they left. I remember breaking down in the taxi the moment I saw them disappear behind the airport's sliding doors.

Now, I was all alone in my grief.

More calls were rejected. Texts weren't replied to and mails weren't answered. My restlessness showed no signs of fading. I couldn't accept that Avantika had moved on. I couldn't accept that it was over. I would wait for her, I had already decided. She would come back.

*'Move on, Deb, you have to. For me. For yourself. Bye. Best of luck for your life. I am leaving for Bangalore.'*

This is what her message said, a day before she had to leave for Bangalore. I didn't think a single sentence could be as discomforting as this message was.

From there, it all went downhill. I had asked Shrey to leave me alone and he had done exactly that. The abandonment was complete in the next few days. Shrey left for Germany for a technological start-up with up some guys he knew from IIT, Delhi. Viru and Yogi received their joining letters and they had to start soon. Anyway, they wouldn't have understood what I was going through. Their relationship with me was restricted to birthday treats and such. The last one I gave was when they found out I had secured a job at BHEL. I don't remember getting a treat in return.

Anyway, they weren't friends I could call my own. There were a few people that I called up, who I knew had loved me once, but it made no difference. I didn't want to meet them either. The tendency of thinking that meeting others would mean cutting into the time I could spend with Avantika still hadn't left me. Avantika had sucked out of all my energy, love and optimism.

Talking to anybody didn't help. I ended up in the same damned state. I didn't need a distraction. I didn't need a diversion. I didn't need company. *I needed Avantika.*

It felt like I was being punished for who I was, like life had come a full circle. Every iota of pain I had subjected others to, came back to torment me, like ghosts looking over my shoulder and sneering at me. Every break-up came back to haunt me. Every friendship that I had not respected was back to haunt me. I had never felt responsible or sorry for the troubles of any of my friends. I assumed they were strong enough to deal with them on their own. My insensitivity came back to bite me.

Things went from bad to worse. If only there was a sign that told me she was suffering as much as I did. Everywhere I went, I could see her, feel her in the air, sense her presence, and smell her perfume. *Maybe she is stalking me. Maybe she is behind that pillar to see how I am doing.*

The emptiness of my apartment had started to haunt me. My parents had left me the car and I spent days driving around her flat, hoping to catch a glimpse of her. *Maybe she hadn't gone to Bangalore at all.* Nothing happened. I drove back and forth from North Campus to Greater Kailash, where we first met, more than a dozen times each day, hoping to bump into her. Nothing happened.

I spent hours at the Delhi University metro station, hoping that she would walk by, spot me and then come running into my arms and tell me how sorry she was. Nothing happened. I called up her friends to help me track her. They, too, had no idea where Avantika was. I asked Vernita but Tanmay was tight-lipped about Avantika's whereabouts. I called the office she had joined and the receptionist wouldn't connect my call unless I knew which department she was working in. After three calls, she threatened to call the police and submit my number. I didn't try it again.

Slowly and steadily, my world was falling apart. I reminded myself that I was doing okay before Avantika came along and changed everything. It didn't help. Since the time I met Avantika, things had changed. Everyone around me had ceased to matter. The world around me ceased to matter; I didn't even want people around. And now there was no one. I had never thought I would need anybody else. I had no friends for I never made good ones.

Had I been a drinker, I would have wasted myself day after day. But since I wasn't, I ate with a vengeance. I bloated up and gained a lot of weight. It was as if I was punishing myself. I spent hours staring blankly at the television and eating. I ordered everything home. I couldn't have gone out to eat, for every place reminded me of her and the time we had spent there.

I spent many of those days writing the defunct blog, but ended up writing her name repeatedly. I was glad nobody read it because all my blog posts were on Avantika, on how much I missed her, and how ridiculous it was to break up with her. The few people who used to comment on my blog stopped doing so. I wished they would comment. All the comments on my blog went straight to Avantika's mailbox because she had created the blog. I wished somehow she would stumble on the blog and feel sorry for me. I wasn't even looking for her to come back any more. I just wanted pity. A little acceptance to tell me that she was sorry she had left me.

I kept tracking her on social networking sites to see if there was anybody else in her life. But there was absolutely nothing that would suggest anything. She had not been online for about a month now. As a last resort, I enrolled for the Spirit of Living course, hoping I might just bump into Avantika, even though I knew she was in Bangalore from her last text.

Somewhere during those days, I had accepted that I would never see her again. It felt better when I thought that all the doors had closed in on me. It was better than the times when I felt there was a glimmer of hope. It's better to die in an atmosphere without oxygen than struggle in one with traces of it.

The recognition of pain told me that I had loved her truly and that's something I had never done before.

Not surprisingly, I did not bump into Avantika during the course. When I joined the course, which they claimed to be a spiritual uplifting process, I thought I would trash everything, fight with the members, fight with the teachers, call Sri Guru names, and walk off dramatically. But once the course started, I couldn't do any of that. It may not have been spiritually uplifting for me but I did see people in the most rotten of moods going out with a smile on their faces. Stressed-out couples, out-of-job executives, broken hearts like me, drug addicts, everybody smiled and tried to get rid of their problems.

The course was a glorified meeting of a few miserable people like us dancing, singing, playing and sharing our woes with each other. It worked like a charm on most people. Including me. It wasn't until the fifth day that I opened up and burst into tears and found myself in the arms of a forty-year-old woman who had lost both her children in a gruesome car accident. When she, a woman who had lost two children, told me that everything would be okay, my grief seemed a lot smaller than hers. In the fifteen days of the course, the woman became my best friend. She talked about her kids, a boy and a girl, and I talked about Avantika. Sometimes, we broke down together and sometimes we laughed like little babies on a sugar high. I marvelled at her courage and she told me I had a huge heart. She was a godsend.

I started accepting my break-up. I forgave Spirit of Living. Not because I had started accepting the senseless philosophy (which wasn't as senseless any more) but because I started seeing with my own eyes how much people revered Sri Guru. He was a father figure to millions. I had seen people's faces light up just at the mention of his name. He was like a god to many. I hate to say this, but I started respecting him, even loving him. The only time I wasn't woeful about the break-up was when I looked at his adorable bearded face and his enlightened eyes.

But I did not forget that my break-up, for once, was not my own doing. The course helped and I hate to say that because had it not been for the Spirit of Living I would still be with Avantika!

I called up Smriti, half out of guilt, half to get over Avantika, but just ended up crying. Smriti tolerated me for a while and then asked me not to call her ever again.

Another month passed like that. All my life, I had driven everyone away. Now, it was I who was being driven away, from friends, from family, from Avantika. I had nobody to talk to, nobody to laugh with, nobody to cry with, and nobody to celebrate with. But then again, I wanted nobody, I wanted *her*. I wanted the time she had promised me. Now it was all gone. I had been dumped, unceremoniously, painfully, unreasonably . . . and a lousy job at a public-sector office beckoned.

# 17

'Are you sure you are going to be fine?' Shrey asked. He'd called from Germany, so the call must have cost him a lot. I liked that at least somebody cared. 'I know it's been kind of hard for you. First Avantika and then your family leaving. But it isn't that bad; there are a million girls out there. Go for them. You will be just fine.'

'I hope so, man. Hang up now. It must be costing you a lot,' I said. I didn't want to be sympathized with all the time. It made me feel like a loser, which I probably was.

'Are you crazy? I hacked into their telephone exchange and so actually I am calling from their . . . let me see . . . oh fuck, it's their parliament's line . . . fuck . . . bye. You take care . . .'

'You haven't changed, have you?'

'And you don't need to change. *The girls are waiting*.' He hung up.

Shrey was working with some IITians in a start-up of some kind. They were trying to make a hybrid car in Germany, which could run on biodiesel and sunlight. While Shrey's life kept getting better, things were getting worse for me every passing day. I was the only one going to a government office amongst us. The pay was horrible and I knew the work environment would be too. While I was already cursing BHEL, the office I was destined to work at, Vernita's job had already started a fortnight ago and they were sending her to Thailand for a new employees' retreat. Tanmay had joined his uncle's business and had started preparing for the CAT again.

Viru and Yogi had joined their job in the research and development department of a tractor-manufacturing unit in Punjab. They were back in their homeland. It suited them. *Everybody is happy*, I thought.

Vernita had everything she wanted. Viru and Yogi had each other, their homeland and loads of liquor, I was sure. Shrey was living his dream of being amongst technology maniacs and working on a project that no one believed in. Of the people around me, I had ended up the worst.

Avantika's words rang in my head—*You will never get the pants ironed if you don't take them off.*

I didn't care whether I was going for a job at a government office or a plush investment bank. The only thing that mattered was Avantika. If I didn't have her, nothing else mattered.

The morning of the first day of my job at BHEL was especially tough. I missed her even more now. There was no one to wake me up, no one to pester me and remind me of the little details, and no one to tell me that I would be great and that I had nothing to fear. I dragged myself out of bed, slipped into the shirt and pair of jeans I had bought a few days before. The office bus was right on time and the middle-aged uncles folded their newspapers and boarded the bus. The air inside the office bus was depressing. There were grown men sleeping with their heads on the windowpanes, drooling all over themselves. I decided that I would take the car to work from the next day. It took an hour for the bus to pick more old men and reach the office. The final few jerks woke everyone up in the bus.

I stared at the monstrous office of BHEL standing tall at Bhikhaji Cama Place, New Delhi. It was fifteen storeys tall but looked at least thirty. It was a gigantic building made out of brown stone and cement, placed in what looked like an ascending and descending staircase. *So this is the place*, I told myself. I had lost the drive to sit for any other interviews.

The guard asked for my ID and I fished it out and flashed it as I moved through the automated doors. I had been there before, but always looked at it as a place where losers or old people worked.

I still hadn't come to accept that I was a loser and that I had just lost the woman I loved. The world was there for the taking. I just had to figure out how and whether I wanted it more than I wanted Avantika.

I looked up at the huge board that had all the details about the building.

*Piping. Sixth floor.*

I tried to memorize the data. The building was about five decades old, but it was surprisingly well maintained for a government office. The lift was a little tricky for me, though. Different lifts stopped at different floors, so it took me quite some time to get used to it.

'Is this the piping department?' I asked a bespectacled man who I was sure had spent all his life at BHEL.

He took two full minutes to chew upon what I had asked and answered, 'This is the eighth floor. Piping is the sixth floor. New employee? Tricky lift, eh?'

'Yes. Thank you.'

'You will have to work really hard here. Our principles of integrity and hard work are well known around the globe,' he said and became suddenly strangely demonic. 'And get a haircut. Such long hair is unacceptable.'

'Okay, sir,' I said and left before he could comment on how my falling jeans would further rot the company.

As I jumped alternate stairs to reach the sixth floor, I wondered whether I would end up like him, old, lazy and bitter. I would not. *This is just temporary*, I told myself.

I did intend to leave the job in a few years and go for an MBA at Harvard or Yale. Or the one at ISB. Or maybe go to the Middle East. They needed a lot of mechanical engineers there.

I might even meet Avantika's parents. Not that they would

have liked it if I told them anything. They were Punjabis and they wanted a nice Punjabi boy—rich and fair and tall—for their daughter. But then, I could have been an oil magnate and impressed them out of their wits. Or become the president of the United States. Or just got admitted to a mental asylum.

Just as my mind started to drift off to thoughts of Avantika, another old voice called out. 'Deb?'

'Yes?'

'I am Deepak Malhotra. Deputy general manager, piping. Your dad talked to me. Welcome to BHEL. I hope you like it here.'

Mr Malhotra was one of the better-dressed people in BHEL. Most people there in the office wore the same shirt for a month before putting it out to wash.

'Thank you, sir.'

'Amit is waiting for you in cubicle number five. You are a management trainee under him. He will show you around. If you have any problem, you can see me or Mr Goyal. Cubicle five is the third one from the left along that aisle. Go ahead. Nice meeting you, young man . . . nice jeans,' he chuckled.

He reminded me of my father, who kept asking me how often they dropped down and how I managed to wear them so low.

I decided to love him. He didn't have a paunch, was tall, and had a perfectly trimmed peppered moustache. He was a man of consequence and it showed in his demeanour.

I walked down the aisle of the piping department. It dispelled quite a few doubts I had in my mind. It wasn't as dilapidated as I thought it would be. They were definitely not using MS DOS. The computers were all upgraded. The desks were swanky and clean, with no spit stains on them. The cubicles were nice and spacious, and there were two huge offices in the corners. One for the DGM and another one for the head of the department.

It's another matter that the computers missed people. There was a bunch of people in some corner discussing the new receptionist in the office. Another bunch discussed the cricket match the previous day, while they sipped tea and occasionally ran their hands over their bulging stomachs.

But overall, the office was impressive. I liked it. *I had to*. I reached cubicle five.

'Hello, sir,' I said.

'Hello!' he said as he swirled around his chair to set his eyes on me. I saw his desktop screen. It was Monica Belluci in a gold bikini, and it was signed 'Amit' beneath. He wore a shirt tucked deep inside his hideously faded jeans and wore glasses with a frame that was heavier than him. He had not yet grown out of his fifth-grade hairstyle that his parents had decided for him. A dreadful crew cut. Unlike other desks, his was a tutorial on how to keep a desk organized. For someone like me, who had more books sleeping with me on the bed than stacked on an unused study table, this was new.

I decided to like him, too. Not that I had a choice.

'So you must be Deb?' he asked. He gave the twirling pencil in his hand quite some rotations.

'Yes, sir,' I said.

'I am Amit. Call me Amit. I am no *sir*. I joined last year, so it is cool.'

'Fine, Amit.'

'How many trainees have joined? Any girls? Any hot ones?'

'No, Amit. Not that I know of,' I said. I was little surprised. Not that he looked old, but I didn't expect this question so early in the day. Not from somebody who looked like the king of Nerdsville. He desperately tried to sound urbane, but his small-town upbringing was dripping from every consonant and syllable. The small-town accent was overpowering.

'Not that you know of? If somebody would know that, it's you. Want a tour around the office?'

'I would love one.'

The ice between us broke the very second we met. It lit my dull life suddenly. It was my longest conversation in over a month, apart from the childless woman at the Spirit of Living convention.

He stood up. He wasn't more than five-feet-five and barely had any flesh on him. He was skin stretched over bones. I could have flicked him into orbit.

'Okay, let's go. Let's start from the least glamorous to the most glamorous departments. First on our list is the planning department.'

'The least glamorous?'

'Yes, all the old people work there. They are the reason why most of our projects get delayed. The excruciatingly slow department. It's like a very slow dentist performing a root canal on all your molars,' he said and started to hop off. His imitation Nike shoes were in sharp contrast to mine but he carried them off with unmatched aplomb.

'My father worked in the planning department,' I said. Not that it mattered to me; it was just that he worked hard enough for a government employee and he should get credit for that.

'Oh! Debashish Roy? Now I get it. It just slipped out of my mind. You want me to apologize for what I just said. I won't, because you don't want me to. But yes, your father. He worked really hard and tried to fast track every project. Why do you think he got the transfer?'

'Okay.' Dad never ceased to make me proud. Although working in a PSU after IIT, Delhi, isn't what people expect. If only he'd worked in an multinational, I would have graduated from Purdue.

'No, it's not okay. Count and tell. How many people are at their desks? Quick, you have ten seconds,' he said and started looking at his watch.

'Everybody, I guess.'

'That took eighteen seconds. Eighteen seconds and still a wrong answer. The answer is nobody. You are not at your desk if you are not working. Okay, another question. On how many screens do you see the screensaver on?'

'Everybody's.'

'That's three seconds. And that's the right answer. That also means nobody has touched their computer screens for at least the last ten minutes. And it's just ten thirty. Why do people not take their jobs seriously? Extended Monday morning blues, huh?'

'Yes, maybe.'

'You don't speak much, do you?'

*It's useless trying to blow spit bubbles in the direction opposite to a gale,* I thought. He looked like a nerd but definitely didn't talk like one. I mean, he wasn't a stud but he sounded like a hyperactive, hyper-vocal genius.

Piping, cost engineering, rotatory equipment, civil department etcetera, etcetera. He was desperately trying to explain what each department did, but my brain diligently rejected such useless bits of information.

I felt he told me more about BHEL than people get to know in their entire lives. This office was in sharp contrast to what I had imagined and heard of offices that my college mates were going to. Small-town guys and girls flocked to this place. From where they belonged, there was still a certain amount of prestige associated with government jobs.

'This is the last department. Chemical processes. And that is my dream girl.'

'Who? What? That?' I exclaimed.

'Why? Isn't she good?' he asked with the innocence of a two-year-old who has just sketched his first drawing and is nervous about what his art teacher might say.

I looked at her. She was ten shades darker than I was and I was, by no means, fair. She stood at five feet and wore an awkward, ill-fitting pink suit. She could have passed by me a zillion times and I wouldn't have noticed. She had a sweet face but after Avantika and Vernita, I had set myself high standards.

'I know. You wouldn't like her. You must be going around with sexy, mini-skirted girls. But she is a nice girl.'

'I am not going around with anybody,' I said. I didn't need to say that but I wanted to check whether it still hurt. It did.

'Why? You broke up with your girlfriend? This is the problem with Delhi girls. They are all like this. That's why I like her. She's from my homeland—Bihar. Do you want to meet her?'

Delhi girls? I wondered if it had anything to do with it. Maybe she actually had dumped me for somebody else.

'No, it's fine.'

'It's okay. Don't be shy.' He tugged my hand and pulled me all the way through the aisle to her table. I was standing right in front of her.

'Hi, Astha,' Amit said.

And for a moment, I felt I was back in the time when I first met Avantika. His cheeks had turned the loveliest shade of pink and his milky white complexion didn't help his cause either. He fidgeted and nervously shifted his weight from one foot to another.

'Hi, Amit. You, here?' she said. She pulled her head out from beneath foot-long sheets that had lines, semicircles, three-fourth circles crisscrossing all over it. She fumbled with the sheets thrice before she managed to fold them into neat bundles. I wondered how these guys were so well organized.

'Ummm . . . meet my new management trainee, Deb,' he stammered. For the first time that day, I saw him stumbling for words. He was sweating despite the cold blast from the air conditioner.

'Hello,' she said.

'Good morning, ma'am,' I said.

'Call me Astha.' She sounded sweet, too, a voice that matched her kind, docile face.

'Perfect,' I said.

'Amit, I have some work right now. Lunch break?'

'No problem. See you later then,' he said, still blushing and red like the setting sun.

'Welcome to BHEL,' she said and wiggled her hand. Her palm was darker than the back of my hand.

'Thanks. Bye.' We walked off.

As soon as we were out of her audible and visible range, he started to tug at my shirt and ask, 'Isn't she cute? Isn't she cute?' She was, without any doubt, the first girl Amit had talked to. Amit confirmed that later. Amit jumped around boyishly and waited for my answer. He didn't look a day older than twenty!

'Hey, chill. Yes, she is cute. Are you guys going out?'

'I don't know. I once told her that I *like* her. She didn't answer and we haven't talked about it.'

'What? Why? You said you like her, then why didn't you ask her out?'

'No. What do I say? What if she says no? How do I say that? Where do I take her?' he continued to tug my shirt like a toddler would and his eyes didn't leave me.

'The same way you said, *I like you.*'

'You mean I should mail that?' he asked. His gaze never left me and his tone got more paranoid with every passing second.

'You mailed that? *You mailed that?* Did you actually just *mail* that? And you have never talked about it, you motor mouth?'

*Not again! No mails again!*

'Why? What is wrong with that? She sent me her piping stress sheets and I mailed her back saying I liked them. I even said I loved them.'

'You liked her *designs*? You didn't say you like *her*?'

'NO! Obviously not. Are you crazy? I cannot say that. But I said I *liked* her work. I even said I *loved* it. Isn't that enough?'

'*No, it is not!* How do you plan to eventually kiss her? Or have sex with her? Or will you do it with her designs?' DCE legacy strikes. Sex is all we can think and talk about. I am another ashamed alum of my college. Or is it me who defames the rest of our alums?

'Deb? What are you talking about? There is still a lot of time for that and I will learn when the time comes. How can you even talk about that? It's so . . .' He was visibly scandalized. So was I; I had clearly overstepped a line and said something I shouldn't have.

'Fine, there is a lot of time to go. How old are you? And her?'

'I am twenty-five, she is twenty-four.'

'Oh, great! She is twenty-four already? When do you plan to say something? When she gets married? By Bihar standards, she is already overage, isn't it?'

'Don't say that,' he said and hung his head as if it was his fault. But he was a twenty-five-year-old virgin who was yet to have a proper conversation with a girl. I hadn't met a lot of that kind around me. I knew a lot of people from my college who had started going to prostitutes for they couldn't get laid legitimately.

We had switched places. He was not in charge now. I was. He was the trainee. I was comfortable again, even though I was the *last* person he should be receiving relationship advice from.

'Anyway, we will figure something out,' I said.

'I hope we do. Now tell me, did you like anything in the office?' he asked.

The process department had twice the number of girls than all the other departments, combined. No one was smart enough, though. After Avantika, my tastes had changed, too. I was spoilt. I was hers and I was ruined for other women.

I said nothing.

*The girls are waiting.*

# 18

'Deb, watch out. Open the first file in the second directory in the C drive,' Amit shouted at me in whispers as he walked close behind a big, bulky, drowsy-eyed old man. I still hadn't learnt how to do anything in my first two months at BHEL, except getting coffee for Amit from time to time. I pretty much did whatever he asked me to and stayed out of doing anything productive.

In BHEL, there were no parties, there were no gorgeous girls, and there were no office trips. It was an engineering firm, and as expected, the work environment was depressing, the employees boring, mostly guys, and sad ones—the *ghissu*s. The gender ratio was abysmal. I had passed out from an engineering college to reach another. The same discussions. The same jokes. The same porn preferences.

I had attended a few training sessions taken by senior employees in the first few weeks. They had introduced us to the fundamental concepts of piping and other things that—to my surprise—no one listened to. There were eight new trainees in the piping department. Each one of them was dutifully told by their mentors that all classes were a sham. *You learn everything on the job*, was the buzz around the classes. I did not think it was necessary to talk to anyone else other than Amit and sometimes, Astha.

I did go around the office looking for people I could connect more with to talk to, but I found none. I tried initiating conversations with a few colleagues but soon lost interest. Avantika had left me in deep, *deep* trouble.

Just as I had opened the file, the oldie reached my cubicle and started to stare at my computer screen. He didn't say anything and just stared at the strange combination of pipes that lay in front of me. He bent over and brought his face within microns of the monitor; his armpits stank of sour yogurt.

I had a look at those pipes, and at once, I realized it wasn't my cup of tea. I started sharpening my pencil again.

'So, working hard?' he bawled in my ear.

'Huh? Yes, sir.' I stood and breathed.

'Sharpening pencils won't do. Do something. I know how you got here but don't think it's easy working here. You have to work to survive. You have to be smart and just working hard won't do,' he said as he leaned onto me.

Surviving hadn't been too tough. All it meant was getting coffee and writing semi-mushy mails to Astha on behalf of Amit, which were wrenched out of all their mush once Amit edited them. The training period anywhere in the world is a honeymoon period. And just in case it's a government office, you can be gone for a year and nobody would notice. Unless, of course, your father used to work in the same office.

He continued, 'Get it? How is your dad? In Hyderabad? Whatever. Get back to work and I want to have your first isometric sheet done by Monday. I haven't got even one yet.' He turned to look at Amit and said, 'I want a progress report on Debashish in a few days. Please make sure it is done as soon as possible.'

I was seeing this man for the first time and he had already started to run me into the ground. I just kept myself from sticking that pencil up his hair-infested nose, which had more hair than his barren head.

'Okay, sir.'

He went off.

'Gosh! Now *that* was a narrow escape. He nearly had you in,' Amit said.

'Excuse me? Who the hell *is* he? I didn't think anybody around me could be of any damn consequence. This is a government office! How anyone be so heavy-handed?'

'No. Not anybody. *He* can be. He is just back from a tour. Mr Goyal is the one who was passed over for your dad's promotion. So he won't take kindly to you. He is the HOD.'

'*So?* What can he do? He can't possibly kick me out,' I said. I was an employee of the Government of India. I had to be dead or mentally unstable to lose the job. *Mentally unstable* I was, but he would never know about Avantika.

'He can,' he said. 'Till the time you are a trainee and on probation. This one year, he can. He will take your viva one year from now. He can easily kick you out then. So better be careful.'

*This is just a temporary arrangement*, I reminded myself.

'Nothing will happen, especially when you are here. I am sure you will take care of me.' I swirled around in my new chair. Amit and I were the first ones to get them as I had pestered the hell out of the store in-charge. It was better than what it's description in the catalogue had promised. *The Hamilton Swivel-Tilt Dining Chair features a diamond-shaped back and legs on rolling casters. The top of the back piece is a sleek 'Brushed Faux Medium Cherry' wood, while the frame is a 'Matte Pewter and Bronze' metal. This piece features curved armrests and a swivel and tilt design. Rolling casters provide easy mobility.*

'Deb! You are taking things too lightly. Did you read the manual I gave you yesterday? Obviously, you did not. What do you think you are doing? You haven't even bothered to go to the site once. I tell you, you are going to be in big trouble. And how do you think you will do the pipe section he asked you to complete?'

'How am I? What are *you* here for, genius? You are going to do it, not me.' I broke my record of eight complete three-hundred-and-sixty degree revolutions and pushed even harder. I wasn't taking things lightly. These chairs were little pieces of magic.

'And what do I get this time for doing what you are supposed to do?'

'A gift. A beautiful romantic gift. You want that? Or should I just start the pipe section? Maybe I am taking things too lightly. Maybe I should start working and not help you with Astha at all. We should all do what we are supposed to do and not meddle in other people's affairs at all.' I started to fiddle with the files.

'Okay . . . okay, okay. Don't touch those files; you will mess up the order. I need that. I will do it for you. What are you making for her? Is it expensive? That's not a problem; I will pay you for that. But please make something good. When are we giving it?'

'It will be good. Don't you worry,' I said. This was the usual. During the first two months, I wasn't required to do anything other than type out mundane reports or fill out Excel tables. It was all the mentally numbing work that seniors didn't want to do any more.

All the MTs were required to do that and more. Instead, Amit did everything for me for the return of my services in the Astha project. And that was fair in a way, too. Amit was too smart to be working in a government office. What used to take me hours to do was just a minute's work for him. He tried really hard to teach me certain things, but I was too stubborn about letting nothing affect my ignorance. We were living out a symbiotic relationship. It was the *only* relationship I had at that point and it was what was keeping me sane.

'So, are you shifting in today?' I asked him. I badly needed a roommate. Even now, the moment I stepped out of the office, I was clouded by thoughts of Avantika. The intensity was much less now, though. *Maybe*. It had been three months since I had last contacted her but she was still very much around me all the time . . . I missed her. The laughs, the seductions, the touches, the winks. I missed it all. Still no movement on her social networking profiles. She had gone missing.

Nobody was a better choice than Amit for a roommate. He, too, had nothing much in his life. Everybody in the office who didn't matter hated him. He was too smart for them to handle and for those who mattered, he was a gem. All the seniors loved him. I think they saw a little bit of themselves in him when they had joined, not for the lure of a lazy sinecure job, but the passion to do something. What did they make out of it? Nothing.

Most importantly, I had come to love him. He was a cute lost kid in love, who knew nothing about it. I was the kid in office, who wanted to know nothing about it. A few months had passed and Avantika had left a void I would never be able to fill. Amit tried hard to fill my days and keep me distracted. He had even made me start studying for the CAT examination again.

He knew I would fuck up my career if I were to stay at BHEL for more than year. I knew that too, but ... There were still a few months to go for the exam and Amit was the only one who had the patience to remind me of that every day.

'Yes, I am moving in today. The truck will arrive at eight thirty. Won't it be so cool? Then I can call up Astha whenever I want to and you can tell me what all to say. Thanks, Deb. But I will pay you the rent. You will have to accept that, else I will not shift in.'

'Fuck off, Amit. Either you get the house without the rent or you don't get it.'

'Okay, as you say. But—'

I stopped him. I refused, although the temptation to add to the meagre salary was great, but I had started to love him. Moreover, he was doing me a favour by staying with me.

'Deb ... Deb! Will we call her tonight? I mean, can we?'

'Sure, Amit. Can you now please complete the sheet?' I had been trying to make him call her since I had joined office but he had some or the other inexplicable reason not to call her. *What would I say? I am too nervous? She is too beautiful for me. I am sure she is seeing someone else. What if she doesn't like me over the phone?*

But that night, we finally did. Amit left the office early that day to oversee the shifting. And I spent the rest of the day sharpening pencils. I couldn't break my record on the swivelling chair and hit a plateau at eleven rotations.

~

'What the fuck?' I exclaimed. 'Did you do all that? You know what? You have to be gay to do all this.'

He had cleaned up the entire flat. It wasn't my place any more. The place had been a mess since Mom left. And not only did he clean up the room, he had also replaced all the flowers in the vases and put some where there weren't any. But I should have expected that. He was the only one in the entire office who used a dustbin for pencil shavings. There was even a papier-mâché lamp that he had put in the drawing room. It suited the setting so much it seemed to have grown out of it. Avantika loved papier-mâché lamps.

'Do you like it?' he asked.

'Do I like it? I love it. See, this is the reason I won't take any rent from you. I don't need a housemaid any more.'

'Do you have a housemaid? This place didn't look as if it had been cleaned in ages.'

'No, I do not have one and I don't want one.'

'Never mind, now that I am here. Everything will be just fine,' he said rubbing his hands together.

I hoped so. We spent the next few hours unpacking his stuff and placing it in his new cupboard. The house had started as a modest two-bedroom apartment, but then as we had grown in size, so had the flat. My parents extended our house wherever and however it possibly could until it ended as a huge three-bedroom flat with a humungous balcony, though we never felt it was big enough. Now, I shifted into the master bedroom and Amit shifted into mine.

I was relieved of the unpacking duty when he finally said that I wasn't arranging things, I was stuffing them and adding to his work. I lay back then and watched him arrange his clothes, the idols and the photoframes in neat patterns. I wondered how people like him think. *What makes them think that a perfectly, or almost perfectly arranged closet can be arranged in a better manner? Where does that thought originate? What drives them to do it? What difference does a neat closet make in their lives? If I do it, will it bring Avantika back?* Just as I was slipping into arbitrary thoughts of

Avantika, Amit brought me back to my senses.

'So, do we call her up now? I have been waiting to do this for a year now. Please. Please. I promise to be your pipe-sheet slave all my life. Please do this. If I don't do this today, I won't ever be able to do it again.'

'As if it's me who has stopped you from doing so. Go ahead. Call her.' I tossed the phone to him.

*Are you crazy? A year? It took me three days to call Avantika up! And we had kissed before that!*

Astha and Amit never talked to each other. They had the strangest relationship possible. They liked each other and everyone around them knew that. But they were downright terrified at the mere thought of talking to each other. Even during their lunch meeting, they would transform into dumb, smiling statues after the first few seconds of customary hellos. All my attempts to start a conversation fell on deaf ears.

The only one who would talk was Astha's best friend, Neeti. I knew that Neeti had a crush on me. To make things worse, she made a thousand nails on a blackboard sound like pure symphony. She talked, rather shrilled and shrieked a lot more than required. I had decided I would hold her responsible if Amit and Astha never became a couple. She was irritating. Sweet but irritating.

'Are you sure I should call her? Is this the right time? What if she is not awake? Maybe we shouldn't. Or can I just send a message and ask her? What do I do?' Amit repeated these things as he paced around the room.

'Okay, I will call her. And then you can talk. Is that fine?' I said as I stretched for the first time on my bed. For the last two months, I had been sleeping on the couch because I was too lazy to clear the newspapers and Dominos' boxes strewn across the bed.

'Yes, you can do that. But then don't tell her I am here.'

'Great. Then how do I ask her to talk to you? Telepathy?'

'Okay, do whatever you want to. Do it quick.' He was still shaking the foundations of my flat.

'Hi, Astha!'

'Hi, Deb.'

'What are you doing? I hope you are not busy.'

'No, Neeti and I just finished the dishes.'

Amit had already drifted into his daydreams. This was the longest sentence he had heard from her.

'Okay. Actually, Amit and I were kind of getting bored. So we thought we would bore somebody else too.'

'No, it's okay. You tell me. How are you finding the work? Have you started working yet?'

Amit had shit his pants for all I could guess. I could tell he was feeling insecure. He always did that when he saw other guys talking to her.

'It's good. I was just wondering, I mean, if you aren't doing anything, whether we could meet up. Amit has something really important to tell you.'

'Amit? Really? Actually it's very late. I won't get an auto back home. I . . . am sorry.'

'Don't worry about that. I will drop you home. I don't think that will be problem.'

'Um . . . err . . . Neeti isn't well, too. Can we do this some other time? If he doesn't mind? I am really sorry about today.' Amit stopped pacing and sat down beside me, pretending to read the newspaper, big tears edging his eyes.

'Never mind. It's okay. It wasn't anything important. We will meet up whenever it is convenient for you.'

'I am very sorry I couldn't come,' she said. Amit rolled over the bed, covering his face with the newspaper.

'It's fine. Never mind! Ohh! The match is on. Can I catch you later?'

'Okay, bye. And I am sorry. I am very sorry,' she said.

'It's all right, bye. I hope Neeti gets well soon.'

Click. I disconnected the call and turned to Amit, 'Hey dude! Are you crying?'

'No, I am not,' he squeaked and sniffed.

'Yes, you are. It's okay. She said we would do it some other time. She couldn't help it. Neeti is ill.'

'Shut up. She was lying. First, she said she couldn't come

because she wouldn't get an auto. Then suddenly Neeti fell ill. I tell you, she doesn't like me! What if she already has a boyfriend? Or maybe her parents have already seen a guy for her? Maybe she likes Kumar from the equipment department? Damn, Deb. What do I do? Why did she do this to me? What did I do wrong?' Amit had again slipped into one of his hype-paranoid motor-mouthing sessions.

*Why did Avantika turn me down?*

'Hey. First, you haven't done anything wrong. You haven't *done anything*. And she definitely doesn't have a boyfriend. Or a suitor. Whatever.'

'Then why did she turn me down?' he asked and wiped off discharges from various places. I wondered whether he would allow the yellow stain to become a crust before he wiped it with his shirt again. He didn't.

'She didn't turn you down. She just said we would do it some other time.'

'But why?'

'Maybe it was just too sudden. Maybe she wanted some time to get ready and stuff. You know that, don't you? These girls, you know, they need a lot of time to decide what they have to wear on their first date. That needs a lot of planning. Maybe she didn't want to disappoint you by looking bad on her first date.'

'But she never looks bad. I like her the way she is.' Amit sometimes behaved so cutely that I felt like kissing him. He reminded me of myself, pre-college, pre-make-outs, and pre-night-outs.

*I like you the way you are. Please come back, Avantika.*

'Maybe, but she doesn't know that. Have you told her that? No, you haven't. So how do you expect her to know? You don't even talk to her.'

'No,' he said.

'I know that. I think she wants to look even better when she sees you outside the office. That is the reason she was apprehensive about today.'

'Better?' he exclaimed. He again reminded me of myself when

I used to look at Avantika without even an iota of lust in my eyes, before I first saw her naked. But he was much dumber than I was.

'Yes, better,' I said.

'Deb, you always get the girls you want. That is why you don't understand me. I love her, but there is nothing I can do. I cannot talk to her like you do. I cannot be as cool as you are. I am scared, Deb. Will I ever get her?' he asked as he sobbed softly.

'That is not true, Amit. And you know that. I loved Avantika, but . . .' I trailed off.

'I am sorry, Deb. I forgot. I am very sorry. Let us not talk about this.'

We kept quiet for a while before he started again, 'But tell me, have you ever felt like I am feeling right now?' he asked.

'As in?' I asked. He intended to change the topic, as he saw the life being sucked out of me, but he couldn't do it as well as I would have liked him to.

'I mean, have you had a crush? Like running after somebody and trying to catch her attention? Being helpless in expressing your love? I have never liked somebody the way I like her,' he sighed.

'For better or worse, I was like you in school. I had a ten-year long crush on a girl—Manisha, but I could not get her. I could never tell her. Not in the way I wanted to. You at least exchange hellos. I didn't have the courage to do even that. All I did was to stare at her for days, hoping something would happen. Quite obviously nothing did. Before Avantika came, I always dated girls who resembled her. Small, fair, cute. I thought a lot about her till Avantika came around and changed everything,' I said.

*Ten years? You're kidding me, Deb! You were a loser!* That is what Avantika had said. Manisha had sort of known about my crush as had my entire batch. But in those times, I defined the word— undateable. That would not have changed even if I happened to be the last guy living. But after school, I lost weight, lost my conscience, gained oodles of confidence in the year I had dropped before getting to DCE and dated girls who looked like her with a vengeance. I became directionlessness personified.

'Are you trying to scare me? What will happen to me? I cannot wait ten years. She will get married. What should I do, Deb?' He went paranoid again.

'Chill, Amit. You have me. I didn't.'

'Do you think I will get her?'

'Yes, you will.' I was glad I hadn't got Manisha. I would have never known how beautiful life could be. Not to forget, how sexy and wild too. And painful.

# 19

'Get up. Get up. Get up, Deb! DEB!' It took me quite some time before I realized that it wasn't a dream, that Amit was trying to wake me up. He was actually trying to do that.

'Ahh . . . it's just eight, Amit. Go to sleep,' I yawned.

'The punching time is eight forty. We've got to leave right now!' he said.

'We will be going by car, you asshole. Won't take more than twenty minutes. Let me sleep. Anyway, the guard will punch my card in.'

'What guard?'

'What do you mean *what guard*? He is the one who punches my card. So I can go as late as I want to. Or miss office if I want to.' I turned around to see Amit, as he stood there, dressed and his briefcase in his hand. 'Oh shit! You are ready. It will still take me an hour to find my underwear.'

'Please hurry. I will let the guard punch my card tomorrow, too, but please get up now. Just today. Tomorrow, I promise we will sleep till late. And go as late as you want to, but hurry up. Have you done your sheets? Obviously, you haven't. Have you made the gift? No, you haven't. What the hell do you think you are doing? If you don't want to get kicked out, get up and get ready.'

At last, I felt like hauling my ass up to the office. Getting kicked out of a government-owned firm? Now *that* would have been a failure I would never live down.

We reached the office about five minutes late. The guard was quite surprised to see me so damn early. I handed over Amit's ID to him and instructed him to do the same. It took me quite some time to convince Amit to make the possibly career-damaging move. It is only the punching of your I-card that counts. The accounts department had no idea whether you had been to office or not, if your card was punched every day. I owed the guards at least half my salary.

Just as we settled down at our computers, the sound boomed again. It was the sound I had come to hate the most. It was Mr Goyal again.

'So, Deb? Are you ready with your sheets?' he asked with the same demonic smile running across his face. I could break that face without a speck of guilt.

'Yes, sir, I am almost done with it,' I said. I didn't even know which sheet he was shouting about. But I didn't want him to win.

'Ohh? That's good to hear. Finding it too easy, gentleman? Quite like your dad. He never used to respect the piping department. He, too, found it easy. So, it's easy?'

I knew he was throwing me a challenge and it would be foolish to accept it. But then, this was my father's battle and I didn't want to let him down, even though he probably wouldn't even know about it.

'It is not that tough, that's all I can say.'

'Okay, then I want the full isometrics of the BINA refinery project ready by tomorrow. By nine sharp. Best of luck,' he said and rolled away.

I could now break open his jaw, burst open his tummy and hang him by his sack till it burst open, too. I knew I had won the psychological battle, but he had won the verbal one. There was no way the whole piping floor combined could have completed the work in a day. Let alone, Amit. For me, I would have to be reborn at least a hundred times just to think about doing it. I was told all this by Amit. I did not know what Goyal had asked me to do. It was only after I repeated what Goyal said word for word to a flabbergasted Amit, that I realized what I had put my hands into.

'*Are you mad?* How are you supposed to do it? Okay, how am *I* supposed to do it? That's designing at least twenty-five pipes. *In a day.* Even if I do it at the pace of one an hour, it will still take a whole day. Oh great, we are already an hour short. Why are you looking at me like that? I am not going to do it. Not for anything that you give me. It's *twenty-five* pipes. The whole department takes a month to do that. No, not this time.'

I knew he would do it. His non-stop blabbering meant he was thinking how to go about it.

'Okay, fine. I was thinking of asking Astha and Neeti out tonight,' I said, 'but since you won't do it for anything in the world, let's drop that plan.'

'Were you? Seriously? You were about to ask her again? What if she refuses again? Please do something. You promised you would.' Our symbiotic relationship kicked in again.

'I will do it. But just in case . . .'

'Okay, I will do the pipes. But I won't be able to do all of it. It's a lot to do. But I will try. I promise I will try.'

'Why do you think I care? That bastard knows this can't be done. Just do five or six and that would be enough for me to kick his ass.'

'Fine, but when will you ask them about tonight? I mean, do that early. You know, girls take time for planning their first date and all,' he said, trying to mimic me.

'Ohh! Is that so? Why don't you go and do it yourself, then?' I said.

'Why don't *you* go and do these sheets yourself, then?' he challenged.

'Okay, you win. I am off.' I left for the eighth floor where Astha worked.

The only thing that made my days bearable was the unsaid love between these two. They were these grown kids who had never loved or lusted before. I loved being around them. In a way,

I felt close to Avantika. I, too, loved her a lot. Just that it hadn't worked out. But I wanted this to work out. I knew it wouldn't be easy to convince Astha and Neeti to agree for a date . . . let alone one extending beyond sunset. But the refusal the day before was smoother than what I had expected from a girl who was new to this city known for its inability to treat women with respect. She hadn't been very clever while turning it down, but I had expected it to be worse.

Amit had been trying to convince me for a day date, but I knew that would make no sense. It wouldn't make any difference. Both of them would have found something interesting around them to stare at, rather than actually talk.

I climbed the stairs to the eighth floor. It had been quite some time since I had actually moved out of my small world of office, Amit and my flat. So, for a moment, I did find the girls there bordering on attractive. *The girls are waiting.*

I tried to shrug off thoughts of Shrey. He had been having quite some fun with his equally desperate IIT buddies. He never forgot to mail me about that. I don't think he missed any of the strip clubs in his city and beyond. His propensity to party and still work hard was commendable.

I never replied to his mails.

Astha wasn't at her seat. However, I spotted Neeti at the coffee dispenser.

'Hi, Neeti.'

'Hi, Deb? Sorry we couldn't come yesterday. I wasn't well. First, my stomach was upset, then my throat, and I started to feel feverish but the fever never came. I was so weak. I wish we could have come. Hope you didn't mind. Plus it was so late in the night . . . Can't we do it in the morning time? Weekends. Fun, no? But I am *so* sorry again.'

'It's okay. Do you have any idea where Astha is?' I replied after trying to make sense out of what she had just shrieked.

'Oh, Astha! Look. Think of the devil and here she is. Hi, Astha, Deb was looking for you.'

'Hi, Deb. I am really sorry,' Astha said as she tucked a

few strands of hair behind her ear. She almost dropped the fifty-odd rolls of sheets precariously held beneath both her armpits.

'It's okay. You don't have to apologize.' It had almost become a kind of reflex action for them. I had cancelled a million plans with my friends and could never recall a single time when I had apologized. Maybe *that* was the difference.

'Anyway, now that I see Neeti is doing all right and I know Amit and I will have nothing to do tonight as well, I am asking you out again. And this time you don't have an option. I will pick you up at nine. Right?'

'Perfect. I would be only too happy to come,' Neeti screamed and almost jumped.

'And you, Astha?'

'Yes, sure, Deb. Nine it is.' She couldn't possibly blush with that complexion of hers but had she been any fairer, she would have looked like a ripe tomato. A pink tomato.

I bumped into Amit just as I moved out of the process department. Apparently, he had been there all this while, trying to gauge something from our expressions. 'So, Deb? Did she say yes?' he asked as I walked towards him.

I didn't answer and stared at him with a dull stolid expression. I loved to do that.

'Deb? Please don't do that. Tell me. Say something.'

'You had better get down to work. You have a hell of a lot to do,' I said.

The very next moment he picked up all eighty kilograms of me and shouted the living daylights out of me. Needless to say, he was happy. Very happy indeed.

I left the office early that day. I had promised to make a gift for Astha. Something that he could give her when they went out for the first time. More than for him, I wanted to do this for myself. The gift I was to make for her was the one I had planned to make for Avantika, but never got a chance.

The gift didn't take that long because I had already made it a thousand times in my head and because I didn't actually make it myself. I had a designer friend who used to design packets for bakeries and FMCG companies. He hardly took an hour to put everything together. It was a beautiful small, square paperweight made out of papier-mâché. Five of its six faces had the alphabets used in *Astha* and a paragraph written about the good things in her that started with those letters.

As Avantika and Astha shared three alphabets, the writing part wasn't that tough. It turned out beautifully. It was big enough not to get lost and small enough to be used as a paperweight. It was something that she could keep with her at all times. How I wish I could have gifted it to Avantika.

'Deb, this is beautiful. I didn't know you could make such a thing,' Amit said. I realized it was not just the girls who had a reflex *sorry*, even Amit had a reflexive *thank you*.

'It's okay. But will you please sit down now? We are not leaving before eight and there are still a couple of hours to go.'

'Eight? But they live so far off. Won'e it take at least an hour and a half to reach there?' he said.

'Half an hour, Amit, just half an hour. Sit down and relax. Don't tire yourself out. And I'll be thankful if you start with the work while we are still here,' I said.

'What if there is a traffic jam? What if we get late? A flat tyre? Anything can happen.'

I was about to kill him. He was losing it.

'Late? We have three hours to go. We are already dressed up and I have the car keys in my hand. And you think we will get late? Have you totally lost it?' I shouted.

'Okay, I am sorry. Don't get angry now. Please,' he said and silence took over. Only for while, though. 'Does that mean I still have time to change my shirt?'

'Okay, that's it. Now I *do* have to kill you,' I said and darted towards him. He ran and bolted himself in his room. 'Good for me, Amit. I am not letting you out before nine. I am sorry, I lied.' I bolted the door from outside.

The next few hours were the noisiest ever. Amit kept on shouting for an hour or so and then shut up. He must have slept off, I thought. Or maybe he hadn't. Maybe he was doing the sheets. That's what I hoped for, at least.

'Deb, can't you drive a little faster?' Amit said, tugging constantly at my shirt, as he always did whenever he was nervous. Like a petulant kid.

'Don't you worry, buddy. We will be there by ten.'

'*By ten?* That's an *hour* late. Deb, why don't you ever listen to me? I am older than you. I got late in the morning, too. Why do you do this to me? Don't you like me or what? Okay, leave that. I have a whitener with me. Can we just erase the *love you* part from this paragraph? I mean, isn't it too early? What if she doesn't like it?'

'This is my favourite song. One word more and I will throw you out.' It was my favourite song. The first one Avantika had dedicated to me. *Accidentally in love*—Counting Crows.

I could never figure out why you remember these things when they don't matter anymore. The funny part—you never remembered them when they did matter. Okay, I just lied; Avantika and I celebrated every monthly anniversary, our fiftieth date, the hundredth date, our first kiss, absolutely everything. I had been looking forward to 20 May, the day our relationship started, our one-year anniversary, but Avantika had other plans. She had left me by then. She saved me a lot of money, though.

'Sorry,' Amit said and looked away.

He was such a kid, fifteen not twenty-four. I wished to be him. I wished to be me. I wished to be Avantika's toothbrush or hairbrush.

# 20

'Where are we going?' Neeti shrieked in my ear.

I had begged on my knees until they were scraped but Amit refused to sit in the back seat with Astha. As a result, I had to turn the rearview mirror at an awkward angle so that Amit could see her and vice versa. Everyone was blushing. It was a pink world out there.

'I don't know. You tell me,' I said.

'India Gate! India Gate! India Gate!' Neeti jumped up and down. *The transformation was complete.* I was a babysitter, now stuck with two shy kids and one over-zealous one. I didn't drink or dance. But I loved going to clubs, a thing that I had picked up from Avantika. India Gate was never in my scheme of things. Only forty-year-olds went to India Gate with kids in tow and ate off of plastic plates.

I had a few places in mind but I was sure they wouldn't be interested. They were seven and I was the forty-year-old uncle keeping them together.

It had been two months since I had started earning and I hadn't spent a single paisa. All my expenses were taken care of either by my parents or Amit.

I waited for quite some time for somebody else to speak but

nobody did. Amit and Astha were too busy playing hide-and-seek in the rearview mirror. Shrey would have been blowing kisses by now or kissing her real good, had he been in the back seat.

'India Gate is fine by me. Amit? Astha?' I asked.

'Fine,' Amit said.

We reached India Gate at around 11.30 p.m. I had taken a very long route, as I didn't want too many people hanging around. There weren't a lot of people when we got there. It wasn't a bad choice. In addition, that meant more time with the three of them. Neeti, I was not sure, but I simply loved the other two.

The imposing India Gate looked like it always did—*gigantic, overwhelming and thought-evoking.* I had often thought of reading the names written on it and counting them, but never got the time to do so. I had my entire forties to do that.

The few people who were on the huge lawns were winding up their picnic stuff to leave. I had come here often with Mom and Dad as a kid. The ragpickers had already started picking up the pieces the families had left behind. I, too, was doing the same. *Picking up the pieces.*

We crossed the arched metal ropes that marked the boundary of the lawns and walked towards the lake. I quite liked this place as a kid.

'So, Neeti. We are here. Want some ice cream?' I asked, as I wanted to leave Astha and Amit alone for a while.

'Yes, sure. Let's go. Let's go! I did see the vendors somewhere. Where did they go? Where? Where? Let's go. Where is that?' she asked.

'Over there,' I motioned.

'Let's go,' Amit said.

'Amit, you don't have to accompany us. We just want some time alone. Do you mind?' I asked. And expectedly, he didn't get it. He started giving me the *naughty you* look. But as long as he didn't come with us, I was fine.

'Okay, we will just wait here,' he said. Astha seemed to have found something really interesting about the earthworms crawling about, as she never bothered to look up. She was as nervous as Amit was, if not more.

'They love each other, don't they?' Neeti asked, nudging me rhythmically with her elbow.

'Yeah, I think so. But they never talk. They never meet up. I hope they do that after today.'

'That's why you came alone with me here. Very smart, you are. I always knew it,' she said.

'Yes, very smart,' I said. I tried not to further the eardrum-risking conversation. I looked back to see how Amit was doing. They were facing each other, all right. But I was sure they hadn't exchanged a single word. He was fiddling with the paperweight that jutted out from his back pocket. I wondered if he would muster up the courage to give it to her.

'They are not talking, still? I know. She is always like that. She never speaks in front of him. You know what? I wasn't ill yesterday. She didn't want to come. She is old-fashioned, you know? I am not like that. I wanted to come. But she said it's not right to go out like this. I am always ready. I am very modern.'

I had gotten used to such nonsensical blabbering from her. When I first met her, I thought she was a lunatic. Though she wasn't, she came pretty close to it.

'I hope they do talk,' I said, as we dragged our feet to the ice cream vendor. 'Hey, I am getting a call. Just hold on,' I said.

It was Shrey from a number that could be from anywhere.

'Hey, dude! What's up?' he had already picked up an accent. An American one from Germany and he was using it with unmatched gusto.

'Your accent is, for one,' I said.

'Sorry, yaar! You know, having an accent here helps. With the girls, you know! No one wants to date someone from India. So I give them stories about how I was born in Kenya, and then moved to the States and lived in London for a while. Either they catch me lying or I get lucky! Most of the women here anyway can't speak a word of English!'

'I don't want to know any of that. By the way, where are you calling from this time? Military headquarters?'

'Nope. I am at a German friend's place. And she is *so* hot and has a great ass, man! I am staying at her place for a while. Not that I am going to get lucky or anything, but it's still worth a shot. Worst-case scenario is that I still get to see her prance about in her lingerie. I love how confident these women are about their bodies.'

'So life is great, huh?' I said mockingly.

'Great? It's awesome, man. The project is going great. We have finally managed to incorporate a special electronically controlled gearing mechanism that divides the fuel . . .'

'Why do you think I care? Just cut out that part.'

'Okay, never mind.' Amit would have said sorry after this, I thought. Even Astha.

He continued, 'But the sex is great, man. You should come over some time. Maybe we can set you up with someone. I talk a lot about you and they go all teary eyed when I tell them how perfect your relationship was and how dedicated you were.'

'Sorry, I am not interested.'

'You still haven't got over her, have you? Go out man, have some fun.'

'I am having fun, Shrey,' I said irritably.

'Is that so? Where are you?'

'I'm out with friends . . . and I am having fun,' I said as I walked away from Neeti.

'Guys or chicks?'

'Two couples. Happy?'

'How's your chick?' he asked. I looked at Neeti, who smiled. She wasn't bad if not for her badly buckled jeans, frilly top and eighties' make-up. And the way she spoke. Or behaved.

'She is good.'

'Have you slept with her, yet?'

'Why are you sounding like Viru?'

'No, seriously. Go out there and give her the time of her life. You are Deb, after all. She is waiting, man. All the girls are waiting.

By the way, I called Viru, too. Yogi was there as well. They still share a room. They said they miss you.'

*I didn't care.* They almost didn't exist for me. But it did make me feel better. I made a mental note of calling them, though I never did.

'Have to hang up now. Bye.'

'Bye, Shrey.'

'Sleep with her. Do it for me. And yes, I saw Suhel's profile yesterday. He has put up his picture with Vandana up there. Bloody asshole. Though Vandana has got a little chubbier. Anyway, bye.'

'Bye.'

Click. He was fucking around to death, but I still didn't wish to be him, I wished to be Amit. I wished to be Avantika's mirror. Even her doormat wouldn't be bad. Ceiling fan would have been better. At least I would be able to look at better things.

*Shrey still loved Vandana*, I thought as I walked back to Neeti. That is all that matters, I told myself. At the end of the day, that's all that matters.

'Deb, I think they talked. I saw them. He gave her something when you were talking. So sweet, no? What was that? Do you know what he gave her? Did you help him get it for her? Did you?' she asked, her excitement level not dipping a teeny-weeny bit.

'Nothing. Let them see.'

I couldn't actually tell whether they were talking but she was alternating between looking at the gift and him. Eye contact was a huge step forward. And that meant I had to stay away from them for a lot longer.

'Deb? Deb! Tell me! How many girls have you gone out with? How many?'

'There have been a few,' I answered, not striving for any real conversation.

'I expected this. Never mind, how many have you kissed? What does it feel like? Do you think they will do that today? Tell, tell, tell. I am *so* curious!'

It came back. *The girls are waiting.* I was trying to keep this away from my mind. But Neeti was as easy as they come. *Should*

*I do it?* I could have got her to do anything within days. It had been months since I had even talked to anybody other than these two girls.

'It feels good. Why do you think everybody keeps doing it all the time?'

'You are *so* lucky. You must have done it so many times. Tell me no, how do you do it?'

This was going to be a long evening.

'It's pretty easy if you ask, and doesn't matter how you do it as long as you are in love.'

*Pointless slobbering of tongues.*

'Okay, tell me more! When did you do it the first time? Where did you do it? You are not telling me anything. This is not fair. Tell, please no, please no, please no,' she screeched.

'I don't remember,' I said.

'What do you mean you don't *remember*? Try Deb, try! Okay, when was your first kiss? Where did you do it? How was it? I am sure you remember that. Now don't lie, you have to tell me something. I am your friend, no? Pleeeease!'

I remembered every second of it. If my memory allowed a little more, I could have told her how many times I exhaled that night. 'I don't know. That's too personal,' I said as I stretched out on the lawns. The starless sky wasn't as enamouring as it had been on the night of the Farewell. *Nothing was.*

'I am sorry to have asked.' That happened to be her shortest screech that day.

'Don't be.'

I turned to see how Amit was doing. They were doing better. They still weren't talking to each other, but their eyes were locked for sure. They sat on the bench close to the lake under a big tree. There couldn't have been a more ideal place. Smriti and I once had sex there, at five in the morning. We had driven all night to find a place where we could park and make out. We didn't find any and we were running into cops everywhere. My car windows weren't tinted, so that didn't help us either. Eventually, we came to that place, in dire need of a walk after the long drive. We had no intentions of doing anything out there as it was almost morning. But our fate, horny as it was, had other plans. As we sat on the bench, the hug gave way to groping and within a few moments my unzipped jeans were around my knees while she was literally naked, breathing heavily and moaning as I pushed myself into her, clawing in deep at her thighs. I had bundled her skirt in a lump near her waist and pulled her top right up to her neck. A few morning walkers were close by, but we carried on. Maybe we didn't care that they were there or perhaps the risk of somebody spotting us egged me on. It had started raining then. We carried on until the rain became a little hard to handle. We had to rush back to the car parked alongside the railing. Half naked. The car had fogged up from the inside due to the rain. And we finished our unfinished business. We had forgotten her thong on that bench. We decided to leave them behind. That day was right up there in my list of make-outs. Any such list is incomplete without a session in the open.

'Deb, why are you so lost? I know I am not interesting enough. I am sorry for boring you. Okay, you tell me what we should do now? Anything that you want. Okay, I will tell you something. You know Kumar from the equipment department? You know, no?'

'Yes, I know. Everybody knows him. The one who hits on everybody, I know.'

'No, you don't know then. He doesn't hit on everybody. I think he likes me. He comes to my desk at least twenty times a day. He likes me, no? What do you think? Does he like me?'

'Yes, I really think he does.' It still wasn't helping.

I looked at Amit. His eyes were still set on Astha. I wondered if he was blinking. Or if Astha was blinking any less than a million times a second. It didn't seem real. Every second that Amit spent staring at Astha meant an extra second of humiliation from Mr Goyal. *Twenty-five sheets.*

'Yes, Neeti. He is good. I think you should go around with him.'

'But I don't want to. I don't love him. I know he is good, but maybe he is not lucky enough,' she gave out a punctuated he-he giggle.

'Maybe you will start loving him. Go out and try him at least,' I said.

'But Deb, I don't love him. I love somebody else,' she said. For the first time I saw a hint of sadness in her eyes. It wasn't actually sadness. Her eyes had just lost their twinkle and weren't wide open like always. That is, she seemed normal in those moments.

'Who is it?' I asked. Although I said this, I knew what the answer would be. I started hoping she wouldn't come out with it. But knowing her, I knew she would even tell me everything and beyond.

'It's you, Deb.'

*What a surprise.* I should have stayed quiet.

'Won't you say anything? At least say something. Something. Please say something, no?'

'Neeti, I am not ready for this. And for you right now. I am sorry. This can't happen.'

'Deb, we can at least try. You just told me, *Go out with Kumar . . . maybe you will start loving him.* Please at least give it a try, no? Deb? If it is not good, we will break up. I promise.'

Did I just have to make life tougher for myself? It was probably the first time I was turning down a girl. Life had been strange. When I loved break-ups and crushes, I had to fight for them. Now that I didn't need them, they were in plenty.

'No, Neeti. I have been through all this and I just know that it will not work out. I am not the guy for you. It is just an infatuation. It will go away. Don't you worry. It will be over in a while. Like this.' I snapped my fingers, trying to be funny. It didn't work. She stared at me as if I had decided that we should abort our love child and eventually I would marry someone else.

'Deb, how can you say that? You don't even know me that well. Give it a try. I will be a good girlfriend, I promise. Please, Deb. Don't do this to me,' she said. I knew her well enough. She was an ear-shattering, dumb, clingy girl with absolutely no sense of how to behave. Inner beauty is eternal but not when it is packaged like Neeti was.

'I am sorry.' I did feel sorry for her. But more than anything, she seemed to be pleading more for an ice cream rather than a relationship. And why would anyone want to be in a relationship with a guy like me?

'Deb, have you decided? Please think about it. Please do. Think about it again. Okay, I will not say anything. You think.'

'I am sorry,' I said.

'Deb, don't be sorry, just think. Close your eyes and think.'

'But—'

'Just think, Deb. Close your eyes.' She covered my eyes with her hand.

I closed my eyes and all I could see was Avantika. Yes, she looked extremely sexy in formals, as she lugged a laptop and went around changing the world in her new office.

'Nothing, Neeti. There can be nothing,' I said. I feared that she might kiss me when she closed my eyes. But she didn't.

'You didn't think! You opened your eyes too soon. I couldn't even kiss you,' she shrieked.

'What?' I exclaimed. I felt like a genius. Though, I missed out on a kiss. Did I want it? Maybe. Maybe not. I missed Avantika, but a kiss is just a kiss, nothing more. No, I didn't want to kiss her.

'Yes, I would have kissed you and then had it felt good . . . that would mean you love me. That's easy, no?' she asked. She *was* a lunatic, after all.

'It doesn't happen that way. You have to be in love to kiss. I am not in love right now and I can't kiss you. It would be wrong and immoral and I don't want to lie.' I didn't believe what I just said. Maybe I had gone insane, too. *You have to be in love to kiss?*

*The girls are waiting.*

'You will love me some day, Deb. I know you will. You just have to,' she said and lay down beside me. We didn't exchange even a word for the next hour or so. Amit and Astha were still in the same state of wordless staring. I wondered if they had died and rigor mortis had set in, cementing them in their place for all of life and beyond. I wondered what it would be like to kiss

Neeti, if I were to forget Avantika for a few seconds. It wouldn't be too good, I knew. *But, what the heck, she isn't coming back to see what I have been up to. She doesn't even care. Maybe in some twisted way, I am getting back at her.*

Another fifteen seconds and I decided against it. There were other considerations. I had lost Vernita to a kiss, though earned myself love, but I couldn't afford to lose an Amit. Or an Astha.

It was already 2 a.m. Just seven hours to the rendezvous with Mr Goyal. I finally decided to call it a night.

'Neeti, I think we should go home now.'

'As you say, Deb.' She still had the deadpan expression on her face. I wished I could make her understand that it was not meant to be.

'I presume nobody needs ice cream here.' I broke their stare.

'Err . . . no, Deb,' Amit said as he woke up from his stupor.

'Shall we leave now? It's getting late. And we have work to do,' I said.

'Shit! It's two? Let's leave. I am sorry, Astha. We have to go.' I had never seen him exchange a sentence so fucking comfortably. I felt like a genius matchmaker. We walked to the car and Astha and Amit climbed into the back seat.

'What happened, Amit? Don't want to see me drive?' I laughed at them.

'No,' he said shyly.

We dropped the girls at their flat and all the way, nobody spoke. In the back seat, they moved their lips continuously as if to say *love you*, but not actually making a sound. Amit tracked Astha right until the time she switched on her flat's light.

'Shall we go now?' I asked him.

'Hmm . . .'he said.

We drove off.

'Amit? Are you *crying*? Oh damn! *You are crying?* What the hell?'

He was sniffing lightly before, but just after I said these words, he burst out crying. I had seen this happen a million times . . . you ask someone who is close to tears if he or she is crying and they will burst out crying within moments.

'No . . .' he said, as he notched up his crying pitch.

'I thought everything was fine. You seemed fine. I thought everything went great. What happened?'

He kept on crying. *Wailing*, to be precise.

'For God's sake, tell me what happened? And stop crying,' I shouted.

'I am sorry, Deb, I can't help it. But, but . . .' he trailed off.

'What? Tell me this very second or I will push you out of the moving car. You can walk your way home from there.'

'I love her so much, but . . .'

'But *what*?' I sensed something was wrong.

'But I want to marry her.' He started crying again.

I feared the worst. What Amit had feared the day before. Maybe her marriage was already fixed with somebody and that was the reason she never spoke to Amit. I dreaded the answer but I gathered the courage to ask him.

'So, what's the problem?'

'Huh? Nothing, I want to marry her. I want to marry her. I want to marry her.'

Another Neeti, I thought. He stopped crying and started looking at me perplexed. I gave him the same expression he threw at me.

'So, what's the catch? Why are you crying? Have her parents already seen someone?'

'No! What are you talking about? NO!' He wiped his tears off with his shirt as he wasn't old enough to use tissues.

'Then why the hell are you crying?' I shouted out of irritation.

'*What if she says no?* I really want to marry her and I can't get married to anyone else,' he shook my hand off the gear stick.

'Is that all? You nearly had me *dead* there.'

'You think that's not a big deal?' he asked.

'Shut up, Amit. I got you till here. Trust me, I will get you there. Forget all that, tell me how many sheets have you done?'

'Sheets? None, till now. I haven't started doing them.'

'You haven't started? What the hell were you doing when I locked you up in the room?'

'I wasn't doing the sheets, I was just thinking about Astha.'

'Are you crazy or what? It's almost three and I have just six hours to go. What the fuck, man! You promised you would do it. This sucks. I am going to be so dead tomorrow.'

'I am sorry, Deb. Don't be so angry now. I swear I will do it. Don't you worry about it; it will be ready by morning. I am sorry.'

'You should be, man. Please do something at least when we get back home.'

'By the way, she loved the gift. Thanks, Deb. I wonder what would have happened if you weren't with me,' Amit said as he sank into his seat and dreams.

'Whatever.'

We reached my place and I crashed moments later.

# 21

*I chose a very opportune time to save Avantika from the goons, let go of Avantika's leg and fall off the cliff so that she could hang on and live. I had insurance and she had cheated me to get it. Even while plunging to a certain death, I couldn't help but think how much I loved her.*

I woke up, startled. It was 8 a.m.

I couldn't see Amit around. Though we had different rooms, we slept in mine because it had the air conditioner. I walked out, rubbed my eyes, looked at my early morning ugly face in the mirror and entered his room. He was awake.

'Good morning, Deb,' he shouted excitedly.

'Easy, Amit. Good morning.' I forgot that I had to be angry with him for the work he hadn't done for me.

'I have good news,' he exclaimed.

'And what is that?'

'I have done all the sheets! The third was a little tricky. Its material was still posing a problem as there is a transition from mild steel to grey cast iron here, so I just used the composite material formula to calculate the maximum stress at those points and used a factor of safety that was high enough ...'

'Cut out the crap. Just tell me how much you have comple ...'

I was still groggy. I stared more intently at him to give me a definite answer, so it hadn't quite registered what he had just said.

It finally did. *All the sheets?*

'WHAT? Did you say *all?* What? Don't tell me you just said all? *All?* Amit, you did it all?' I asked and checked if this was a continuation of the dream I was in before.

'Yes, Deb, I have done it all.'

I was living with a god. I jumped onto his bed and hugged the life out of him. I felt the skeleton crumble to pieces, but I didn't want to let go of him.

'You really did this? How is this humanly possible? How on earth did you do it?' I still wasn't out of shock.

'It wasn't that tough. You see, there is symmetry between the rack pipes and the overhead pipes. The pipes have been designed in such a way that they are interchangeable, only the stresses and bending moments change, that too negligibly. So the calculations have to be just extrapolated with the equation I formulated, which I have written on the eighth sheet. After you do that, it's just the displacements that have to be taken care of. That's when the computer takes over. Wherever the displacement gives a red mark on the data sheet, you just have to provide a dummy support and it's done. And the hanger part was easy, too. There is a set pattern of changes in strains in every part of the pipe. So it wasn't tough. It was the least I could I do . . . and Astha and Neeti helped me. They didn't sleep the whole night. It wouldn't have been possible without them . . .' he said, and I didn't want to interrupt him. He loved those incomprehensible shitty sheets. I envied him. He had a passion and I did not. *Except for a certain Avantika.*

'Amit. I don't need to know any of that.' I still stared at him just as Astha had been doing last night. 'I really love you guys . . . and you really love this bullshit, don't you?'

'Yes, Deb, very much,' he said and balled himself up shyly.

I wouldn't have admitted it even over my dead body, even if I loved those pipes.

'So let's go out there and kick the hell out of Goyal's ass!'

'Sure, Deb. I would love to see you do that,' he said. Just as I turned to look for my underwear, he said, 'I have never had a friend like you.'

'Same here, Amit.'

It was true. I was glad that I had told him. Reciprocated is equal to told. *Of course I loved him.*

We left my flat on time and reached the office an hour too early by my standards. For the first time, I was glad to be sitting on my seat and looking forward to my rendezvous with that bastard.

'Deb, I just called up at his office. He is in a meeting with Mr Malhotra, planning department HOD and some other piping people. He won't be back before eleven. Seems like I had a lot of time. We could have slept for two hours last night,' he said.

'I am sorry, man! You guys had to stay up all night for this bullshit.' I knew he wouldn't have slept; he would have redone them and made them better.

'It's okay, Deb. Just go out there and show them that you are as good as your dad. I know why you accepted what Mr Goyal said and took it up as a challenge. It's for your father. Although your dad would have jumped off this building had he seen you work. But it's okay, no two people are alike. He probably couldn't have got me Astha,' he said.

'I can bet on that.' I got up from my seat.

'Where do you think you are going? It's just nine thirty and he is in a meeting,' he said.

'That's why I am going.' I turned to leave and left five pipe sheets behind.

'Deb! You left these,' he said.

'Seems like you had a lot of time in hand beyond those two hours, too,' I said aloud as I walked towards the meeting room, and crossed my fingers.

'May I come in, sir?' I asked as I knocked and opened the door before they could respond.

I looked straight at Goyal and his face lost colour, as if he had just seen a ghost.

'Can't you see that I am busy? This is a meeting; your

unimportant things can wait,' Mr Goyal barked. I could see the fear in his eyes and I loved it. I moved in for the kill.

'Sir, I thought the twenty-five pipes of BINA refinery that you gave me yesterday to do were important. I thought that's why you asked me to do it in a day. Sorry, sir, I could just do twenty. Sir, if you say so, I will complete the remaining five in an hour or two, if you need them today.' I tried to be as explicit as possible and not miss out on any of the details. As I finished, Goyal's head shrunk to the size of a pea. All the people alternated between staring at him and me. I dropped the sheets where he was sitting and stood there with my hands behind my back, like a dedicated, hardworking employee.

Malhotra broke the silence. 'Mr Goyal? Twenty-five sheets? These are of the BINA refinery project? One day?' he looked at me. 'You did all of it in *one day*?'

A senior manager, Mr Bhatli, looked at Malhotra and spoke, 'Sir, I am not sure about this. But this part was to be done at the senior manager level. Definitely not at the trainee level. Deb, aren't you a trainee? You joined just last month, right? How did you do it? Can I have a look at the sheets, please? Have you got them checked by somebody, to confirm if what you did is correct?'

I picked up the sheets and handed them over to Bhatli. Malhotra and the three senior managers started to peruse the sheets in sheer disbelief. Goyal looked as if he was choking, I could tell.

'What do you have to say about this?' Mr Bhatli said as he handed over a sheet to Malhotra.

'This is pure genius. *One day?* Mr Bhatli, how long would your team have taken to do this?' Malhotra asked.

'Five to six weeks minimum, sir,' he said.

'How did you do it, Deb?' Malhotra asked. I hadn't realized till then that it was really *such* a big deal. I knew it was tough, I didn't know it was an insurmountable task! My ex-girlfriend was a porn star and my roommate was a god. Sweet life.

'Sir, it isn't as tough as it seems to be. You see, there is symmetry between the rack pipes and the overhead pipes. The pipes have been designed in such a way that they are interchangeable, only the stresses and bending moments change, that too negligibly. So the calculations have to be just extrapolated with the equation I formulated, which I have written on the eighth sheet. After you do that, it's just the displacements, which have to be taken care of. That's where the computer takes over. Wherever the displacement gives a red mark on the data sheet, you just have to provide a dummy support and it's done. And the hanger part was easy, too. There is a set pattern of changes in strains in every part of the pipe. So it wasn't tough. But, sir, this wouldn't have been possible if it wasn't for Amit. He is the genius behind this and he is the one who has taught me everything.'

I felt like I was back in college where, during vivas, I used to speak the most nonsensical things with sky-high confidence and the professors would look at me with the same disbelief these people had written all over their faces. Only this time, it was because I was right. *Or Amit was right.*

'Did you hear that, Mr Bhatli? Mr Goyal? This is great work, Deb,' Malhotra said.

'Thank you, sir. But it was Amit who helped me with all of this,' I said.

'Mr Bhatli, I need to see Amit after this meeting,' he said. 'Isn't he the short guy who always has a lot of questions and runs into trouble with the planning department?'

The others nodded.

'Okay, sir. I always thought Amit had the brains. I will do that, sir,' Mr Bhatli said.

'Deb, both of you have done a good job. You can go now. Keep up the good work,' Malhotra said.

I turned, and just as I walked away towards the door, I heard Malhotra say to the others, 'Like father, like son. This chap will go a long way.'

I walked just a little slower to the door to listen to what the others had to say. I smiled.

Mr Goyal could have taken credit for spotting my talent, but I guess he was a dumbass after all. *Not a patch on my dad,* not even close. I was proud of my father and I was sure he would be proud of me too. The news would reach him, I thought. It did. But he knew me better than the Bhatlis and Malhotras.

His message read—

*Congratulations. Heard about you. I don't know what you are doing, but keep doing it. Because whatever it is, it's working. Miss you, son. Hope to see you soon.*

That felt good, anyway. Amit was busy the whole day, as expected. He wouldn't get an out-of-turn promotion, as the system didn't allow that. But he wouldn't miss one for sure. The government system doesn't account for geniuses, anyway.

~

'Hi, Neeti. What's up?'

I had nothing to do, so better than talking to a cell phone snap of Avantika, I thought it would be better to talk to Neeti. I hated to admit it, but it felt good talking to her. Or knowing that somebody cared . . . who, incidentally, could also go on and kiss me outside a relationship. I did start to think about what Shrey had said. Was it the best way to forget Avantika? Moreover, I feared my organ might turn vestigial out of sheer redundancy. I needed a distraction!

'Hi, Deb.' She looked and sounded miserable. I hadn't expected that. I thought she would go on mauling my ear with her stupid relationship chatter even the next day.

'Are you busy? Can we talk? Actually, I have nothing to do, with Amit being all busy and stuff. And I am tired of sharpening pencils. I hope you are not still upset. I hope you understand. We can work this out.'

'You think so?' she said, raising her eyebrows up to her hairline. She did sound sexy in short sentences. Well . . . kind of. It was a welcome change.

'Yes, I do. A date of sorts? You mind?' I lied.

'Okay, whatever you say, Deb . . . I don't have much work to do, anyway. I never do, you know. Okay, let's see. Let's go to Vasant

Vihar, I have heard a lot about it, you know? But I've never gone there. Can we please go there? Of course, if you don't mind.' She was getting back to her usual self. Long sentences, often unnecessary and delivered in a high-pitched tone.

'Sure, why not!' We left the office.

I quite loved it that way. Unlike the private firms, you can move in and move out any time you want to, especially if you don't give a shit about the work. Nobody can ever kick you out. And age turns out to be the biggest qualification.

We went to Vasant Vihar, which was a twenty-minute drive from my office. In its day, it used to be the most happening place in the city. But with its overwhelming popularity, wannabes had started to flock to the place, girls started to get eve-teased and the place lost its charm. But the regulars still kept coming here.

I couldn't say that I had a great evening, but after a long time, I'd gone out to a place, if you didn't count the India Gate outing. Even Neeti, after the previous night's ordeal, was not saying as much as she was used to. She was a little depressed and that was the first time I felt she was not that hard to bear. But she was definitely likeable . . . not that I had many people to compare her with.

'Bye, Neeti. Thanks for lunch. If you see Amit, just tell him I have left. And do think about the night-out. Please?'

'Okay, Deb, will do that. Don't worry. Even I am excited about it. Thank you.'

'My pleasure,' I said as I walked away.

'Deb,' she called out. 'I am so glad we came out today. Thank you. If you need anything, just remember, I will always be there for you.' She turned back, with glazed eyes. She ran off. I was sad to know that she was into me. That day, she had acted and spoken like a grown-up. She wasn't that bad, after all.

I went back home early that day and spent the rest of the afternoon sleeping, after wrapping up some things I had to do. I waited for Amit to come back. After months, I would be going on a night-out. It was an unsettling feeling; nervousness taking over some of my senses. I wondered what he would think of it.

'Hi, Deb! You know what?' Amit said as I opened the door for him.

'No, I don't. Do I have a choice of not listening? I am just a little bit sleepy. We were out on a night-out last night, remember?' I said. I didn't realize that, when I was saving Avantika's life from villains in my dreams, it was Amit who had stayed up the whole night.

'Shut up and listen, Deb. I was given the responsibility of heading the whole piping job for the new refinery project that's going to start in December. And it's going to be so exciting. And you are working with me, so you should start working now. It is so amazing,' he said as he arranged his shoes in a perfect line and pulled his jeans another notch higher.

'Amit! No extra pay and extra work? Who does that? Okay, I am sorry, *you* do that. I am happy for you but I will stick to getting coffee for you,' I said. More work also meant more pencils to sharpen for me and I didn't quite relish that.

'Deb, there is something I want to talk to you about. Don't mind, but it is serious. Can we do it right now?' I had never seen such an expression on his face except once, when I caught him shagging. Until that day I had thought he never masturbated, but what do you know . . .

'Yes, sure. Let's go and sit in your room. I have just used a mosquito spray in mine.' We moved to his room.

'Deb, I want to talk about Neeti. You know much more about relationships than I do. But Astha told me about what happened between the two of you. Neeti cried the whole night and couldn't stop talking about it. And Astha didn't like it. And all of a sudden you went out with her today. Why, Deb? You've never done that before. I do not doubt you. I really like you. But I also really like Neeti and I can't see her or Astha cry. I am sorry if I am wrong. But I thought it would be wrong not to tell you about this. I am very sorry.'

'Don't be. I can understand your concern.'

I did. I wasn't hearing this for the first time. I was thankful I hadn't kissed her the previous night. Even though she was looking quite kissable by fifth-grade standards, I did not do it. It was like a second shot, and I had done well at that. It wasn't tough, I thought.

'So, why did you go out with her today?' he asked.

'You will know soon,' I said. In those moments, I felt I had grown up and become responsible all of a sudden. I wasn't the same brash, sick bastard I had once been and I felt good about it. I didn't kiss her, not because she wasn't my type or because I suspected she had dropped a few screws as a child. It was because I loved the little man and let him know that. I had learnt something. I had made a friend and I valued him. It was strange to actually look beyond the obvious. I felt like a sage. I had been so wrong before. I missed Vernita, even Tanmay and Avantika. One changes with time, from fighting for a window seat to the time when you are old and prefer an aisle seat closer to the washroom. I had chosen the aisle closer to Amit, letting go of the window to Neeti's life.

'Deb, there is also something else I wanted to tell you. Please don't be angry about it. I am sorry I did that. But that day when you locked me up in your room, I read your personal diary. There was a link you had bookmarked. I am sorry, but I couldn't help it,' he said. He was more apologetic than I would have been had I actually ruined her life. I don't think I would have been apologetic at all. My insensate tool desperately needed to get in somewhere.

'I would have been very angry . . .'

'Deb, I am really sorry. I didn't mean to see it. You just kept . . .'

'Amit! Will you let me finish? I don't have a diary. What you must have read was a blog I once maintained. I forgot its password so I stopped writing,' I explained.

I had not forgotten it. The password was—*Ilovedeb*. I hated it enough not to type it and loved it enough not to change it.

'You forgot your own password? You are kidding me. I am sorry, I told you. You don't have to lie to me. I have seen recent posts too.'

'Shut up, man. You know the Gitanjali I told you about? She was the only reader I had, amongst a few others. She kept trashing it, so I stopped writing. I was just a really bad writer. Yes, I knew the password but I didn't feel like writing any more. That's about it. Now chill. It's no big deal.' I said.

'Whose story is it?'

'Mine,' I said, trying to recollect what all I had written. I remember Gitanjali refusing to read it any further. *Do not depress me, Deb, and for god's sake, get over her.*

'You really loved M, didn't you? Why did you address her by an alphabet *M* and not her real name? Okay, I think I shouldn't ask that. But do you still love her?'

'I still do.' I said. I loved the girl I called 'M' in the blog. It was Avantika.

The doorbell rang.

'I will get that,' I said as I jumped out of his bed.

'Who is that?' he shouted.

'I have something for you. Quick!'

He came out shouting: 'Deb, I told you not to order from outside today. I called the tiffin service earlier and they will deliver the food soon.'

I opened the door and let them in.

'Who is that?' he asked and then saw them. 'Shit! What? What are you doing here? Deb, did you know they would come? What a surprise, Astha! Deb!' He looked at me, and seeing me unmoved by all that was happening, continued, 'Oh so you knew. Why didn't you tell me? It is such a big surprise. Hi, Astha! Sorry. I didn't expect this.'

'Hi, Amit! Hi, Deb! I didn't know about this too. Neeti dragged me here,' she said.

Seeing them talk felt like a better achievement than seeing Mr Goyal lose his balls. After all, it was my doing and I was proud of it.

'Okay, before we waste any more time, we have planned something for the two of you. We now know something about the two of you that you would take ages to tell each other. So, we thought we would just speed up the process for you. Welcome to your room for tonight.'

And I swung open the supposedly mosquito-infested room

and for a few seconds, I admired my second attempt at something mushy and love-laden. The room was filled with white and red balloons bobbing in it with a huge cake bang in the middle of the bed. Two massive teddy bears (Amit told me she liked them!) on either side of the cake with a bunch of roses in their hands completed the picture. There were frills criss-crossing the walls. The room was lit up with scores of aromatic candles.

It was my first expense since I had started earning and it was worth it. It might have been silly, but it was infinitely romantic. Piping sheets were much easier to pull off.

Amit and Astha waded into the room through all those balloons, awestruck at what they saw. I just loved it. Neeti winked at me in appreciation. The wink brought back memories of *her*. I had set this room for her, just that she wasn't here. But her wink was here and I was here, only she wasn't.

I switched on the light. A gigantic poster awaited them, done beautifully in sparkling blue over a huge red sheet. It read:

*The day Astha and Amit decide to marry each other. Cheers to you guys.*

*—Neeti and Deb*

'Takes care of your dad's worries, doesn't it?' I whispered into Astha's ear. Apparently, she too had been crying the previous night for the same reason that Amit had been. Only a lot harder and Neeti told me that it had been troubling her for a while. Her parents were pressing her to get married for quite some time now and she was running out of reasons for why she couldn't get married. All this while, she had wanted to know how strongly Amit felt about her.

I was the happiest person that night out of all present in that room.

It seemed like their vocal chords had given way.

'Okay, I am bolting the door from outside. You are not going home tonight. And we won't open the door till the time you've done justice to the cake and the balloons and the candles. Bye now and don't you worry. Dinner is served and it's in the microwave right there,' I said and before they could shake themselves enough to say anything to me, Neeti and I rushed out and bolted them in. *No sounds this time around. He won't struggle to come out of that room now.*

Neeti and I pinned our ears to the door for the next half an hour or so to catch any kind of sound and we couldn't hear anything. We hadn't quite expected them to make out, but these guys weren't even talking. We both ate, sitting on the floor, right outside their door, just in case. Neeti drifted off before I could thank her for the cutest dinner I had ever had. I picked her up, placed her on Amit's bed, and saw her ensconced comfortably there. She looked beautiful sleeping. I was glad I had kept my hands off her. Or was I? I missed being in a relationship. It sucked to be single and alone when other people were happy being in love.

I fell asleep after a little while.

This time, I came in the way of a bullet that pierced my heart and saved Avantika. *Yet again.* I woke up and walked up to their door. I saw more through prior knowledge than my still not fully opened eyes.

I creaked open the door.

'Good morning, Deb!' they said in unison. Quite clearly, they had not slept the night before. The balloons were still in their places. They were sitting on the floor facing each other. Like Neeti and I were last night, trying to eavesdrop.

'Good morning, people. And why the hell do you think my parents invested in that huge bed? It's for sleeping!'

'Deb, we didn't want to disturb it. It is so beautiful. Moreover we had no camera in this room and we didn't want to let the most memorable moment of our lives go uncaptured. Thank you, Deb. Thank you very much. And I am sorry for doubting your intentions towards Neeti,' Amit said.

'I am sorry too, Deb. I was the one who started it. I am really sorry,' Astha added.

'It's fine, guys! So tell me. What did you decide? I hope we won't be disappointed by whatever you have decided,' I said.

'I hope not. We are leaving for Bihar tonight to talk to her father. Can you believe that, Deb? We are *actually* going tonight. I think I beat you there; I am meeting Astha's father within two days of my first date. *Deb, I am actually going!* Don't look at me like that,' Amit shrieked and burst with a heady concoction of pride, elation and goddamned happiness.

'Is this true, Astha?' He had actually beaten me to it and I was so happy he had. Anyway, I wouldn't have dreamt of doing anything like that, maybe except in Avantika's case.

'Yes, Deb.' She was stripped naked in front of me. That's how she made me feel, at least, when she looked away shyly and blushed.

We hugged and shouted our tops off and woke up Neeti in the ensuing commotion. When she heard the news, she gave a shriek so loud that I wouldn't have been surprised if a couple of hyenas had turned up at my door.

It was hard to believe that they were actually getting married. One date and that is all they took. It was the kind of love that gets written about. A love pure and pristine, with no doubts or hesitation. All they took was one night to decide that they wanted to be with each other for the rest of their lives.

It was just in the nick of time, or Astha's father would have selected a husband for her. And two broken hearts in one house was the last thing I wanted.

They were at my place the whole day. They clicked pictures and discussed what they had to do when they reached Bhagalpur, her village in Bihar. Neeti and I, in the meanwhile, packed Amit's bags.

'You know what, Deb? I have never seen a guy like you. You are such a good friend. You are so caring, so sweet. I am obviously sad that we couldn't be what they are. But we are still more than good friends, no? And I am so happy about that. You are perfect, Deb,' Neeti said. 'Now what is that? You are stuffing the undergarments in the same compartment as the toothbrush? Give them to me. Let me do it.'

*So much for being perfect.*

Finally, the time came for them to leave. It was heart-warming to see how they couldn't keep their eyes off each other. While I belonged to the group of people who call themselves progressive and think a couple should date and get to know each other better before they take a huge step in a relationship, I couldn't find a single speck of doubt in *their* decision. Isn't this how love should be? When the decisions are easy and there are no pretensions? Maybe that's the difference between being in a relationship and being in love.

Just as they reached the main gate, they all shouted out in unison. 'Three cheers for our best friend, Deb.'

And they went on to do the *Hip Hip* thing, which I always felt shouldn't be done more than twice; it becomes a drag the third time. But I loved it that time. I finally had friends, those who stayed up all night for me, that too for some silly challenge I had picked up.

We all hugged and thanked each other for being wonderful friends and they left.

I was alone again. They would not be back for a week at least, I was sure. So I had decided I would skip office for a week and wallow in self-pity. Also, I had been a good man for the last three days and I wanted to soak in my own goodness.

'I will pay you back some day, for you are my best friend ever,' Amit told me and left.

Quite embarrassingly, he left me feeling loved, missed and in tears.

# 22

I spent the next few days lazing around at my place. Six days and fourteen hours to be exact. But without Amit, I didn't feel like going to office. Anyway, with the guard doing his duty, I didn't need to. I tried to rearrange my things, but gave up soon after realizing that I couldn't do any better with the room after what Amit had done.

I called up Neeti more than a few times to lend an ear to her shrieks, but even she wasn't that free any more. I had watched all the porn I had. I snooped on Amit's computer. It was cleaner than a nun's.

Pipes were his only love, after Astha. I regretted not to have learnt anything about piping. At least I would have had something to do. It was supposedly the ideal life I had always imagined myself in. I had no expenses, I was doing nothing and I was responsible for nothing. All I needed was Avantika.

I hadn't quite gotten over her. It wasn't that I was exercising my tear glands every day, but I still thought about her all the time. I daydreamed for hours on end and imagined us together in the future. At times, I did feel like contacting her, but I knew that would only add to the pain.

I always believed that one fine day she would return to my

life . . . with a new boyfriend in tow and eventually drive me to suicide. That would be perfect. Two ex-boyfriends in different jails and one dead. Sri Guru would be right too, then. She would then be the cause of *all* our sorrows.

But that was just one aspect. I daydreamed about a million times during those months about the zillion ways in which we could cross each other's paths again some time, any time in the next many decades. And then walk into the sunset hand-in-hand, boyfriends, husbands, teenage kids, cancer notwithstanding.

*I desperately needed to move on.*

Just as I was about to drift off again, the bell rang. It was a courier. The details were missing on the package and I had no idea where it had come from. I signed the sheet and the courier guy handed me a big brown envelope. I tore it open and found a big spiral-bound document, which was about two hundred pages thick. I dreaded the thought that it had something to do with the pipes for the BINA refinery project and someone needed some clarification on it. Now that Amit was not reachable, I had no idea how I'd answer them.

*'Deb, the dummy support you have provided here, do you think it will take the stress?' . . . 'Deb, we ran it on Caesar 2 and it is showing some major deviations. Would you kindly check it and tell us?'*

I reached for the cell phone to switch it off. As I did so, I flicked the first page open, expecting semicircles and 3-D cylinders to jump up at my face and torment me.

I couldn't have been more wrong.

**Our Story**—it screamed in big letters. *To Deb*, it said below.

I flicked through the page to reach the index. I read it. Twenty-one chapters labelled neatly. I spotted names that were familiar to me on the pages. *Deb, Shrey, Avantika, Tanmay . . .*

It was me. It was my story. They were *my* incidents. Everything that had happened to me was right there, in my hands. Somebody had recorded it and documented it. It was my life. On paper. The words had me by the collar and transported me to the times they were set in. Everything started happening again and a montage ran in front of my eyes. I watched everything go by: Smriti and I near India Gate, Shrey having a smoke, me standing naked in Splash, kissing Avantika on the stairs, Mom and Dad leaving for Hyderabad . . . everything. It all came back and I was dumbstruck.

I started to flip through the pages, not to read, but just to see what all was in there.

Everything. Every *goddamned* thing.

The words came out and struck me. They were all either said or written by me. Some time or the other. Each one of them. It was my blog on paper, only instead of fake names and fake places, real names had been used. No details were skipped and it was a comprehensive throwback of my life. The blog was haphazard and the timeline of the posts were awry, but on the paper in my hands, it was painfully chronological.

I skipped to the last chapter.

*Deb and Amit.*

It was Amit! I couldn't believe it. Is this why he had asked me questions about my past life? Is this why he had spent hours listening to me talk about Smriti and Shrey? Is this why he had wanted to know about my relationship? Is this why he was interested in my blog and had so many questions about it? I remember him asking so many questions after he had apologized for having stumbled across my blog.

Was this how he was paying me back? He had strung it all together. I *so* loved the little man. I switched on my phone to call him up, but there was no answer.

I was trembling as I turned the first page to read from those pages. *Chapter One.* I was still numb. I had barely known him for a few months and I didn't think he could do this for me.

My eyes welled up as I started reading it. Everything I had ever told him was in it. He remembered everything, every word, and every sentence. I started living every moment again. He had hung on to every word that I told him. Everything that I ever loved, ever wanted, ever hated, ever felt. It was right there, in front of me. Amit was beyond pipes. He was my best friend. I would not give him up for a thousand jobs and a million girlfriends.

I was on the last chapter. It had been seven hours since I had begun reading it, never looking up unless it was for sniffing my fluids in. I was reading everything thrice and often even more than that. A lot of things were blog posts I had written on my own, but everything was so beautifully knit together that every new sentence made me nostalgic. However strange it had been to listen to my stories of my girlfriends, he hadn't missed a single thing I had told him. It often reminded me of things I didn't remember myself. He had given me the good times back.

I finished the last chapter. *Deb and Amit.*

I read the last line of it. *Deb, thanks for everything. You are the best.*

I cried a little more and thought about Amit a little more. I thanked god for having found a friend like him and prayed for his success and well-being. I was exhausted, physically and emotionally. The experience of knowing you have a friend who would be with you, come hell or high water, was overwhelming. I drifted off.

*Our Story* lay open on my bed.

I was woken up by the front door swinging open slowly.

# 23

There was nobody at the door. I had forgotten to bolt the door after the courier guy had delivered the brown envelope.

I went with groggy eyes to close the door. As I locked the door from inside, she called out. My mind imploded with possibilities and questions even as I tried to come to grips with reality.

*Think Deb, think. What does she want? What do you want? What does she want? Why is she here?*

She must have walked in when she saw the door open and now was standing right in front of me. 'Deb, come here,' she said.

She stood there in a black shirt and deep blue jeans, both of which clung to her body. I could have fed on her for days. Just when I started walking towards her, she ran up to me and ploughed into me, pushing me against the wall. She stapled me to the wall, my hands outstretched and pinned to the wall, palms up. She stared deep and hard, came close and licked my lips once. She bit my lips and I tilted her backwards until the first drops of blood seeped out from my pursed lips. She looked hungry and so was I. She thrust her lips and tongue into my mouth, and hurt me with every bite. We fought for dominance, sucked and bit wherever we could. She slipped her hand down and grabbed hold of my thing, and tried to push her hand back along it. It sent me into the throes of ecstasy.

'Like it?' she asked as I pulled back from the kiss, grimacing in pain. She let go of me and stepped back. She unbuttoned her shirt but didn't take it off. She unzipped her jeans slightly but didn't take them off either.

'Strip,' she commanded. 'I want you out of those clothes right now.'

I stripped. Out of my shirt and out of my shorts. And everything else. She moved further away as I moved towards her. Her smirk teased me. She had me naked and looking for cover. She didn't need any. She looked gorgeous in her unbuttoned shirt.

'What do you want?' she asked in the wickedest sense possible. She was staring where I was the hardest as if mocking its size, presence and helplessness.

'I want you.' I was breathing heavily by then.

'I don't think you will be up to it.'

'I definitely will.' I grabbed her and she dug her teeth deep into my neck, pushed herself into me and grabbed hold of my ass, digging her nails in, and squeezed it. She climbed onto me, her legs wrapped around my waist and I carried her to my room. I dropped her on the bed, on the bound pages of *Our Story*. She invited me with a naughty smirk on her face. I slipped off her shirt. I pinned her to the bed and kept her from grabbing hold of what was erect and rendering me paralysed till she was naked. I pulled off her jeans.

'Like it?' she said again. I was too frenzied to appreciate her lingerie.

'I don't think so. I like you better naked.' I grabbed it by my teeth and pulled it off slowly, never taking my eyes off her. She looked down on me, her eyes half closed and asking for it. I pulled it off slowly and bent over her.

She tried covering her breasts naughtily but I pulled her hands away to take one hard look at her. She was naked. I went down on her and fed on her body. Her eyes never left mine as her hands guided my head to places she wanted me to touch and lick and eat. Her moans told me I was doing what she wanted me to do. In those moments, I was her slave and she could have me do anything that she thought right. I ate her to my heart's content and I relished it.

We crashed the television, we rolled over my laptop. I fought, I grabbed, I groaned. I was inside her. She bit, she clawed, she moaned. The more we became one, the harder she moaned, the more I groaned. Our passion spent, I rolled away from her, leaving her body blue and battered. I was exhausted. We had our first sex . . . and I realized there were a lot of things a girl can do than just lie there and let the guy do all the work. It was delightful.

'I was scared,' she said.

'About what?' as I outlined her breasts with my fingers. They looked gorgeous with my love bites on them. We had been barbaric.

'I thought you wouldn't be this good,' she said and grimaced as I pressed the biggest love bite I had ever given her. It was a huge bluish mark on the inside of her left breast.

'I was always this good,' I said and squeezed her right breast hard enough to get a shriek out of her.

'I don't think so, Deb,' she said, clenching her teeth.

'What made you come back, Avantika?' I asked.

'What we just did.'

'*This?* Which means you missed it. It proves my point. I was good.' I had expected something else. I wanted her to tell me she still loved me.

'Maybe. Or that I found no one better.' She laughed out. She was still so gorgeous. She sat up and tied hair into a neat bun. Girls look better after sex, Shrey once told me. *So true.*

'I don't need any of that,' I said and kissed her thigh, ready for another go, but I needed some answers first.

'Easy, Deb. Just sit beside me,' she said as she fished something out from her bag.

'Here.' She handed out some sheets to me.

It said—*Chapter 22.*

*What?*

'Deb, this is our story,' she said.

'Wh . . . at? Fuck. It was you? *It was you?* What for? It was you? I thought it was Amit! How could it be you? How do you know? But the last chapter about Amit and me? How did you know about that? Oh Avantika, I love you. But why?'

For the third time, the flapping of the tongue. *How does she know about Amit? She is a witch.*

'Hear me out, Deb. I have answers for everything. A few days back, someone from Bramha Publications read your blog and mailed me. They said they really liked your blog and wanted your story in book form. I thought I wouldn't do it, but I missed you so much and I thought it would let me be close to you again. So I started writing and I wrote it for them. I sent them the first few chapters and they really liked it and wanted me to complete the book. This is what it is. The last chapter of our story. The end of our story. The end of me,' she said and started to look the other way. She had tears in her eyes.

*The end of me?*

The last part shook me to the roots and the pages fell out of my hands, trembling, shaking, reaching out to her.

'*The end of . . . you?*' I asked as I fixed my eyes on her and choked on my own words.

'I am dying, Deb. I am dying.' She broke down, turning away from me and dug her face into my lap.

'What do you mean? What . . . What are you saying? Tell me you are kidding. What . . .' I went blank as I grabbed hold of her and made her look at me.

She looked up, her eyes filled up with all the sadness in the world, held my face with her hands and said, 'I have cancer, Deb. The drugs killed me. They killed me. Doctors say I have just a few months to live. That is why I came back. To spend my last few days with you. Please don't leave me, Deb. I want to live. With you. Please Deb. Don't let me die. I don't want to die. Please Deb, save me, please save me,' she broke down and sank into my lap.

'Huh?'

I lost my senses. I felt numb. I looked at her. She was dying. *Avantika was dying.* The person I had dreamt of spending my life with, was right there in front of me. *Dying.* In my lap, begging me to save her, to give her the life I promised I would. She was right there, asking for what she deserved. She wanted me to keep her alive, save her, love her. She was back with me, just as I wanted. But only to go forever, leaving me behind, forever, alone . . . with the guilt that I couldn't save her. She would be gone in a matter of days and I would see her crumble and die in front of me. But I was helpless. I had failed. I felt cheated. I felt punished for the times I had wronged other people. But why *her*? Why not *me*? Why would anyone punish her?

I mustered up courage to look at her again. She hugged me as if to never leave. I never wanted to let her go. She was beautiful. But I noticed things I was too lost in her to see before. Her eyes were tired. They had lost the twinkle, those eyes in which I used to get lost for hours, eyes that said more than her lips, eyes that winked naughtily, eyes that saw a great guy in me. She had gone weak, her muscles were wasted, and her wrists barely had any flesh on them. She was all bones, her collarbones were prominent, her thighs were thin and scrawny and she looked terrible.

The love bites, which stood out, were on pale yellow skin, not on the glowing skin I used to touch on one pretext or the other. She barely had any strength when we made love, I remembered. I held her face, wet with my tears and hers, and noticed the change. Those pink lips had gone pale, that complexion had lost its radiance. She was sick, and it showed. There was hair lying everywhere I saw. Chemotherapy makes you lose hair, I had heard. I imagined her like other cancer patients, bald and strapped to a chair with needles dipping into her veins. I cried.

I looked around to see *Our Story* scattered beneath her hair, beneath her dying body. Beneath a dying me. Beneath a dying *us*.

I wanted to die. I wanted to die before her. I wanted to die with her.

'Avantika, what did the doctors say?' I asked as tears flooded my eyes.

'A few months. Last stage, Deb. A few months is all that is left for me now . . .'

I grabbed her and we cried out aloud. She broke away from my embrace and started kissing away my tears. Just as I had done on the first night-out.

It had been hours. I lay there looking at her, still in denial that she would be gone. I had lived these three months of separation, hoping that some day, some damned day, she would come back to me and we would be what we were again. She was back. But . . .

She spoke. 'Deb . . .'

I hung on to every word she said. If I survived this, I would need every bit of her memory to carry on. I wanted to tell her how much I loved her. I wanted to hear the same from her. As many times as life would allow her. I would need her to say that she loved me with every breath she took. I would need whatever was left of her.

She locked my eyes in a gaze and said, 'Deb, they said . . . I will die in a few months . . . if I . . .'

'If . . . ?'

'If I don't get enough of you, my sweetheart!'

'*WHAT?*' I let out, shocked.

And there it was, then. *Her wink!* She winked. And burst out laughing!

'What the fuck? What the bloody . . . *Are you crazy?*' I shouted at her as I jumped on the bed. How could I forget, this was Avantika! Was this a joke? Damn!

'Aww . . . I am not going to leave your worthless life so soon, Deb.'

'You are an ass, you know that? Damn you! Were you out of your mind? I could have died, you bloody witch!' I shouted and swore happily.

'Why? You have cancer or what?' she stood up and hugged me. She laughed.

'No, I don't. But I have a great fucking girlfriend without whom I cannot live. And if she ever dies, I will go with her,' I said, looked at her and kissed her nose. Then, we cried a little more.

'Okay, Avantika. Does cancer spread through sex? Because I am ready to do it again, baby.'

'I don't think so,' she smiled and winked. I pushed her onto the bed. I forgot about Chapter 22. Whatever it was, it couldn't be better than this.

We spent the whole day on the bed making-out whenever I was capable of it. It got wilder with each time and that's where the hair on the bed came from. Apparently, her weight loss was because of her aim to reduce to size zero. I categorically told her that it was absolutely unnecessary and she was perfect the way she was. She couldn't hold her laughter once I told her what I had imagined. *Deb and the Cancer Story*, it would forever stay.

'Deb, you have twenty missed calls on your phone. Pick it up.' I picked it up and she put me on loudspeaker. It was the guard from my office.

'Deb *sahab*? Deb *sahab*! I have been calling you since the evening. They caught me punching the cards today. They have taken both your cards. What do I do, Deb *sahab*? The vigilance team wants to talk to me tomorrow. What do I say, Deb *sahab*?' he asked frantically. There was a reason to be frantic. Suspension was a given for such an offence. I knew Goyal was behind it. Nobody otherwise gave a shit about who punched your card. He wouldn't let this one go, I thought. Bastard.

'Arjunji, it's nothing to worry about. Tell them you just punched my card. Not a word about Amitji. Get that? Just my card and tell them I asked you to hand over Amit's card to him as he forgot it on his desk. Just tell them that, I will handle the rest,' I said.

'Okay, Deb *sahab*. Thank you.' He hung up.

'Avantika, can I have the laptop? If there is anything left of it, I mean!' I said.

'Why? Seems like you pretty much lost the job, didn't you?'

'Seems like it.'

'I am so unlucky for you! If we are to be together, I think you will have to make do without a job!' she chuckled. 'So what are you going to do now?'

'Nothing much, drop some shit on people before I leave. That won't save my job, but it will save my face, I guess.'

I didn't care about the job. I had Avantika. Jobs would follow. Although we hadn't exchanged a word about our relationship, I just knew she was there to stay. And there were plenty of jobs out there.

I typed out a long resignation letter addressed to Mr Malhotra. I accused Mr Goyal for mental harassment and all Amit's not-so-loved colleagues for making life hell for me, as they couldn't stand me being so smart. Therefore, I had no choice but to start working from home. Mr Malhotra would believe me as he had already seen the results.

'So what do you think? Will it work?' she asked.

'It has to. If not, Dad will pull me out of this mess. So, it's not a big deal. I have you now. Nothing else matters.' I hugged her.

It got to me later that I had done a pretty good job with the letter. The vigilance team was off me and I still had the job. But I resigned anyway. I would have sounded guilty if I had not. I couldn't have possibly disappointed Dad. I wanted him and everyone else to feel that I was a victim of office politics and I didn't want to continue any more. Amit wasn't touched and that was all I cared about. Astha's parents wouldn't accept an out-of-work suitor. Goyal missed another promotion.

'So Avantika, you still haven't told me . . . what brings you back?' I asked.

'Sri Guru,' she said.

'Not again. He was the reason we were in this shit in the first place. Nothing would have gone wrong had he not meddled.'

'Shut up, Deb. At least now I know that I cannot live without you. And for sure that you love me as much as I do.'

'Big deal. I could have told you that. Anyway, continue,' I said, happily irritated.

'I was back to my alcohol habit. The only time I didn't drink was when I was writing this book. I was fucking myself over, all over again. It was then that I met Sri Guru again and realized I was running away from something that is truly mine. I was running away from my responsibility. *You.* I am ready to take that now. If something happens to you, I will make sure I set it right. If it is because of me that you see the bad times, it will be because of me that you will see the good ones,' she finished.

Thankfully. I never got her philosophical nonsense.

'You bet! Whatever. I generally don't get this bullshit philosophy of yours. What I do get though, is that you are a great kisser. Can we do it again?' I leant forward to get what was truly *mine.*

She leant away. 'Before everything else, you should thank Amit. He read your blog and mailed me, days after I met Sri Guru. He seemed to know a lot about me. That is when it all started to fall into place. He told me about you guys, and everything you did for them. I thought if these guys get treated so well, I should be in for super-special treatment!'

'Ohh! Yup, I missed that. That is how those chapters came up. This is how you knew all the details? But can we kiss first?' I leant forward and she leant away again. 'Now what? You still have something else? AIDS? Hepatitis? Whatever it is, I don't mind. Can we kiss?'

She again fished something out from her bag.

'Yes, there is something else too. Here goes. The first cheque from Bramha Publications. *Our Story* is being published this year. Like that?' She smiled and handed over the cheque to me. I read it aloud. It wasn't much, but it was an assurance that it would be published. My story? Our story? Why would anyone be interested in reading that? Why would anyone want to know about a loser like me? It was unbelievable.

'What the . . . ? Shit, this is unreal, man! I so fucking love you! I so, so, so, so, so damn love you! Can we please kiss now?' I jumped onto her, pinning her on the bed.

'We have to. The last chapter ends with a kiss.'

We kissed.

# Epilogue

And that, folks, is where my story ends. There was a lot of kissing, jumping on the bed, partying out, eating out that followed when Amit and Astha came back, but let us keep it for some other time.

Avantika had her posting shifted to Delhi and I was still looking for a job. We decided that being together was more important than job satisfaction. Or even having a job for that matter.

Shrey was to come to Delhi in December, with his German girlfriend in tow. He could even speak a little bit of German. It was cute to see them fight in a mixture of wretched English and equally bad German. He was in love again. When they came, they wrecked my place, which Amit had so lovingly decorated now that Astha was a regular visitor. Shrey, among other things, made Astha and Amit kiss. Their first kiss, a month before they got married. I remember how happy we were that day.

Viru and Yogi came for a visit, too, and promptly asked all of us to treat them, for all of us had a reason to celebrate. I loved them all; they loved me back. Deb was back. Good times were back.

Life had turned a full circle. A screwed one, but a complete one.

~

Just in case you are interested in what happens a couple of years down the line and are wondering if the good times lasted. Here it is . . .

Shrey, too, bought a copy of my book. *Pirated*. But he made quite some money in Germany and ordered the legal one. He was doing well, too. He almost married the German girl he was dating and was disinherited from his family. He became the youngest person to donate to the National Physical Laboratory. He hacked Suhel's account and somehow got him fired; that is what he tells me.

Tanmay and Vernita got married, too, after Vernita got pregnant. Vernita still works in that investment bank and earns a fortune. Tanmay, meanwhile, got through the IIMs and is travelling around the world on internships. Vernita talks to me now, occasionally. We never discuss the kiss. No matter how much I try to. She acts as if it never happened.

Viru and Yogi worked their way up right to the top before they were fired. For sleeping with their boss's wife. Together. It was her birthday party that got a little out of hand. They are now setting up their own auto-manufacturing unit. Together. The treat for that is still due but I don't foresee it coming any time soon.

And my best buddy now, Amit, has just shifted to the Middle East with Astha and their one-year-old son, Dev. His kid is already doing math sums. They are doing quite well, too. We mail each other every day. In his last mail, he sent me the snap of his latest asset. An Audi.

And yes, Neeti. She got married to Kumar last year. Shawar is out of prison now and being a good boy. Paritosh is still rotting.

And as for me—Avantika and I are still together. Avantika got me a job at her office and I am doing well. As her junior. The last place we made out was our boss's cabin. It was her idea. Though

Avantika now complains that I spend way too much time with my friends. Now that her Bengali classes are over, I am taking her to meet my mom soon.

My book did hit the stands and sank without a trace.

And of course I love you!

*Imagination seldom runs wild, but when it does, you have a book.*